EROTIC TALES

Ilona Staller, otherwise known as La Cicciolina, is a former porn star who became an Italian MP. Her strong views on sex and the erotic make her famous across the world. She is married to the artist Jeff Koons and lives in Munich.

EROTIC TALES

Introduced by La Cicciolina

PAN BOOKS
LONDON, SYDNEY AND AUCKLAND

First published 1993 by Michael O'Mara Books Limited

This edition published 1994 by Pan Books Limited
a division of Pan Macmillan Publishers Limited
Cavaye Place London SW10 9PG
and Basingstoke

Associated companies throughout the world

ISBN 0 330 32783 6

1 3 5 7 9 8 6 4 2

A CIP catalogue record for this book is available from
the British Library

Printed and bound in Great Britain by
Cox & Wyman Ltd, Reading, Berkshire

Contents

LA CICCIOLINA

Eroticism

ONCE upon a time the word 'erotic' was associated with 'sin'. Erotic fantasies and sexual desire had to be repressed. Of course, prohibition bred transgression. Taboos were there to be broken. Intellectuals identified freedom to explore their sexual desires as part of freedom of expression. On the other hand, they despised pornography for its treatment of women as objects, not human beings to be treated with respect.

I believe that I have helped resolve that contradiction. I have taken desire beyond materialism, beyond orgasm, beyond love to discover the reality of eroticism. In 1976, my voice caused millions of Italians to dream of the erotic. My voice, in my radio programme called 'Do you want to go to bed with me?', was enough to drive my listeners into erotic frenzy. I made people dream of love and desire, the unimaginable delights of love.

Just one year later, through photographs in magazines often erotic and sometimes explicit, my audience discovered my body. I acted in erotic films and displayed my sex like a full-blown rose. The public outcry became even more noisy when I met my audiences at stage shows. I took nudity out of the ghetto of seedy nightclubs into the bright lights of conventional theatres. This was a new way of celebrating eroticism. Soon, even television was prepared to accept my erotic performance. I was able to prove that beyond pornography lies true eroticism and the desire for a new world.

The stories in this book show that what is erotic is impossible to limit or define. The erotic universe is infinite, without boundaries, beyond the horizons of the rational world. Love is not the same as eroticism which stimulates emotions through shock and raw sensation. In fact, eroticism may conflict with love, turning it into a game. A look, a glimpse of forbidden stocking, can be erotic particularly when love is being stifled by the problems of ordinary life which so often induce frustration and provoke anger. True love—simple and genuine, can be seen as boring because it does not need fantasy to fuel it. And yet I believe beyond fear, beyond fantasy, beyond eroticism, is love.

ILONA STALLER

DANIEL DEFOE

from

Moll Flanders

'Moll Flanders', Daniel Defoe's story of a whore, was published in 1722. This story of incest, adultery and bigamy was considered to be obscene despite the heroine's deathbed repentance.

BY this means I had, as I have said above, all the advantages of education that I could have had if I had been as much a gentlewoman as they were with whom I lived; and in some things I had the advantage of my ladies, though they were my superiors; but they were all the gifts of nature, and which all their fortunes could not furnish. First, I was apparently handsomer than any of them; secondly, I was better shaped; and, thirdly, I sang better, by which I mean I had a better voice; in all which you will, I hope, allow me to say, I do not speak my own conceit of myself, but the opinion of all that knew the family.

I had with all these the common vanity of my sex, viz. that being really taken for very handsome, or, if you please, for a great beauty, I very well knew it, and had as good an opinion of myself as anybody else could have of me; and particularly I loved to hear anybody speak of it, which could not but happen to me sometimes, and was a great satisfaction to me.

Thus far I have had a smooth story to tell of myself and in all this part of my life I not only had the reputation of living in a very good family, and a family noted and respected everywhere for

virtue and sobriety, and for every valuable thing; but I had the
character too of a very sober, modest, and virtuous young woman,
and such I had always been; neither had I yet any occasion to think
of anything else, or to know what a temptation to wickedness
meant.

But that which I was too vain of was my ruin, or rather my
vanity was the cause of it. The lady in the house where I was had
two sons, young gentlemen of very promising parts and of extraordinary behaviour, and it was my misfortune to be very well with
them both, but they managed themselves with me in a quite different manner.

The eldest, a gay gentleman that knew the town as well as the
country, and though he had levity enough to do an ill-natured
thing, yet had too much judgment of things to pay too dear for his
pleasures; he began with that unhappy snare to all women, viz.
taking notice upon all occasions how pretty I was, as he called it,
how agreeable, how well-carriaged, and the like; and this he contrived so subtly, as if he had known as well how to catch a woman
in his net as a partridge when he went a-setting; for he would contrive to be talking this to his sisters when, though I was not by, yet
when he knew I was not so far off but that I should be sure to hear
him. His sisters would return softly to him, 'Hush, brother, she
will hear you; she is but in the next room.' Then he would put it
off and talk softlier, as if he had not known it, and begin to
acknowledge he was wrong; and then, as if he had forgot himself,
he would speak aloud again, and I, that was so well pleased to hear
it, was sure to listen for it upon all occasions.

After he had thus baited his hook, and found easily enough
the method how to lay it in my way, he played an opener game;
and one day, going by his sister's chamber when I was there,
doing something about dressing her, he comes in with an air of
gaiety. 'Oh, Mrs Betty,' said he to me, 'how do you do, Mrs Betty?
Don't your cheeks burn, Mrs Betty?' I made a curtsy and blushed,
but said nothing. 'What makes you talk so, brother?' says the
lady. 'Why,' says he, 'we have been talking of her below-stairs this

half-hour.' 'Well,' says his sister, 'you can say no harm of her, that I
am sure, so 'tis no matter what you have been talking about.' 'Nay,'
says he, ''tis so far from talking harm of her, that we have been talking a great deal of good, and a great many fine things have been
said of Mrs Betty, I assure you; and particularly, that she is the
handsomest young woman in Colchester; and, in short, they begin
to toast her health in the town.'

'I wonder at you, brother,' says the sister. 'Betty wants but one
thing, but she had as good want everything, for the market is
against our sex just now; and if a young woman have beauty,
birth, breeding, wit, sense, manners, modesty, and all these to
an extreme, yet if she have not money, she's nobody, she had as
good want them all, for nothing but money now recommends a
woman; the men play the game all into their own hands.'

Her younger brother, who was by, cried, 'Hold, sister, you run
too fast; I am an exception to your rule. I assure you, if I find a
woman so accomplished as you talk of, I say, I assure you, I would
not trouble myself about the money.'

'Oh,' says the sister, 'but you will take care not to fancy one,
then, without the money.'

'You don't know that neither,' says the brother.

'But why, sister,' says the elder brother, 'why do you exclaim so
at the men for aiming so much at the fortune? You are none of
them that want a fortune, whatever else you want.'

'I understand you, brother,' replies the lady very smartly; 'you
suppose I have the money, and want the beauty; but as times go
now, the first will do without the last, so I have the better of my
neighbours.'

'Well,' says the younger brother, 'but your neighbours, as you
call them, may be even with you, for beauty will steal a husband
sometimes in spite of money, and when the maid chances to be
handsomer than the mistress, she oftentimes makes as good a market, and rides in a coach before her.'

I thought it was time for me to withdraw and leave them, and
I did so, but not so far but that I heard all their discourse, in

which I heard abundance of fine things said of myself, which
served to prompt my vanity, but, as I soon found, was not the way
to increase my interest in the family, for the sister and the younger
brother fell grievously out about it; and as he said some very dis-
obliging things to her upon my account, so I could easily see that
she resented them by her future conduct to me, which indeed was
very unjust to me, for I had never had the least thought of what she
suspected as to her younger brother; indeed, the elder brother, in
his distant, remote way, had said a great many things as in jest,
which I had the folly to believe were in earnest, or to flatter myself
with the hopes of what I ought to have supposed he never intended, and perhaps never thought of.

It happened one day that he came running upstairs, towards the
room where his sisters used to sit and work, as he often used to do;
and calling to them before he came in, as was his way too, I, being
there alone, stepped to the door, and said, 'Sir, the ladies are not
here, they are walked down the garden.' As I stepped forward to
say this, towards the door, he was just got to the door, and clasping
me in his arms, as if it had been by chance, 'Oh, Mrs Betty,' says
he, 'are you here? That's better still; I want to speak with you more
than I do with them'; and then, having me in his arms, he kissed
me three or four times.

I struggled to get away, and yet did it but faintly neither, and he
held me fast, and still kissed me, till he was almost out of breath,
and then, sitting down, says, 'Dear Betty, I am in love with you.'

His words, I must confess, fired my blood; all my spirits flew
about my heart and put me into disorder enough, which he might
easily have seen in my face. He repeated it afterwards several times,
that he was in love with me, and my heart spoke as plain as a voice,
that I liked it; nay, whenever he said, 'I am in love with you,' my
blushes plainly replied, 'Would you were, sir.'

However, nothing else passed at that time; it was but a surprise,
and when he was gone I soon recovered myself again. He had
stayed longer with me, but he happened to look out at the
window and see his sisters coming up the garden, so he took his

leave, kissed me again, told me he was very serious, and I should hear more of him very quickly, and away he went, leaving me infinitely pleased, though surprised; and had there not been one misfortune in it, I had been in the right, but the mistake lay here, that Mrs Betty was in earnest and the gentleman was not.

From this time my head ran upon strange things, and I may truly say I was not myself, to have such a gentleman talk to me of being in love with me, and of my being such a charming creature, as he told me I was; these were things I knew not how to bear, my vanity was elevated to the last degree. It is true I had my head full of pride, but, knowing nothing of the wickedness of the times, I had not one thought of my own safety or of my virtue about me; and had my young master offered it at first sight, he might have taken any liberty he thought fit with me; but he did not see his advantage, which was my happiness for that time.

After this attack it was not long but he found an opportunity to catch me again, and almost in the same posture; indeed, it had more of design in it on his part, though not on my part. It was thus: the young ladies were all gone a-visiting with their mother; his brother was out of town; and as for his father, he had been at London for a week before. He had so well watched me that he knew where I was, though I did not so much as know that he was in the house; and he briskly comes up the stairs and, seeing me at work, comes into the room to me directly, and began just as he did before, with taking me in his arms, and kissing me for almost a quarter of an hour together.

It was his younger sister's chamber that I was in, and as there was nobody in the house but the maids below-stairs, he was, it may be, the ruder; in short, he began to be in earnest with me indeed. Perhaps he found me a little too easy, for God knows I made no resistance to him while he only held me in his arms and kissed me; indeed, I was too well pleased with it to resist him much.

However, as it were, tired with that kind of work, we sat down, and there he talked with me a great while; he said he was charmed

with me, and that he could not rest night or day till he had told me
how he was in love with me, and, if I was able to love him again,
and would make him happy, I should be the saving of his life, and
many such fine things. I said little to him again, but easily discovered that I was a fool, and that I did not in the least perceive what
he meant.

Then he walked about the room, and taking me by the hand, I
walked with him; and by and by, taking his advantage, he threw
me down upon the bed, and kissed me there most violently; but,
to give him his due, offered no manner of rudeness to me, only
kissed me a great while. After this he thought he had heard somebody come upstairs, so he got off from the bed, lifted me up,
professing a great deal of love for me, but told me it was all an honest affection, and that he meant no ill to me; and with that he put
five guineas into my hand, and went away downstairs.

I was more confounded with the money than I was before with
the love, and began to be so elevated that I scarce knew the ground
I stood on. I am the more particular in this part, that if my story
comes to be read by any innocent young body, they may learn
from it to guard themselves against the mischiefs which attend an
early knowledge of their own beauty. If a young woman once
thinks herself handsome, she never doubts the truth of any man
that tells her he is in love with her; for if she believes herself
charming enough to captivate him, 'tis natural to expect the effects
of it.

This young gentleman had fired his inclination as much as he
had my vanity, and, as if he had found that he had an opportunity
and was sorry he did not take hold of it, he comes up again in half
an hour or thereabouts, and falls to work with me again as before,
only with a little less introduction.

And first, when he entered the room, he turned about and shut
the door. 'Mrs Betty,' said he, 'I fancied before somebody was
coming upstairs, but it was not so; however,' adds he, 'if they
find me in the room with you, they shan't catch me a-kissing of
you.' I told him I did not know who should be coming upstairs,

for I believed there was nobody in the house but the cook and the other maid, and they never came up those stairs. 'Well, my dear,' says he, "tis good to be sure, however'; and so he sits down, and we began to talk. And now, though I was still all on fire with his first visit, and said little, he did as it were put words in my mouth, telling me how passionately he loved me, and that though he could not mention such a thing till he came to his estate, yet he was resolved to make me happy then, and himself too; that is to say, to marry me, and abundance of such fine things, which I, poor fool, did not understand the drift of, but acted as if there was no such thing as any kind of love but that which tended to matrimony; and if he had spoke of that, I had no room, as well as no power, to have said no; but we were not come that length yet.

We had not sat long, but he got up, and, stopping my very breath with kisses, threw me upon the bed again; but then being both well warmed, he went farther with me than decency permits me to mention, nor had it been in my power to have denied him at that moment, had he offered much more than he did.

However, though he took these freedoms with me, it did not go to that which they call the last favour, which, to do him justice, he did not attempt; and he made that self-denial of his a plea for all his freedoms with me upon other occasions after this. When this was over, he stayed but a little while, but he put almost a handful of gold in my hand, and left me, making a thousand protestations of his passion for me, and of his loving me above all the women in the world.

It will not be strange if I now began to think, but, alas! it was but with very little solid reflection. I had a most unbounded stock of vanity and pride, and but a very little stock of virtue. I did indeed cast sometimes with myself what my young master aimed at, but thought of nothing but the fine words and the gold; whether he intended to marry me, or not to marry me, seemed a matter of no great consequence to me; nor did my thoughts so much as suggest to me the necessity of making any capitulation for myself, till he came to make a kind of formal proposal to me, as you shall hear presently.

Thus I gave up myself to a readiness of being ruined without the least concern, and am a fair memento to all young women whose vanity prevails over their virtue. Nothing was ever so stupid on both sides. Had I acted as became me, and resisted as virtue and honour required, this gentleman had either desisted his attacks, finding no room to expect the accomplishment of his design, or had made fair and honourable proposals of marriage; in which case, whoever had blamed him, nobody could have blamed me. In short, if he had known me, and how easy the trifle he aimed at was to be had, he would have troubled his head no farther, but have given me four or five guineas, and have lain with me the next time he had come at me. And if I had known his thoughts, and how hard he thought I would be to be gained, I might have made my own terms with him; and if I had not capitulated for an immediate marriage, I might for a maintenance till marriage, and might have had what I would; for he was already rich to excess, besides what he had in expectation; but I seemed wholly to have abandoned all such thoughts as these, and was taken up only with the pride of my beauty, and of being beloved by such a gentleman. As for the gold, I spent whole hours in looking upon it; I told the guineas over and over a thousand times a day. Never poor vain creature was so wrapt up with every part of the story as I was, not considering what was before me, and how near my ruin was at the door; indeed, I think I rather wished for that ruin than studied to avoid it.

In the meantime, however, I was cunning enough not to give the least room to any in the family to suspect me, or to imagine that I had the least correspondence with this young gentleman. I scarce ever looked towards him in public, or answered if he spoke to me when anybody was near us; but for all that, we had every now and then a little encounter, where we had room for a word or two, and now and then a kiss, but no fair opportunity for the mischief intended; and especially considering that he made more circumlocution than, if he had known my thoughts, he had occasion for; and the work appearing difficult to him, he really made it so.

But as the devil is an unwearied tempter, so he never fails to find opportunity for that wickedness he invites to. It was one evening that I was in the garden, with his two younger sisters and himself, and all very innocently merry, when he found means to convey a note into my hand, by which he directed me to understand that he would to-morrow desire me publicly to go of an errand for him into the town, and that I should see him somewhere by the way.

Accordingly, after dinner, he very gravely says to me, his sisters being all by, 'Mrs Betty, I must ask a favour of you.' 'What's that?' says his second sister. 'Nay, sister,' says he very gravely, 'if you can't spare Mrs Betty to-day, any other time will do.' Yes, they said, they could spare her well enough, and the sister begged pardon for asking, which they did but of mere course, without any meaning. 'Well, but, brother,' says the eldest sister, 'you must tell Mrs Betty what it is; if it be any private business that we must not hear, you may call her out. There she is.' 'Why, sister,' says the gentleman very gravely, 'what do you mean? I only desire her to go into the High Street' (and then he pulls out a turnover), 'to such a shop'; and then he tells them a long story of two fine neckcloths he had bid money for, and he wanted to have me go and make an errand to buy a neck to the turnover that he showed, to see if they would take my money for the neckcloths; to bid a shilling more, and haggle with them; and then he made more errands, and so continued to have such petty business to do, that I should be sure to stay a good while.

When he had given me my errands, he told them a long story of a visit he was going to make to a family they all knew, and where was to be such-and-such gentlemen, and how merry they were to be, and very formally asks his sisters to go with him, and they as formally excused themselves, because of company that they had notice was to come and visit them that afternoon; which, by the way, he had contrived on purpose.

He had scarce done speaking to them, and giving me my errand, but his man came up to tell him that Sir W— H—'s coach stopped at the door; so he runs down, and comes up again immediately. 'Alas!' says he aloud, 'there's all my mirth spoiled at once; Sir W— has sent his coach for me, and desires to speak with me upon some earnest business.' It seems this Sir W— was a gentleman who lived about three miles out of town, to whom he had spoken on purpose the day before, to lend him his chariot for a particular occasion, and had appointed it to call for him, as it did, about three o'clock.

Immediately he calls for his best wig, hat, and sword, and ordering his man to go to the other place to make his excuse—that was to say, he made an excuse to send his man away—he prepares to go into the coach. As he was going, he stopped a while, and speaks mightily earnestly to me about his business, and finds an opportunity to say very softly to me, 'Come away, my dear, as soon as ever you can.' I said nothing, but made a curtsy, as if I had done so to what he said in public. In about a quarter of an hour I went out too; I had no dress other than before, except that I had a hood, a mask, a fan, and a pair of gloves in my pocket; so that there was not the least suspicion in the house. He waited for me in the coach in a back lane, which he knew I must pass by, and had directed the coachman whither to go, which was to a certain place, called Mile End, where lived a confidant of his, where we went in, and where was all the convenience in the world to be as wicked as we pleased.

When we were together he began to talk very gravely to me, and to tell me he did not bring me there to betray me; that his passion for me would not suffer him to abuse me; that he resolved to marry me as soon as he came to his estate; that in the meantime, if I would grant his request, he would maintain me very honourably; and made me a thousand protestations of his sincerity and of his affection to me; and that he would never abandon me, and, as I may say, made a thousand more preambles than he need to have done.

However, as he pressed me to speak, I told him I had no reason to question the sincerity of his love to me after so many protestations, but—and there I stopped, as if I left him to guess the rest. 'But what, my dear?' says he, 'I guess what you mean: what if you should be with child? Is not that it? Why, then,' says he, 'I'll take care of you and provide for you, and the child too; and that you may see I am not in jest,' says he, 'here's an earnest for you,' and with that he pulls out a silk purse, with an hundred guineas in it, and gave it me. 'And I'll give you such another,' says he, 'every year till I marry you.'

My colour came and went, at the sight of the purse and with the fire of his proposal together, so that I could not say a word, and he easily perceived it; so putting the purse into my bosom, I made no more resistance to him, but let him do just what he pleased, and as often as he pleased; and thus I finished my own destruction at once, for from this day, being forsaken of my virtue and my modesty, I had nothing of value left to recommend me, either to God's blessing or man's assistance.

But things did not end here. I went back to the town, did the business he publicly directed me to, and was at home before anybody thought me long. As for my gentleman, he stayed out, as he told me he would, till late at night, and there was not the least suspicion in the family either on his account or on mine.

We had, after this, frequent opportunities to repeat our crime—chiefly by his contrivance—especially at home, when his mother and the young ladies went abroad a-visiting, which he watched so narrowly as never to miss; knowing always beforehand when they went out, and then failed not to catch me all alone, and securely enough; so that we took our fill of our wicked pleasure for near half a year; and yet, which was the most to my satisfaction, I was not with child.

But before this half-year was expired, his younger brother, of whom I have made some mention in the beginning of the story, falls to work with me; and he, finding me alone in the garden one evening, begins a story of the same kind to me, made good honest professions of being in love with me, and, in short, proposes fairly and honourably to marry me, and that before he made any other offer to me at all.

I was now confounded, and driven to such an extremity as the like was never known; at least not to me. I resisted the proposal with obstinacy; and now I began to arm myself with arguments. I laid before him the inequality of the match; the treatment I should meet with in the family; the ingratitude it would be to his good father and mother, who had taken me into their house upon such generous principles, and when I was in such a low condition; and, in short, I said everything to dissuade him from his design that I could imagine, except telling him the truth, which would indeed have put an end to it all, but that I durst not think of mentioning.

But here happened a circumstance that I did not expect indeed, which put me to my shifts; for this young gentleman, as he was plain and honest, so he pretended to nothing with me but what was so too; and, knowing his own innocence, he was not so careful to make his having a kindness for Mrs Betty a secret in the house, as his brother was. And though he did not let them know that he had talked to me about it, yet he said enough to let his sisters perceive he loved me, and his mother saw it too, which, though they took no notice of it to me, yet they did to him, and immediately I found their carriage to me altered, more than ever before.

I saw the cloud, though I did not forsee the storm. It was easy, I say, to see that their carriage to me was altered, and that it grew worse and worse every day; till at last I got information among the servants that I should, in a very little while, be desired to remove.

[*Moll marries a gentleman-tradesman who proves to be a spendthrift and deserts her when all their money is gone. She finds herself in Bath, 'a place of gallantry enough; expensive, and full of snares', where she lodges with a woman who does not 'keep an ill house, as we call it, yet had none of the best principles in herself.'*]

We had lived thus near three months, when the company beginning to wear away at the Bath, he talked of going away, and fain he
would have me to go to London with him. I was not very easy in
that proposal, not knowing what posture I was to live in there, or
how he might use me. But while this was in debate he fell very
sick; he had gone out to a place in Somersetshire, called Shepton,
where he had some business, and was there taken very ill, and so ill
that he could not travel; so he sent his man back to Bath, to beg
me that I would hire a coach and come over to him. Before he
went, he had left all his money and other things of value with me,
and what to do with them I did not know, but I secured them as
well as I could, and locked up the lodgings and went to him,
where I found him very ill indeed; however, I persuaded him to
be carried in a litter to the Bath, where there was more help and
better advice to be had.

He consented, and I brought him to the Bath, which was about
fifteen miles, as I remember. Here he continued very ill of a
fever, and kept his bed five weeks, all which time I nursed him and
tended him myself, as much and as carefully as if I had been his
wife; indeed, if I had been his wife I could not have done more. I
sat up with him so much and so often, that at last, indeed, he
would not let me sit up any longer, and then I got a pallet-bed into
his room, and lay in it just at his bed's feet.

I was indeed sensibly affected with his condition, and with the
apprehension of losing such a friend as he was, and was like to be
to me, and I used to sit and cry by him many hours together.
However, at last he grew better, and gave hopes that he would
recover, as indeed he did, though very slowly.

Were it otherwise than what I am going to say, I should not be
backward to disclose it, as it is apparent I have done in other cases
in this account; but I affirm, that through all this conversation,
abating the freedom of coming into the chamber when I or he was
in bed, and abating the necessary offices of attending him night
and day when he was sick, there had not passed the least immod-
est word or action between us. Oh that it had been so to the last!

After some time he gathered strength and grew well apace, and I would have removed my pallet-bed, but he would not let me, till he was able to venture himself without anybody to sit up with him, and then I removed to my own chamber.

He took many occasions to express his sense of my tenderness and concern for him; and when he grew quite well, he made me a present of fifty guineas for my care, and as he called it, for hazarding my life to save his.

And now he made deep protestations of a sincere inviolable affection for me, but all along attested it to be with the utmost reserve for my virtue and his own. I told him I was fully satisfied of it. He carried it that length that he protested to me, that if he was naked in bed with me, he would as sacredly preserve my virtue as he would defend it if I was assaulted by a ravisher. I believed him, and told him I did so; but this did not satisfy him; he would, he said, wait for some opportunity to give me an undoubted testimony of it.

It was a great while after this that I had occasion, on my own business, to go to Bristol, upon which he hired me a coach, and would go with me, and did so; and now indeed our intimacy increased. From Bristol he carried me to Gloucester, which was merely a journey of pleasure, to take the air; and here it was our hap to have no lodging in the inn but in one large chamber with two beds in it. The master of the house going up with us to show his rooms, and coming into that room, said very frankly to him, 'Sir, it is none of my business to inquire whether the lady be your spouse or no, but if not, you may lie as honestly in these two beds as if you were in two chambers,' and with that he pulls a great curtain which drew quite across the room and effectually divided the beds. 'Well,' says my friend, very readily, 'these beds will do, and as for the rest, we are too near akin to lie together, though we may lodge near one another'; and this put an honest face on the thing too. When we came to go to bed, he decently went out of the room till I was in bed, and then went to bed in the bed on his own side of the room, but lay there talking to me a great while.

At last, repeating his usual saying, that he could lie naked in the bed with me and not offer me the least injury, he starts out of his bed. 'And now, my dear,' says he, 'you shall see how just I will be to you, and that I can keep my word,' and away he comes to my bed.

I resisted a little, but I must confess I should not have resisted him much if he had not made those promises at all; so after a little struggle, as I said, I lay still and let him come to bed. When he was there he took me in his arms, and so I lay all night with him, but he had no more to do with me, or offered anything to me, other than embracing me, as I say, in his arms, no, not the whole night, but rose up and dressed him in the morning, and left me as innocent for him as I was the day I was born.

This was a surprising thing to me, and perhaps may be so to others, who know how the laws of nature work; for he was a strong, vigorous, brisk person; nor did he act thus on a principle of religion at all, but of mere affection; insisting on it, that though I was to him the most agreeable woman in the world, yet, because he loved me, he could not injure me.

I own it was a noble principle, but as it was what I never understood before, so it was to me perfectly amazing. We travelled the rest of the journey as we did before, and came back to the Bath, where, as he had opportunity to come to me when he would, he often repeated the moderation, and I frequently lay with him, and he with me, and although all the familiarities between man and wife were common to us, yet he never once offered to go any farther, and he valued himself much upon it. I do not say that I was so wholly pleased with it as he thought I was, for I own I was much wickeder than he, as you shall hear presently.

We lived thus near two years, and only with this exception, that he went three times to London in that time, and once he continued there four months, but, to do him justice, he always supplied me with money to subsist me very handsomely.

Had we continued thus, I confess we had had much to boast of; but as wise men say, it is ill venturing too near the brink of a

command, so we found it; and here again I must do him the
justice to own that the first breach was not on his part. It was one
night that we were in bed together warm and merry, and
having drunk, I think, a little more wine that night, both of us,
than usual, though not in the least to disorder either of us, when,
after some other follies which I cannot name, and being clasped
close in his arms, I told him (I repeat it with shame and horror of
soul) that I could find in my heart to discharge him of his engagement for one night, and no more.

He took me at my word immediately, and after that there was
no resisting him; neither indeed had I any mind to resist him any
more, let what would come of it.

Thus the government of our virtue was broken, and I
exchanged the place of friend for that unmusical, harsh-sounding
title of whore. In the morning we were both at our penitentials; I
cried very heartily, he expressed himself very sorry; but that was all
either of us could do at that time, and the way being thus cleared,
and the bars of virtue and conscience thus removed, we had the
less difficulty afterwards to struggle with.

It was but a dull kind of conversation that we had together for
all the rest of that week; I looked on him with blushes, and every
now and then started that melancholy objection, 'What if I should
be with child now? What will become of me then?' He encouraged me by telling me, that as long as I was true to him, he would
be so to me; and since it was gone such a length (which indeed he
never intended), yet if I was with child, he would take care of that,
and of me too. This hardened us both. I assured him if I was with
child, I would die for want of a midwife rather than name him as
the father of it; and he assured me I should never want if I should
be with child. These mutual assurances hardened us in the thing,
and after this we repeated the crime as often as we pleased, till at
length, as I had feared, so it came to pass, and I was indeed with
child.

JOHN CLELAND

from

Fanny Hill

or Memoirs of a
Woman of Pleasure

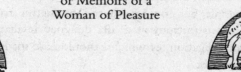

*'Fanny Hill' was written by John Cleland in 1748-9 while he was imprisoned
in the Fleet for debt. It is perhaps the most famous of all erotic novels.*

NOR was this worthy act of justice long delayed: I had it too much
at heart. Mr H— had, about a fortnight before, taken into his service a tenant's son, just come out of the country, a very handsome
young lad, scarce turned of nineteen, fresh as a rose, well shaped
and clever-limbed: in short, a very good excuse for any woman's
liking, even though revenge had been out of the question; any
woman, I say, who was disprejudiced and had wit and spirit
enough to prefer a point of pleasure to a point of pride.

Mr H— had clapped a livery upon him; and his chief employ
was, after being shown my lodgings, to bring and carry letters or
messages between his master and me; and as the situation of all
kept ladies is not the fittest to inspire respect even to the meanest
of mankind, and perhaps less of it from the most ignorant, I could
not help observing that this lad, who was, I suppose, acquainted
with my relation to his master by his fellow servants, used to eye
me in that bashful confused way, more expressive, more moving,
and readier caught at by our sex than any other declarations
whatever: my figure had, it seems, struck him, and modest and
innocent as he was, he did not himself know that the pleasure he

took in looking at me was love, or desire; but his eyes, naturally wanton, and now inflamed by passion, spoke a great deal more than he durst have imagined they did. Hitherto, indeed, I had only taken notice of the comeliness of the youth, but without the least design. My pride alone would have guarded me from a thought that way, had not Mr H—'s condescension with my maid, where there was not half the temptation in point of person, set me a dangerous example; but now I began to look on this stripling as every way a delicious instrument of my designed retaliation upon Mr H—, of an obligation for which I should have made a conscience to die in his debt.

In order then to pave the way for the accomplishment of my scheme, for two or three times that the young fellow came to me with messages, I managed so as without affectation to have him admitted to my bedside, or brought to me at my toilet, where I was dressing; and by carelessly showing or letting him see as if without meaning or design, sometimes my bosom rather more bare than it should be; sometimes my hair, of which I had a very fine head, in the natural flow of it while combing; sometimes a neat leg, that had unfortunately slipped its garter, which I made no scruple of tying before him, easily gave him the impressions favourable to my purpose, which I could perceive to sparkle in his eyes and glow in his cheeks. Then certain slight squeezes by the hand, as I took letters from him, did his business completely.

When I saw him thus moved and fired for my purpose, I inflamed him yet more, by asking him several leading questions; such as had he a mistress?—was she prettier than me?—could he love such a one as I was?—and the like; to all which the blushing simpleton answered to my wish, in a strain of perfect nature, perfect undebauched innocence, but with all the awkwardness and simplicity of country breeding.

When I thought I had sufficiently ripened him for the laudable point I had in view, one day that I expected him at a particular hour, I took care to have the coast clear for the reception I designed him. And, as I had laid it, he came to the dining-room door, tapped at it, and, on my bidding him come in, he did so and shut the door after him. I desired him then to bolt it on the inside, pretending it would not otherwise keep shut.

I was then lying at length on that very couch, the scene of Mr H——'s polite joys, in an undress which was with all the art of negligence flowing loose, and in a most tempting disorder: no stays, no hoop—no encumbrance whatever; on the other hand, he stood at a little distance that gave me a full view of a fine featured, shapely, healthy, country lad, breathing the sweets of fresh blooming youth: his hair, which was of a perfect shining black, played to his face in natural side-curls and was set out with a smart tuck-up behind; new buckskin breeches that, clipping close, showed the shape of a plump well-made thigh, white stockings, garter-laced livery, shoulder-knot, altogether composed a figure in which the beauties of pure flesh and blood appeared under no disgrace from the lowness of a dress, to which a certain spruce neatness seems peculiarly fitted.

I bid him come towards me and give me his letter, at the same time throwing down carelessly a book I had in my hands. He coloured, and came within reach of delivering me the letter, which he held out awkwardly enough for me to take, with his eyes riveted on my bosom, which was, through the designed disorder of my handkerchief, sufficiently bare and rather shaded than hidden.

I, smiling in his face, took the letter, and immediately catching gently hold of his shirt-sleeve, drew him towards me, blushing and almost trembling; for surely his extreme bashfulness and utter inexperience called for at least all these advances to encourage him. His body was now conveniently inclined towards me, and just softly chucking his smooth beardless chin, I asked him, if he was afraid of a lady?—and with that taking and carrying his hand to my breasts, I pressed it tenderly to them. They were now finely furnished and raised in flesh, so that, panting with desire, they rose and fell, in quick heaves, under his touch: at this, the boy's eyes began to lighten with all the fires of inflamed nature, and his cheeks flushed with a deep scarlet; tongue-tied with joy, rapture, and bashfulness, he could not speak, but then his looks, his emotion, sufficiently satisfied me that my train had taken, and that I had no disappointment to fear.

My lips, which I threw in his way, so as that he could not escape kissing them, fixed, fired and emboldened him, and now, glancing my eyes towards that part of his dress which covered the essential object of enjoyment, I plainly discovered the swell and commotion there, and as I was now too far advanced to stop in so fair a way, and was indeed no longer able to contain myself or wait the slower progress of his maiden bashfulness (for such it seemed, and really was), I stole my hand upon his thighs, down one of which I could both see and feel a stiff hard body, confined by his breeches, that my fingers could discover no end to. Curious then, and eager to unfold so alarming a mystery, playing, as it were, with his buttons, which were bursting ripe from the active force within, those of his waistband and foreflap flew open at a touch, when out it started; and now, disengaged from the shirt, I saw with wonder and surprise, what? not the plaything of a boy, not the weapon of a man, but a maypole of so enormous a standard that, had proportions been observed, it must have belonged to a young giant; its prodigious size made me shrink again. Yet I could not, without pleasure, behold and even ventured to feel such a length! such a breadth of animated ivory, perfectly well turned and fashioned, the proud stiffness of which distended its skin, whose smooth polish and velvet softness might vie with that of the most delicate of our sex, and whose exquisite whiteness was not a little set off by a sprout of black curling hair round the root, through the jetty sprigs of which the fair skin showed as, in a fine evening, you may have remarked the clear light ether, through the branchwork of distant trees, overtopping the summet of a hill. Then the broad and bluish-casted incarnate of the head and blue serpentines of its veins altogether composed the most striking assemblage of figure and colours in nature; in short, it stood an object of terror and delight.

But what was yet more surprising, the owner of this natural

curiosity (through the want of occasions in the strictness of his home breeding, and the little time he had been in town not having afforded him one) was hitherto an absolute stranger, in practice at least, to the use of all that manhood he was so nobly stocked with; and it now fell to my lot to stand his first trial of it, if I could resolve to run the risks of its disproportion to that tender part of me which such an over-sized machine was very fit to lay in ruins.

But it was now of the latest to deliberate; for by this time, the young fellow, overheated with the present objects, and too high-mettled to be longer curbed in by that modesty and awe which had hitherto restrained him, ventured, under the stronger impulse and instructive promptership of nature alone, to slip his hands, trembling with eager impetuous desires, under my petticoats, and seeing, I suppose, nothing extremely severe in my looks to stop, or dash him, he feels out and seizes gently the centre-spot of his ardours. Oh then! the fiery touch of his fingers determines me, and my fears melting away before the growing intolerable heat, my thighs disclose of themselves and yield all liberty to his hand; and now, a favourable movement giving my petticoats a toss, the avenue lay too fair, too open to be missed; he is now upon me. I had placed myself with a jet under him, as commodious and open as possible to his attempts, which were untoward enough, for his machine, meeting with no inlet, bore and battered stiffly against me in random pushes, now above, now below, now beside its point, till, burning with impatience from its irritating touches, I guided gently with my hand this furious fescue to where my young novice was now to be taught his first lesson of pleasure. Thus he nicked at length the warm and insufficient orifice; but he was made to find no breach practicable, and mine, though so often entered, was still far from wide enough to take him easily in.

By my direction, however, the head of his unwieldy machine was so crucially pointed that, feeling him foreright against the tender opening, a favourable motion from me met his timely thrust, by which the lips of it, strenuously dilated, gave way to his thus assisted impetuosity, so that we might both feel that he had gained a lodgment; pursuing then his point, he soon, by violent and, to me, most painful piercing thrusts, wedges himself at least so far in as to be now tolerably secure of his entrance: here he stuck; and I now felt such a mixture of pleasure and pain as there is no giving a definition of. I dreaded, alike, his splitting me farther up or his withdrawing: I could not bear either to keep or part with him; the sense of pain, however, prevailing, from his prodigious size and stiffness, acting upon me in those continued rapid thrusts with which he furiously pursued his penetration, made me cry out gently: 'Oh, my dear, you hurt me!' This was enough to check the tender respectful boy, even in his mid-career; and he immediately drew out the sweet cause of my complaint, whilst his eyes eloquently expressed at once his grief for hurting me and his reluctance at dislodging from quarters of which the warmth and closeness had given him a gust of pleasure that he was now desire-mad to satisfy, and yet too much a novice not to be afraid of my withholding his relief, on account of the pain he had put me to.

But I was myself far from being pleased with his having too much regarded my tender exclaims, for now more and more fired with the object before me, as it still stood with the fiercest erection, unbonneted and displaying its broad vermillion head, I first gave the youth a re-encouraging kiss, which he repaid me with a fervour that seemed at once to thank me and bribe my farther compliance, and I soon replaced myself in a posture to receive, at all risks, the renewed invasion, which he did not delay an instant; for, being presently remounted, I once more felt the smooth hard gristle forcing an entrance, which he achieved rather easier than before. Pained, however, as I was, with his efforts of gaining a complete admission, which he was so regardful as to manage by gentle degrees, I took care not to complain. In the meantime, the soft strait passage gradually loosens, yields, and, stretched to its utmost bearing by the stiff, thick, in-driven engine, sensible at once to the ravishing pleasure of the feel and the pain of the distension, let him in about half way, when all the most nervous activity he now exerted to further his penetration gained him not an inch of his purpose; for, whilst he hesitated there, the crisis of pleasure overtook him, and the close compressure of the warm surrounding fold drew from him the ecstatic gush, even before mine was ready to meet it, kept up by the pain I had endured in the course of the engagement, from the unsufferable size of his weapon, though it was not as yet in above half its length.

I expected then, but without wishing it, that he would draw, but was pleasingly disappointed; for he was not to be let off so. The well-breathed youth, hot-mettled, and flush with genial juices, was now fairly in for making me know my driver. As soon, then, as he had made a short pause, waking, as it were, out of the trance of pleasure (in which every sense seemed lost for a while, whilst, with his eyes shut and short quick breathings, he had yielded down his maiden tribute), he still kept his post, yet unsated with enjoyment, and solacing in these so new delights, till his stiffness, which had scarce perceptibly remitted, being thoroughly recovered to him, who had not once unsheathed, he proceeded afresh to cleave and open to himself an entire entry into me, which was not a little made easy to him by the balsamic injection with which he had just plentifully moistened the whole internals of the passage. Redoubling, then, the active energy of his thrusts, favoured by the fervid appetency of my motions, the soft oiled wards can no longer stand so effectual a picklock, but yield and open him an entrance: and now, with conspiring nature and my industry, strong to aid him, he pierces, penetrates, and at length, winning his way inch by inch, gets entirely in, and finally, a home-made thrust, sheathes it up to the guard; on the information of which, from the close join-ture or our bodies (insomuch that the hair on both sides perfectly interweaved and encurled together), the eyes of the transported youth sparkled with more joyous fires, and all his looks and motions acknowledged excess of pleasure, which I now began to share, for I felt him in my very vitals! I was quite sick with delight! stirred beyond bearing with its furious agitations within me, and gorged and crammed even to a surfeit: thus I lay gasping, panting, under him, till his broken breathings, faultering accents, eyes twinkling with humid fires, lunges more furious, and an increased stiffness gave me to hail the approaches of the second period:—it came—and the sweet youth, overpowered with ecstasy, died away in my arms, melting in a flood that shot in genial warmth into the innermost recesses of my body, every conduit of which, dedicated to that pleasure, was on flow to mix with it. Thus we continued for some instants, lost, breathless, senseless of everything and in every part but those favourite ones of nature, in which all that we enjoyed of life and sensation was now totally concentered.

When our mutual trance was a little over, and the young fellow had withdrawn that delicious stretcher with which he had most plentifully drowned all thoughts of revenge in the sense of actual pleasure, the widened wounded passage refunded a stream of pearly liquids, which flowed down my thighs, mixed with streaks of blood, the marks of the ravage of that monstrous machine of his, which had now triumphed over a kind of second maidenhead. I stole, however, my handkerchief to those parts and wiped them as dry as I could, whilst he was readjusting, and buttoning up.

I made him now sit down by me, and as he had gathered courage from such extreme intimacy, he gave me an aftercourse of pleasure, in a natural burst of tender gratitude and joy, at the new scenes of bliss I had opened to him; scenes positively so new that he had never before had the least acquaintance with that mysterious mark, the cloven stamp of female distinction, though nobody better qualified than he to penetrate into its deepest recesses or do it nobler justice. But when, by certain motions, certain unquietnesses of his hands, that wandered not without design, I found he languished for satisfying a curiosity natural enough, to view and handle those parts which attract and concentre the warmest force of imagination, charmed as I was to have any occasion of obliging and humouring his young desires, I suffered him to proceed as he pleased, without check or control, to the satisfaction of them.

Easily, then, reading in my eyes the full permission of myself to all his wishes, he scarce pleased himself more than me, when, having insinuated his hands under my petticoat and shift, he presently removed those bars to the sight by slily lifting them upwards, under favour of a thousand kisses, which he thought, perhaps, necessary to divert my attention to what he was about. All my drapery being now rolled up to my waist, I threw myself into such a posture upon the couch as gave up to him, in full view, the whole region of delight, and all the luxurious landscape round it. The transported youth devoured everything with his eyes and tried with his fingers to lay more open to his sight the secrets of that dark and delicious deep: he opens the folding lips, the softness of which, yielding entry to anything of a hard body, close round it, and oppose the sight; and feeling further, meets with, and wonders at, a soft fleshy excrescence, which, limber and relaxed after the late enjoyment, now grew, under the touch and examination of his fiery fingers, more and more stiff and considerable, till the titillating ardours of that so sensible part made me sigh as if he had hurt me. On which he withdrew his curious probing fingers, asking me pardon, as it were, in a kiss that rather increased the flame *there*.

Novelty ever makes the strongest impressions, and in pleasures especially: no wonder then that he was swallowed up in raptures of admiration of things so interesting by their nature, and now seen and handled for the first time. On my part, I was richly overpaid for the pleasure I gave him, in that of examining the power of those objects thus abandoned to him, naked and free to his loosest wish, over the artless, natural stripling: his eyes streaming fire, his cheeks glowing with a florid red, his fervid frequent sighs, whilst his hands convulsively squeezed, opened, pressed together again the lips and sides of that deep flesh-wound or gently twitched the over-growing moss; and all proclaimed the excess, the riot of joys, in having his wantonness thus humoured. But he did not long abuse my patience, for the objects before him had now put him by all his, and coming out with that formidable machine of his, he lets the fury loose, and pointing it directly to the pouting-lipped mouth that bid him sweet defiance in dumb-show, squeezes in the head, and driving with refreshed rage, breaks in and plugs up the whole passage of that soft pleasure-conduit, where he makes all shake again, and put once more all within me into such an uproar as nothing could still but a fresh inundation from the very engine of those flames, as well as from all the springs with which nature floats that reservoir of joy, when risen to its floodmark.

I was now so bruised, so battered, so spent with this over-match that I could hardly stir or raise myself, but lay palpitating, till the ferment of my senses subsiding by degrees, and the hour striking at which I was obliged to dispatch my young man, I tenderly advised him of the necessity there was for parting, which I felt as much displeasure at as he could do, who seemed eagerly disposed to keep the field, and to enter on a fresh action; but the danger was too great, and after some hearty kisses of leave and recommendations of secrecy and discretion, I forced myself to force him away, not without assurances of seeing him again, to the same purpose, as soon as possible, and thrust a guinea into his hands: not more, lest, being too flush of money, a suspicion or discovery might arise from thence, having everything to fear from the dangerous indiscretion of that age in which young fellows would be too irresistible, too charming, if we had not that terrible fault to guard against.

HENRY FIELDING

from

Tom Jones

Henry Fielding's 'Tom Jones' was published in London in 1749. Tom is in love with Sophia. 'Her shape was not only exact, but delicate, and the nice proportion of her arms promised the truest symmetry in her limbs.' However, Sophia has a rival in 'poor Molly'.

THE citadel of Jones was now taken by surprise. All those considerations of honour and prudence which our hero had lately with so much military wisdom placed as guards over the avenues of his heart, ran away from their posts, and the god of love marched in, in triumph.

* * *

But though this victorious deity easily expelled his avowed enemies from the heart of Jones, he found it more difficult to supplant the garrison which he himself had placed there. To lay aside all allegory, the concern for what must become of poor Molly greatly disturbed and perplexed the mind of the worthy youth. The superior merit of Sophia totally eclipsed, or rather extinguished, all the beauties of the poor girl; but compassion instead of contempt succeeded to love. He was convinced the girl had placed all her affections, and all her prospect of future happiness, in him only. For this he had, he knew, given sufficient occasion, by the utmost profusion of tenderness towards her: a tenderness which he had taken every means to persuade her he would always maintain.

She, on her side, had assured him of her firm belief in his promise, and had with the most solemn vows declared, that on his fulfilling or breaking these promises, it depended, whether she should be the happiest or most miserable of womankind. And to be the author of this highest degree of misery to a human being, was a thought on which he could not bear to ruminate a single moment. He considered this poor girl as having sacrificed to him everything in her little power; as having been at her own expense the object of his pleasure; as sighing and languishing for him even at that very instant. Shall then, says he, my recovery, for which she hath so ardently wished; shall my presence, which she hath so eagerly expected, instead of giving her that joy with which she hath flattered herself, cast her at once down into misery and despair? Can I be such a villain? Here, when the genius of poor Molly seemed triumphant, the love of Sophia towards him, which now appeared no longer dubious, rushed upon his mind, and bore away every obstacle before it.

At length it occurred to him, that he might possibly be able to make Molly amends another way; namely, by giving her a sum of money. This, nevertheless, he almost despaired of her accepting, when he recollected the frequent and vehement assurances he had received from her, that the world put in balance with him would make her no amends for his loss. However, her extreme poverty, and chiefly her egregious vanity (somewhat of which hath been already hinted to the reader), gave him some little hope, that, notwithstanding all her avowed tenderness, she might in time be brought to content herself with a fortune superior to her expectation, and which might indulge her vanity, by setting her above all her equals. He resolved therefore to take the first opportunity of making a proposal of this kind.

One day, accordingly, when his arm was so well recovered that he could walk easily with it slung in a sash, he stole forth, at a season when the squire was engaged in his field exercises, and visited his fair one. Her mother and sisters, whom he found taking their tea, informed him first that Molly was not at home; but afterwards the eldest sister acquainted him, with a malicious smile, that she was above stairs a-bed. Tom had no objection to this situation of his mistress, and immediately ascended the ladder which led towards her bed-chamber; but when he came to the top, he, to his great surprise, found the door fast; nor could he for some time obtain any answer, from within; for Molly, as she herself afterwards informed him, was fast asleep.

The extremes of grief and joy have been remarked to produce very similar effects; and when either of these rushes on us by surprise, it is apt to create such a total perturbation and confusion, that we are often thereby deprived of the use of all our faculties. It cannot therefore be wondered at, that the unexpected sight of Mr Jones should so strongly operate on the mind of Molly, and should overwhelm her with such confusion, that for some minutes she was unable to express the great raptures, with which the reader will suppose she was affected on this occasion. As for Jones, he was so entirely possessed, and as it were enchanted, by the presence of his beloved object, that he for a while forgot Sophia, and consequently the principal purpose of his visit.

This, however, soon recurred to his memory; and after the first transports of their meeting were over, he found means by degrees to introduce a discourse on the fatal consequences which must attend their amour, if Mr Allworthy, who had strictly forbidden him ever seeing her more, should discover that he still carried on this commerce. Such a discovery, which his enemies gave him reason to think would be unavoidable, must, he said, end in his ruin, and consequently in hers. Since therefore their hard fates had determined that they must separate, he advised her to bear it with resolution, and swore he would never omit any opportunity, through the course of his life, of showing her the sincerity of his affection, by providing for her in a manner beyond her utmost expectation, or even beyond her wishes, if ever that should be in his power; concluding at last, that she might soon find some man who would marry her, and who would make her much happier than she could be by leading a disreputable life with him.

Molly remained a few moments in silence, and then bursting into a flood of tears, she began to upbraid him in the following words: 'And this is your love for me, to forsake me in this manner, now you have ruined me! How often, when I have told you that all men are false and perjury alike, and grow tired of us as soon as ever they have had their wicked wills of us, how often have you sworn you would never forsake me! And can you be such a perjury man after all? What signifies all the riches in the world to me without you, now you have gained my heart, so you have—you have— ? Why do you mention another man to me? I can never love any other man as long as I live. All other men are nothing to me. If the greatest squire in all the country would come a suiting to me tomorrow, I would not give my company to him. No, I shall always hate and despise the whole sex for your sake—'

She was proceeding thus, when an accident put a stop to her tongue, before it had run out half its career. The room, or rather garret, in which Molly lay, being up one pair of stairs, that is to say, at the top of the house, was of a sloping figure, resembling the great Delta of the Greeks. The English reader may perhaps form a better idea of it, by being told that it was impossible to stand upright anywhere but in the middle. Now, as this room wanted the conveniency of a closet, Molly had, to supply that defect, nailed up an old rug against the rafters of the house, which enclosed a little hole where her best apparel, such as the remains of that sack which we have formerly mentioned, some caps, and other things with which she had lately provided herself, were hung up and secured from the dust.

This enclosed place exactly fronted the foot of the bed, to which, indeed, the rug hung so near, that it served in a manner to supply the want of curtains. Now, whether Molly, in the agonies of her rage, pushed this rug with her feet; or Jones might touch it; or whether the pin or nail gave way of its own accord, I am not certain; but as Molly pronounced those last words, which are recorded above, the wicked rug got loose from its fastening, and discovered everything hid behind it; where among other female utensils appeared—with shame I write it, and with sorrow will it be read—the philosopher Square, in a posture (for the place would not near admit his standing upright) as ridiculous as can possibly be conceived.

The posture, indeed, in which he stood, was not greatly unlike that of a soldier who is tied neck and heels; or rather resembling the attitude in which we often see fellows in the public streets of London, who are not suffering but deserving punishment by so standing. He had a nightcap belonging to Molly on his head, and his two large eyes, the moment the rug fell, stared directly at Jones; so that when the idea of philosophy was added to the figure now discovered, it would have been very difficult for any spectator to have refrained from immoderate laughter.

I question not but the surprise of the reader will be here equal to that of Jones; as the suspicions which must arise from the appearance of this wise and grave man in such a place, may seem so inconsistent with that character which he hath, doubtless, maintained hitherto, in the opinion of every one.

But to confess the truth, this inconsistency is rather imaginary than real. Philosophers are composed of flesh and blood as well as other human creatures; and however sublimated and refined the theory of these may be, a little practical frailty is as incident to them as to other mortals. It is, indeed, in theory only, and not in practice, as we have before hinted, that consists the difference: for though such great beings think much better and more wisely, they always act exactly like other men. They know very well how to subdue all appetites and passions, and to despise both pain and pleasure; and this knowledge affords much delightful contemplation, and is easily acquired; but the practice would be vexatious and trouble-some; and, therefore, the same wisdom which teaches them to know this, teaches them to avoid carrying it into execution.

Mr Square happened to be at church on that Sunday, when, as the reader may be pleased to remember, the appearance of Molly in her sack had caused all that disturbance. Here he first observed her, and was so pleased with her beauty, that he prevailed with the young gentlemen to change their intended ride that evening, that he might pass by the habitation of Molly, and by that means might obtain a second chance of seeing her. This reason, however, as he did not at that time mention to any, so neither did we think proper to communicate it then to the reader.

Among other particulars which constituted the unfitness of things in Mr Square's opinion, danger and difficulty were two. The difficulty therefore which he apprehended there might be in corrupting this young wench, and the danger which would accrue to his character on the discovery, were such strong dissuasives, that it is probable he at first intended to have contented himself with the pleasing ideas which the sight of beauty furnishes us with. These the gravest men, after a full meal of serious meditation, often allow themselves by way of dessert: for which purpose, certain books and pictures find their way into the most private recesses of their study, and a certain liquorish part of natural philosophy is often the principal subject of their conversation.

But when the philosopher heard, a day or two afterwards, that the fortress of virtue had already been subdued, he began to give a larger scope to his desires. His appetite was not of that squeamish kind which cannot feed on a dainty because another hath tasted it. In short, he liked the girl the better for the want of that chastity, which, if she had possessed it, must have been a bar to his pleasures; he pursued and obtained her.

The reader will be mistaken, if he thinks Molly gave Square the preference to her younger lover: on the contrary, had she been confined to the choice of one only, Tom Jones would undoubtedly have been, of the two, the victorious person. Nor was it solely the consideration that two are better than one (though this had its proper weight) to which Mr Square owed his success: the absence of Jones during his confinement was an unlucky circumstance; and in that interval some well-chosen presents from the philosopher so softened and unguarded the girl's heart, that a favourable opportunity became irresistible, and Square triumphed over the poor remains of virtue which subsisted in the bosom of Molly.

It was now about a fortnight since this conquest, when Jones paid the above-mentioned visit to his mistress, at a time when she and Square were in bed together. This was the true reason why the mother denied her as we have seen; for as the old woman shared in the profits arising from the iniquity of her daughter, she encouraged and protected her in it to the utmost of her power; but such was the envy and hatred which the elder sister bore towards Molly, that, notwithstanding she had some part of the booty, she would willingly have parted with this to ruin her sister and spoil her trade. Hence she had acquainted Jones with her being above-stairs in bed, in hopes that he might have caught her in Square's arms. This, however, Molly found means to prevent, as the door was fastened; which gave her an opportunity of conveying her lover behind that rug or blanket where he now was unhappily discovered.

Square no sooner made his appearance than Molly flung herself back in her bed, cried out she was undone, and abandoned herself to despair. This poor girl, who was yet but a novice in her business, had not arrived to that perfection of assurance which helps off a town lady in any extremity; and either prompts her with an excuse, or else inspires her to brazen out the matter with her husband, who, from love of quiet, or out of fear of his reputation— and sometimes, perhaps, from fear of the gallant, who, like Mr Constant in the play, wears a sword—is glad to shut his eyes, and content to put his horns in his pocket. Molly, on the contrary, was silenced by this evidence, and very fairly gave up a cause which she had hitherto maintained with so many tears, and with such solemn and vehement protestations of the purest love and constancy.

As to the gentleman behind the arras, he was not in much less consternation. He stood for a while motionless, and seemed equally at a loss what to say, or whither to direct his eyes. Jones, though perhaps the most astonished of the three, first found his tongue; and being immediately recovered from those uneasy sensations which Molly by her upbraidings had occasioned, he burst into a loud laughter, and then saluting Mr Square, advanced to take him by the hand, and to relieve him from his place of confinement.

Square being now arrived in the middle of the room, in which part only he could stand upright, looked at Jones with a very grave countenance, and said to him, 'Well, sir, I see you enjoy this mighty discovery, and, I dare swear, take great delight in the thoughts of exposing me; but if you will consider the matter fairly, you will find you are yourself only to blame. I am not guilty of corrupting innocence. I have done nothing for which that part of the world which judges of matters by the rule of right, will condemn me. Fitness is governed by the nature of things, and not by customs, forms, or municipal laws. Nothing is indeed unfit which is not unnatural.'—'Well reasoned, old boy,' answered Jones; 'but why dost thou think that I should desire to expose thee? I promise thee, I was never better pleased with thee in my life; and unless thou hast a mind to discover it thyself, this affair may remain a profound secret for me.'—'Nay, Mr Jones,' replied Square, 'I would not be thought to under-value reputation. Good fame is a species of the Kalon, and it is by no means fitting to neglect it. Besides, to murder one's own reputation is a kind of suicide, a detestable and odious vice. If you think proper, therefore, to conceal any infirmity of mine (for such I may have, since no man is perfectly perfect), I promise you I will not betray myself. Things may be fitting to be done, which are not fitting to be boasted of; for by the perverse judgment of the world, that often becomes the subject of censure, which is, in truth, not only innocent but laudable.'—'Right!' cries Jones. 'What can be more innocent than the indulgence of a natural appetite? or what more laudable than the propagation of our species?'—'To be serious with you,' answered Square, 'I profess they always appeared so to me.'— 'And yet,' said Jones, 'you was of a different opinion when my affair with this girl was first discovered.'—'Why, I must confess,' says Square, 'as the matter was misrepresented to me, by that parson Thwackum, I might condemn the corruption of innocence: it was that, sir, it was that—and that—for you must know, Mr Jones, in the consideration of fitness, very minute circumstances, sir, very minute circumstances cause great alteration.'—'Well,' cries Jones, 'be that as it will, it shall be your own fault, as I have promised you, if you ever hear any more of this adventure. Behave kindly to the girl, and I will never open my lips concerning the matter to any one. And, Molly, do you be faithful to your friend, and I will not only forgive your infidelity to me, but will do you all the service I can.' So saying, he took a hasty leave, and, slipping down the ladder, retired with much expedition.

Square was rejoiced to find this adventure was likely to have no worse conclusion; and as for Molly, being recovered from her confusion, she began at first to upbraid Square with having been the occasion of her loss of Jones; but that gentleman soon found the means of mitigating her anger, partly by caresses, and partly by a small nostrum from his purse, of wonderful and approved efficacy in purging off the ill humours of the mind, and in restoring it to a good temper.

She then poured forth a vast profusion of tenderness towards her new lover; turned all she had said to Jones, and Jones himself, into ridicule; and vowed, though he once had the possession of her person, that none but Square had ever been master of her heart.

*   *   *

The infidelity of Molly, which Jones had now discovered, would, perhaps have vindicated a much greater degree of resentment than he expressed on the occasion; and if he had abandoned her directly from that moment, very few, I believe, would have blamed him.

Certain, however, it is, that he saw her in the light of compassion; and though his love to her was not of that kind which could give him any great uneasiness at her inconstancy, yet was he not a little shocked on reflecting that he had himself originally corrupted her innocence; for to this corruption he imputed all the vice into which she appeared now so likely to plunge herself.

This consideration gave him no little uneasiness, till Betty, the elder sister, was so kind, some time afterwards, entirely to cure him by a hint, that one Will Barnes, and not himself, had been the first seducer of Molly; and that the little child, which he had hitherto so certainly concluded to be his own, might very probably have an equal title, at least to claim Barnes for its father.

Jones eagerly pursued this scent when he had first received it; and in a very short time was sufficiently assured that the girl had told him truth, not only by the confession of the fellow, but at last by that of Molly herself.

This Will Barnes was a country gallant, and had acquired as many trophies of this kind as any ensign or attorney's clerk in the kingdom. He had, indeed, reduced several women to a state of utter profligacy, had broke the hearts of some, and had the honour of occasioning the violent death of one poor girl, who had either drowned herself or, what was rather more probable, had been drowned by him.

Among other of his conquests, this fellow had triumphed over the heart of Betty Seagrim. He had made love to her long before Molly was grown to be a fit object of that pastime; but had afterwards deserted her, and applied to her sister, with whom he had almost immediate success. Now Will had, in reality, the sole possession of Molly's affection, while Jones and Square were almost equally sacrifices to her interest and to her pride.

Hence had grown that implacable hatred which we have before seen raging in the mind of Betty; though we did not think it necessary to assign that cause sooner, as envy itself alone was adequate to all the effects we have mentioned.

Jones was become perfectly easy by possession of this secret with regard to Molly; but as to Sophia, he was far from being in a state of tranquillity; nay, indeed, he was under the most violent perturbation; his heart was now, if I may use the metaphor, entirely evacuated, and Sophia took absolute possession of it. He loved her with an unbounded passion, and plainly saw the tender sentiments she had for him; yet could not this assurance lessen his despair of obtaining the consent of her father, nor the horrors which attended his pursuit of her by any base or treacherous method.

The injury which he must thus do to Mr Western, and the concern which would accrue to Mr Allworthy, were circumstances that tormented him all day, and haunted him on his pillow at night. His life was a constant struggle between honour and inclination, which alternately triumphed over each other in his mind. He often resolved, in the absence of Sophia, to leave her father's house, and to see her no more; and as often, in her presence, forgot all those resolutions, and determined to pursue her at the hazard of his life, and at the forfeiture of what was much dearer to him.

This conflict began soon to produce very strong and visible effects: for he lost all his usual sprightliness and gaiety of temper, and became not only melancholy when alone, but dejected and absent in company; nay, if ever he put on a forced mirth, to comply with Mr Western's humour, the constraint appeared so plain, that he seemed to have been giving the strongest evidence of what he endeavoured to conceal by such ostentation.

It may, perhaps, be a question, whether the art which he used to conceal his passion, or the means which honest nature employed to reveal it, betrayed him most: for while art made him more than ever reserved to Sophia, and forbad him to address any of his discourse to her, nay, to avoid meeting her eyes, with the utmost caution; nature was no less busy in counter-plotting him. Hence, at the approach of the young lady, he grew pale; and if this was sudden, started. If his eyes accidentally met hers, the blood rushed into his cheeks, and his countenance became all over scarlet. If common civility ever obliged him to speak to her, as to drink her health at table, his tongue was sure to falter. If he touched her, his hand, nay his whole frame, trembled. And if any discourse tended, however remotely, to raise the idea of love, an involuntary sigh seldom failed to steal from his bosom. Most of which accidents nature was wonderfully industrious to throw daily in his way.

All these symptoms escaped the notice of the squire: but not so of Sophia. She soon perceived these agitations of mind in Jones, and was at no loss to discover the cause; for indeed she recognized it in her own breast. And this recognition is, I suppose, that sympathy which hath been so often noted in lovers, and which will sufficiently account for her being so much quicker-sighted than her father.

But, to say the truth, there is a more simple and plain method of accounting for that prodigious superiority of penetration which we must observe in some men over the rest of the human species, and one which will serve not only in the case of lovers, but of all others. From whence is it that the knave is generally so quick-sighted to those symptoms and operations of knavery, which often dupe an honest man of a much better understanding? There surely is no general sympathy among knaves; nor have they, like freemasons, any common sign of communication. In reality, it is only because they have the same thing in their heads, and their thoughts are turned the same way. Thus, that Sophia saw, and that Western did not see, the plain symptoms of love in Jones can be no wonder, when we consider that the idea of love never entered into the head of the father, whereas the daughter, at present, thought of nothing else.

When Sophia was well satisfied of the violent passion which tormented poor Jones, and no less certain that she herself was its object, she had not the least difficulty in discovering the true cause of his present behaviour. This highly endeared him to her, and raised in her mind two of the best affections which any lover can wish to raise in a mistress—these were, esteem and pity—for sure the most outrageously rigid among her sex will excuse her pitying a man whom she saw miserable on her own account; nor can they blame her for esteeming one who visibly, from the most honourable motives, endeavoured to smother a flame in his own bosom, which, like the famous Spartan theft, was preying upon and consuming his very vitals. Thus his backwardness, his shunning her, his coldness, and his silence, were the forwardest, the most diligent, the warmest, and most eloquent advocates; and wrought so violently on her sensible and tender heart, that she soon felt for him all those gentle sensations which are consistent with a virtuous and elevated female mind; in short, all which esteem, gratitude, and pity, can inspire in such towards an agreeable man—indeed, all which the nicest delicacy can allow. In a word, she was in love with him to distraction.

One day this young couple accidentally met in the garden, at the end of the two walks which were both bounded by that canal in which Jones had formerly risqued drowning to retrieve the little bird that Sophia had there lost.

This place had been of late much frequented by Sophia. Here she used to ruminate, with a mixture of pain and pleasure, on an incident which, however trifling in itself, had possibly sown the first seeds of that affection which was now arrived to such maturity in her heart.

Here then this young couple met. They were almost close together before either of them knew anything of the other's approach. A bystander would have discovered sufficient marks of confusion in the countenance of each; but they felt too much themselves to make any observation. As soon as Jones had a little recovered his first surprise, he accosted the young lady with some of the ordinary forms of salutation, which she in the same manner returned; and their conversation began, as usual, on the delicious beauty of the morning. Hence they past to the beauty of the place, on which Jones launched forth very high encomiums. When they came to the tree whence he had formerly tumbled into the canal, Sophia could not help reminding him of that accident, and said, 'I fancy, Mr Jones, you have some little shuddering when you see that water.'—'I assure you, madam,' answered Jones, 'the concern you felt at the loss of your little bird will always appear to me the highest circumstance in that adventure. Poor little Tommy! there is the branch he stood upon. How could the little wretch have the folly to fly away from that state of happiness in which I had the honour to place him? His fate was a just punishment for his ingratitude.'—'Upon my word, Mr Jones,' said she, 'your gallantry very narrowly escaped as severe a fate. Sure the remembrance must affect you.'—'Indeed, madam,' answered he, 'if I have any reason to reflect with sorrow on it, it is, perhaps, that the water had not been a little deeper, by which I might have escaped many bitter heart-aches that Fortune seems to have in store for me.'— 'Fie, Mr Jones!' replied Sophia; 'I am sure you cannot be in earnest now. This affected contempt of life is only an excess of your complacence to me. You would endeavour to lessen the obligation of having twice ventured it for my sake. Beware the third time.' She spoke these last words with a smile, and a softness inexpressible. Jones answered with a sigh, 'He feared it was already too late for caution'; and then looking tenderly and steadfastly on her, he cried, 'Oh, Miss Western! can you desire me to live? Can you wish me so ill?' Sophia, looking down on the ground, answered with some hesitation, 'Indeed, Mr Jones, I do not wish you ill.'—'Oh, I know too well that heavenly temper,' cries Jones, 'that divine goodness, which is beyond every other charm.'—'Nay, now,' answered she, 'I understand you not. I can stay no longer.'—'I— I would not be understood!' cries he; 'nay, I can't be understood. I know not what I say. Meeting you here so unexpectedly, I have been unguarded: for Heaven's sake pardon me, if I have said anything to offend you. I did not mean it. Indeed, I would rather have died—nay, the very thought would kill me.'—'You surprise me,' answered she. 'How can you possibly think you have offended me?'—'Fear, madam,' says he, 'easily runs into madness; and there is no degree of fear like that which I feel of offending you. How can I speak then? Nay, don't look angrily at me; one frown will destroy me. I mean nothing. Blame my eyes, or blame those beauties. What am I saying? Pardon me if I have said too much. My heart overflowed. I have struggled with my love to the utmost, and have endeavoured to conceal a fever which preys on my vitals, and will, I hope, soon make it impossible for me ever to offend you more.'

Mr Jones now fell a trembling as if he had been shaken with the fit of an ague. Sophia, who was in a situation not very different from his, answered in these words: 'Mr Jones, I will not affect to misunderstand you; indeed, I understand you too well; but, for Heaven's sake, if you have any affection for me, let me make the best of my way into the house. I wish I may be able to support myself thither.'

Jones, who was hardly able to support himself, offered her his arm, which she condescended to accept, but begged he would not mention a word more to her of this nature at present. He promised he would not; insisting only on her forgiveness of what love, without the leave of his will, had forced from him: this, she told him, he knew how to obtain by his future behaviour; and thus this young pair tottered and trembled along, the lover not once daring to squeeze the hand of his mistress, though it was locked in his.

CHODERLOS DE LACLOS

from

Les Liaisons Dangereuses

Letters from the Vicomte de Valmont
to the Marquise de Merteuil

Choderlos de Laclos wrote 'Les Liaisons Dangereuses' in 1782. It tells, through letters, of the Vicomte de Valmont's ruthless seduction of a beautiful, innocent young woman.

IT was not until Saturday that she came circling about me and stammered a few words; but spoken in so low a tone and so stifled by shame, that it was impossible for me to hear them. But the blushing they caused allowed me to guess their sense. Up till then I had remained proud; but softened by so amusing a repentance I promised to go to the pretty penitent the same evening; and this grace on my part was received with all the gratitude due to so great a benefit.

As I never lose sight of your plans or of mine, I resolve to profit by this occasion to find out exactly what the child is worth and to accelerate her education. But to carry out this labour with more liberty, I needed to change the place of our rendez-vous; for a mere closet, which separated your pupil's room from her mother's, could not inspire her with sufficient confidence to allow her to display herself freely. I had therefore promised myself to make some noise 'innocently', which would cause her sufficient fear to persuade her to take a surer refuge in the future; she spared me that trouble too.

The little person laughs easily; and to encourage her gaiety I

related to her, during our intervals, all the scandalous adventures
which came into my head; and to make them more attractive and
the better to hold attention, I laid them all to the credit of her
Mamma; whom I amused myself in this way by covering with
vices and ridicule.

It was not without reason that I made this choice; it encouraged
my timid pupil better than anything else and at the same time
inspired her with a most profound contempt for her mother. I
have long noticed that, if this method is not always necessary for
seducing a girl, it is indispensable and often the most efficacious
way, when you wish to deprave her; for she who does not respect
her mother will not respect herself, a moral truth which I think so
useful that I was very glad to furnish an example in support of the
precept.

However, your pupil, who was not thinking of morality, was
suffocated with laughter every instant; and at last she once almost
laughed out loud. I had no difficulty in making her believe that she
had made 'a terrible noise'. I feigned a great terror which she
easily shared. To make her remember it better I did not allow
pleasure to reappear, and left her alone three hours earlier than
usual; so, on separating, we agreed that from the next day onwards
the meeting should be in my room.

I have received her there twice; and in this short space the
scholar has become almost as learned as the master. Yes, truly, I
have taught her everything, including the complaisances! I only
excepted the precautions.

Occupied thus all night, I make up for it by sleeping a large part
of the day; and as the present society of the *Château* has nothing to
attract me, I scarcely appear in the drawing-room for an hour
during the day. Today I even decided to eat in my room and I
only mean to leave it after this for short walks. These fantasies are
supposed to be on account of my health. I declared that I was
'overcome with vapours'; I also announced that I was rather fever-
ish. It costs me nothing but the speaking in a slow, colourless voice.
As to the change in my face, rely upon your pupil. 'Love will see

to that'. I spend my leisure in thinking of means to regain my ungracious lady, of the advantages I have lost, and also in composing a kind of catechism of sensuality for the use of my scholar. I amuse myself by naming everything by the technical word; and I laugh in advance at the interesting conversation this will furnish between her and Gercourt on the first night of their marriage. Nothing could be more amusing than the ingeniousness with which she already uses the little she knows of this speech! She does not imagine that anyone can speak otherwise. The child is really seductive! The contrast of naïve candour with the language of effrontery makes a great effect; and, I do not know why, only fantastic things please me now.

* * *

She is conquered, that proud woman who dared to think she could resist me! Yes, my friend, she is mine, entirely mine; after yesterday she has nothing left to grant me.

I am still too full of my happiness to be able to appreciate it, but I am astonished by the unsuspected charm I felt. Is it true then that virtue increases a woman's value even in her moment of weakness—But let me put that puerile idea away with old woman's tales. Does one not meet almost everywhere a more or less well-feigned resistance to the first triumph? And have I not found elsewhere the charm of which I speak? But yet it is not the charm of love; for after all, if I have sometimes had surprising moments of weakness with this woman resembling that pusillanimous passion, I have always been able to overcome them and return to my principles. Even if yesterday's scene carried me, as I now think, a little further than I intended; even if I shared for a moment the agitation and ecstasy I created; that passing illusion would now have disappeared, and yet the same charm remains. I confess I should even feel a considerable pleasure in yielding to it, if it did not cause me some anxiety. Shall I, at my age, be mastered like a schoolboy, by an involuntary and unsuspected sentiment? No; before everything else, I must combat and thoroughly examine it.

And perhaps I have already a glimpse of the cause of it! At least the idea pleases me and I should like it to be true.

Among the crowd of women for whom I have hitherto filled the part and functions of a lover, I had never met one who had not at least as much desire to yield to me as I had to bring her to doing so; I had even accustomed myself to call 'prudes' those who only came half way to meet me, in opposition to so many others whose provocative defence never covers but imperfectly the first advances they have made.

Here on the contrary I found a first unfavourable prejudice, supported afterwards by the advice and reports of a woman who hated me but who was clear-sighted; I found a natural and extreme timidity strengthened by an enlightened modesty; I found an attachment to virtue, controlled by religion, able to count two years of triumph already, and then remarkable behaviour inspired by different motives but all with the object of avoiding my pursuit.

It was not then, as in my other adventures, a merely more or less advantageous capitulation which it is more easy to profit by than to feel proud of; it was a complete victory achieved by a hard campaign and decided by expert manoeuvres. It is therefore not surprising that this success, which I owe to myself alone, should become more valuable to me; and the excess of pleasure I feel even yet is only the soft impression of the feeling of glory. I cling to this view which saves me from the humiliation of thinking I might depend in any way upon the very slave I have enslaved myself; that I do not contain the plenitude of my happiness in myself; and that the faculty of enjoying it in all its energy should be reserved to such or such a woman, exclusive of all others.

These sensible reflections shall guide my conduct in this important occasion; and you may be sure I shall not allow myself to be so enchained that I cannot break these new ties at any time, by playing with them, and at my will. But I am already talking to you of breaking off and you still do not know the methods by which I acquired the right to do so; read then, and see what wisdom is exposed to in trying to help folly. I observed my words and the replies I obtained so carefully that I hope to be able to report both with an exactness which will content you.

You will see by the copies of the two enclosed letters who was the mediator I chose to bring me back to my fair one and what zeal the holy person used to unite us. What I must still inform you of—a thing I learned from a letter intercepted as usual—is that the fear and little humiliation of being abandoned had rather upset the austere devotee's prudence and had filled her heart and head with sentiments and ideas which, though they lacked common sense, were none the less important. It was after these preliminaries, necessary for you to know, that yesterday, Thursday, the 28th, a day fixed beforehand by the ungrateful person herself, that I presented myself before her as a timid and repentant slave, and left a crowned conqueror.

It was six o'clock in the evening when I arrived at the fair recluse's house, for, since her return, her doors have been shut to everyone. She tried to rise when I was announced; but her trembling knees did not allow her to remain in that position: she sat down at once. As the servant who had brought me in had some duty to perform in the room, she seemed to be made impatient by it. We filled up this interval with the customary compliments. But not to lose any time, every moment of which was precious, I carefully examined the locality; and there and then I noted with my eyes the theatre of my victory. I might have chosen a more convenient one, for there was an ottoman in the same room. But I noticed that opposite it there was a portrait of her husband; and I confess I was afraid that with such a singular woman one glance accidently directed that way might destroy in a moment the work of so many exertions. At last we were left alone and I began.

After having pointed out in a few words that Father Anselme must have informed her of the reasons for my visit, I complained of the rigorous treatment I had received from her; and I particularly dwelt upon the 'contempt' which had been shown me. She defended herself, as I expected; and as you would have expected too, I founded the proofs of it on the suspicion and fear I had inspired, on the scandalous flight which had followed upon them, the refusal to answer my letters, and even the refusal to receive them, etc., etc. As she was beginning a justification (which would have been very easy) I thought I had better interrupt; and to obtain forgiveness for this brusque manner I covered it immediately by a flattery: 'If so many charms have made an impression on my heart,' I went on, 'so many virtues have made no less a mark upon my soul. Seduced no doubt by the idea of approaching them I dared to think myself worthy of doing so. I do not reproach you for having thought otherwise; but I am punished for my error.' As she remained in an embarrassed silence, I continued: 'I desired, Madame, either to justify myself in your eyes or to obtain from you forgiveness for the wrongs you think I have committed, so that at least I can end in some peace the days to which I no longer attach any value since you have refused to embellish them.'

Here she tried to reply, however: 'My duty did not permit me.' And the difficulty of finishing the lie which duty exacted did not permit her to finish the phrase. I therefore went on in the most tender tones: 'It is true then that it was from me you fled?' 'My departure was necessary.' 'And what took you away from me?' 'It was necessary.' 'And for ever?' 'It must be so.' I do not need to tell you that during this short dialogue the tender prude was in a state of oppression and her eyes were not raised to me.

I felt I ought to animate this languishing scene a little; so getting up with an air of pique, I said: 'Your firmness restores me all of my own. Yes, Madame, we shall be separated, separated even more than you think; and you shall congratulate yourself upon your handiwork at leisure.' She was a little surprised by this tone of reproach and tried to answer. 'The resolution you have taken . . .' said she. 'Is only the result of my despair,' I replied with vehemence. 'It is your will that I should be unhappy; I will prove to you that you have succeeded even beyond your wishes.' 'I desire your happiness,' she answered. And the tone of her voice began to show a rather strong emotion. So, throwing myself at her feet, I exclaimed in that dramatic tone of mine you know: 'Ah! cruel woman, can there exist any happiness for me which you do not share? Ah! Never! Never!' I confess that at this point I had greatly been relying on the aid of tears; but either from a wrong disposition or perhaps only from the painful and continual attention I was giving to everything, it was impossible for me to weep.

Fortunately I remembered that any method is equally good in subjugating a woman, and that it sufficed to astonish her with a great emotion for the impression to remain both deep and favourable. I made up therefore by terror for the sensibility I found lacking; and with that purpose, only changing the inflection of my voice and remaining in the same position, I continued: 'Yes, I make an oath at your feet, to possess you or die.' As I spoke the last words our eyes met. I do not know what the timid person saw or thought she saw in mine, but she rose with a terrified air, and escaped from my arms, which I had thrown round her. It is true I did nothing to detain her; for I have several times noticed that scenes of despair carried out too vividly become ridiculous as soon as they become long, or leave nothing but really tragic resources which I was very far from desiring to adopt. However, as she escaped from me, I added in a low and sinister tone, but loud enough for her to hear: 'Well, then! Death!'

I then got up; and after a moment of silence I cast wild glances upon her which, however much they seemed to wander, were none the less clear-sighted and observant. Her ill-assured bearing, her quick breathing, the contraction of all her muscles, her trembling half-raised arms, all proved to me that the result was such as I had desired to produce; but, since in love nothing is concluded except at very close quarters, and we were rather far apart, it was above all things necessary to get closer together. To achieve this, I passed as quickly as possible to an apparent tranquillity, likely to calm the effects of this violent state, without weakening its impression.

My transition was: 'I am very unfortunate. I wished to live for your happiness, and I have disturbed it. I sacrifice myself for your tranquillity, and I disturb it again.' Then in a composed but restrained way: 'Forgive me, Madame; I am little accustomed to the storms of passion and can repress their emotions but ill. If I am wrong to yield to them, remember at least that it is for the last time. Ah! Calm yourself, calm yourself, I beseech you.' And during this long speech, I came gradually nearer. 'If you wish me to be calm,' said the startled beauty, 'you must yourself be more tranquil.' 'Well, then, I promise it,' said I. And I added in a weaker voice: 'If the effort is great, at least it will not be for long. But,' I went on immediately in a distraught way, 'I came, did I not, to return you your letters? I beg you, deign to receive them back. This painful sacrifice remained for me to accomplish; leave me nothing that can weaken my courage.' And taking the precious collection from my pocket, I said: 'There it is, that deceitful collection of assurances of your friendship! It attached me to life,' I went on. 'So give the signal yourself which must separate me from you for ever.'

Here the frightened Mistress yielded entirely to her tender anxiety. 'But, M. de Valmont, what is the matter, and what do you mean? Is not the step you are taking today a voluntary one? Is it not the fruit of your own reflections? And are they not those which have made you yourself approve the necessary course I adopted from a sense of duty?' 'Well,' I replied, 'that course decided mine.' 'And what is that?' 'The only one which, in separating me from you, can put an end to my own.' 'But tell me, what is it?' Then I clasped her in my arms, without her defending herself in the least; and, judging from this forgetfulness of conventions, how strong and powerful her emotion was, I said, risking a tone of enthusiasm: 'Adorable woman, you have no idea of the love you inspire; you will never know to what extent you were adored, and how much this sentiment is dearer to me than my existence! May all your days be fortunate and tranquil; may they be embellished by all the happiness of which you have deprived me! At least reward this sincere wish with a regret, with a tear; and believe that the last of my sacrifices will not be the most difficult for my heart. Farewell.'

While I was speaking, I felt her heart beating violently; I observed the change in her face; I saw above all that she was suffocated by tears but that only a few painful ones flowed. It was at that moment only that I feigned to go away; but, detaining me by force, she said quickly: 'No, listen to me.' 'Let me go,' I answered. 'You will listen to me, I wish it.' 'I must fly from you, I must.' 'No,' she cried. At this last word she rushed or rather fell into my arms in a swoon. As I still doubted of so lucky a success, I feigned a great terror; but with all my terror I guided, or rather, carried her towards the place designed beforehand as the field of my glory; and indeed she only came to her senses submissive and already yielded to her happy conqueror.

Hitherto, my fair friend, I think you will find I adopted a purity of method which will please you; and you will see that I have departed in no respect from the true principles of this war, which we have often remarked is so like the other. Judge me then as you would Frederic or Turenne. I forced the enemy to fight when she wished only to refuse battle; by clever manoeuvres I obtained the choice of battlefield and of dispositions; I inspired the enemy with confidence, to overtake her more easily in her retreat; I was able to make terror succeed confidence before joining battle; I left nothing to chance except from consideration of a great advantage in case of success and from the certainty of other resources in case of defeat; finally, I only joined action when I had an assured retreat by which I could cover and retain all I had conquered before. I think that is everything that can be done; but now I am afraid of growing softened in the delights of Capua, like Hannibal. This is what happened afterwards.

I expected so great an event would not take place without the usual tears and despair; and if I noticed at first a little more confusion, and a kind of interior meditation, I attributed both to her prudishness; so, without troubling about these slight differences which I thought were purely local, I simply followed the highroad of consolations; being well persuaded that, as usually happens, sensations would aid sentiment, and that a single action would do more than all the words in the world, which however, I did not neglect. But I found a really frightening resistance, less from its excess than from the manner in which it showed itself.

Imagine a woman seated, immovably still and with an unchanging face, appearing neither to think, hear, or listen; a woman whose fixed eyes flowed with quite continual tears which came without effort. Such was Madame de Tourvel while I was speaking; but if I tried to recall her attention to me by a caress, even by the most innocent gesture, immediately there succeeded to this apparent apathy, terror, suffocation, convulsions, sobs, and at intervals a cry, but all without one word articulated.

These crises returned several times and always with more strength; the last was so violent that I was entirely discouraged and for a moment feared I had gained a useless victory. I fell back on the usual commonplaces, and among them was this: 'Are you in despair because you have made me happy?' At these words the adorable woman turned towards me; and her face, although still a little distraught, had yet regained its heavenly expression. 'Your happiness!' said she. You can guess my reply. 'You are happy then?' I redoubled my protestations. 'And happy through me?' I added praises and tender words. While she was speaking, all her limbs relaxed; she fell back limply, resting on her armchair; and abandoning to me a hand which I had dared to take, she said: 'I feel that idea console and relieve me.'

You may suppose that having found my path thus, I did not leave it again; it was really the right, and perhaps the only one. So when I wished to attempt a second victory I found some resistance at first, and what had passed before made me circumspect; but having called to my aid that same idea of happiness I soon found its results favourable. 'You are right,' said the tender creature, 'I cannot endure my existence except as it may serve to make you happy. I give myself wholly up to it; from this moment I give myself to you and you will experience neither refusals nor regret from me.'

It was with this naïve or sublime candour that she surrendered to me her person and her charms, and that she increased my happiness by sharing it. The ecstasy was complete and mutual; and, for the first time, my own outlasted the pleasure. I only left her arms to fall at her knees, to swear an eternal love to her; and, I must admit it, I believed what I said. Even when we separated, the idea of her did not leave me and I had to make an effort to distract myself.

MARQUIS DE SADE

from

Justine

or Good Conduct Well Chastised

Donatien-Alphonse-Francois de Sade, the Marquis de Sade, wrote 'Justine' in 1791. It has caused outrage ever since.

I HAD about me a woman, probably forty years old, as celebrated for her beauty as for the variety and number of her villainies; she was called Dubois and, like the unlucky Thérèse, was on the eve of paying the capital penalty, but as to the exact form of it the judges were yet mightily perplexed: having rendered herself guilty of every imaginable crime, they found themselves virtually obliged to invent a new torture for her, or to expose her to one whence we ordinarily exempt our sex. This woman had become interested in me, criminally interested without doubt, since the basis of her feelings, as I learned afterward, was her extreme desire to make a proselyte of me.

Only two days from the time set for our execution, Dubois came to me; it was at night. She told me not to lie down to sleep, but to stay near her side. Without attracting attention, we moved as close as we could to the prison door. 'Between seven and eight,' she said, 'the Conciergerie will catch fire, I have seen to it; no question about it, many people will be burned; it doesn't matter, Thérèse,' the evil creature went on, 'the fate of others must always be as nothing to us when our own lives are at stake; well, we are going to escape here, of that you can be sure; four men—my confederates—will join us and I guarantee you we will be free.'

I have told you, Madame, that the hand of God which had just punished my innocence, employed crime to protect me; the fire began, it spread, the blaze was horrible, twenty-one persons were consumed, but we made a successful sally. The same day we reached the cottage of a poacher, an intimate friend of our band who dwelt in the forest of Bondy.

'There you are, Thérèse,' Dubois says to me, 'free. You may now choose the kind of life you wish, but were I to have any advice to give you, it would be to renounce the practice of virtue which, as you have noticed, is the courting of disaster; a misplaced delicacy led you to the foot of the scaffold, an appalling crime rescued you from it; have a look about and see how useful are good deeds in this world, and whether it is really worth the trouble immolating yourself for them. Thérèse, you are young and attractive, heed me, and in two years I'll have led you to a fortune; but don't suppose I am going to guide you there along the paths of virtue: when one wants to get on, my dear girl, one must stop at nothing; decide, then, we have no security in this cottage, we've got to leave in a few hours.'

'Oh Madame,' I said to my benefactress, 'I am greatly indebted to you, and am far from wishing to disown my obligations; you saved my life; in my view, 'tis frightful the thing was achieved through a crime and, believe me, had I been the one charged to commit it, I should have preferred a thousand deaths to the anguish of participating in it; I am aware of all the dangers I risk in trusting myself to the honest sentiments which will always remain in my heart; but whatever be the thorns of virtue, Madame, I prefer them unhesitatingly and always to the perilous favours which are crime's accompaniment. There are religious principles within me which, may it please Heaven, will never desert me; if Providence renders difficult my career in life, 'tis in order to compensate me in a better world. That hope is my consolation, it sweetens my griefs, it soothes me in my sufferings, it fortifies me in distress, and causes me confidently to face all the ills it pleases

God to visit upon me. That joy should straightway be extinguished in my soul were I perchance to besmirch it with crime, and together with the fear of chastisements in this world I should have the painful anticipation of torments in the next, which would not for one instant procure me the tranquillity I thirst after.'

'Those are absurd doctrines which will have you on the dung heap in no time, my girl,' said Dubois with a frown; 'believe me: forget God's justice, His future punishments and rewards, the lot of those platitudes lead us nowhere but to death from starvation. O Thérèse, the callousness of the Rich legitimates the bad conduct of the Poor; let them open their purse to our needs, let humaneness reign in their hearts and virtues will take root in ours; but as long as our misfortune, our patient endurance of it, our good faith, our abjection only serves to double the weight of our chains, our crimes will be their doing, and we will be fools indeed to abstain from them when they can lessen the yoke wherewith their cruelty bears us down. Nature has caused us all to be equals born, Thérèse; if fate is pleased to upset the primary scheme of the general law, it is up to us to correct its caprices and through our skill to repair the usurpations of the strongest. I love to hear these rich ones, these titled ones, these magistrates and these priests, I love to see them preach virtue to us. It is not very difficult to forswear theft when one has three or four times what one needs to live; it is not very necessary to plot murder when one is surrounded by nothing but adulators and thralls unto whom one's will is law; nor is it very hard to be temperate and sober when one has the most succulent dainties constantly within one's reach; they can well contrive to be sincere when there is never any apparent advantage in falsehood . . . But we, Thérèse, we whom the barbaric Providence you are mad enough to idolize, has condemned to slink in the dust of humiliation as doth the serpent in grass, we who are beheld with disdain only because we are poor, who are tyrannized because we are weak; we who must quench our thirst with gall and who, wherever we go tread on the thistle always, you would have us shun crime when its hand alone opens up unto us the door to life, maintains us in it, and is our only protection when our life is threatened; you would have it that, degraded and in perpetual abjection, while this class dominating us has to itself all the blessings of fortune, we reserve for ourselves naught but pain, beatings, suffering, nothing but want and tears, brandings and the gibbet. No, no, Thérèse, no; either this Providence you reverence is made only for our scorn, or the world we see about us is not at all what Providence would have it. Become better acquainted with your Providence, my child, and be convinced that as soon as it places us in a situation where evil becomes necessary, and while at the same time it leaves us the possibility of doing it, this evil harmonizes quite as well with its decrees as does good, and Providence gains as much by the one as by the other; the state in which she has created us is equality: he who disturbs is no more guilty than he who seeks to re-establish the balance; both act in accordance with received impulses, both have to obey those impulses and enjoy them.'

I must confess that if ever I was shaken it was by this clever woman's seductions; but a yet stronger voice, that of my heart to which I gave heed, combatted her sophistries; I declared to Dubois that I was determined never to allow myself to be corrupted. 'Very well!' she replied, 'become what you wish, I abandon you to your sorry fate; but if ever you get yourself hanged, which is an end you cannot avoid, thanks to the fatality which inevitably saves the criminal by sacrificing the virtuous, at least remember before dying never to mention us.'

While we were arguing thus, Dubois' four companions were drinking with the poacher, and as wine disposes the malefactor's heart to new crimes and causes him to forget his old, our bandits no sooner learned of my resolution than, unable to make me their accomplice, they decided to make me their victim; their principles, their manners, the dark retreat we were in, the security I thought they enjoyed, their drunkenness, my age, my innocence— everything encouraged them. They get up from table, they confer in whispers, they consult Dubois, doings whose lugubrious mystery makes me shiver with horror, and at last there comes an order to me then and there to satisfy the desires of each of the four; if I go to it cheerfully, each will give me a crown to help me along my way; if they must employ violence, the thing will be done all same; but the better to guard their secret, once finished with me they will stab me, and will bury me at the foot of yonder tree.

I need not paint the effect this cruel proposition had upon me, Madame, you will have no difficulty understanding that I sank to my knees before Dubois, I besought her a second time to be my protectress: the low creature did but laugh at my tears:

'Oh by God!' quoth she, 'here's an unhappy little one. What! you shudder before the obligation to serve four fine big boys one after another? Listen to me,' she added, after some reflection, 'my sway over these dear lads is sufficiently great for me to obtain a reprieve for you upon condition you render yourself worthy of it.'

'Alas! Madame, what must I do?' I cried through my tears; command me; I am ready.'

'Join us, throw in your lot with us, and commit the same deeds, without show of the least repugnance; either that, or I cannot save you from the rest.' I did not think myself in a position to hesitate; by accepting this cruel condition I exposed myself to further dangers, to be sure, but they were the less immediate; perhaps I might be able to avoid them, whereas nothing could save me from those with which I was actually menaced.

'I will go everywhere with you, Madame,' was my prompt answer to Dubois, 'everywhere, I promise you; shield me from the fury of these men and I shall never leave your side while I live.'

'Children,' Dubois said to the four bandits, 'this girl is one of the company, I am taking her into it; I ask you to do her no ill, don't put her stomach off the *métier* during her first days in it; you see how useful her age and face can be to us; let's employ them to our advantage rather than sacrifice them to our pleasures.'

But such is the degree of energy in man's passions nothing can subdue them. The persons I was dealing with were in no state to heed reason: all four surrounded me, devoured me with their fiery glances, menaced me in a still more terrible manner; they were about to lay hands on me, I was about to become their victim.

'She has got to go through with it,' one of them declared 'it's too late for discussion: was she not told she must give proof of virtues in order to be admitted into a band of thieves? and once a little used, won't she be quite as serviceable as she is while a virgin?'

I am softening their expressions, you understand, Madame, I am sweetening the scene itself; alas! their obscenities were such that your modesty might suffer at least as much from beholding them unadorned as did my shyness.

A defenseless and trembling victim, I shuddered; I had barely strength to breathe; kneeling before the quartet, I raised my feeble arms as much to supplicate the men as to melt Dubois' heart . . .

'An instant,' said one who went by the name of Coeur-de-fer and appeared to be the band's chief, a man of thirty-six years, of a bull's strength and bearing the face of a satyr; 'one moment friends: it may be possible to satisfy everyone concerned; since this little girl's virtue is so precious to her and since, as Dubois states it very well, this quality otherwise put into action could become worth something to us, let's leave it to her; but we have got to be appeased; our mood is warm, Dubois, and in the state we are in d'ye know, we might perhaps cut your own throat if you were to stand between us and our pleasures; let's have Thérèse instantly strip as naked as the day she came into the world, and next let's have her adopt one after the other all the positions we are pleased to call for, and meanwhile Dubois will sate our hungers, we'll burn our incense upon the altars' entrance to which this creature refuses us.'

'Strip naked!' I exclaimed, 'Oh Heaven, what is it thou doth require of me? When I shall have delivered myself thus to your eyes, who will be able to answer for me? . . .'

But Coeur-de-fer, who seemed in no humour either to grant me more or to suspend his desires, burst out with an oath and struck me in a manner so brutal that I saw full well compliance was my last resort. He put himself in Dubois' hands, she having been put by his in a disorder more or less the equivalent of mine and, as soon as I was as he desired me to be, having made me crouch down upon all fours so that I resembled a beast, Dubois took in hand a very monstrous object and led it to the peristyles of first one and then the other of Nature's altars, and under her guidance the blows it delivered to me here and there were like those of a battering ram thundering at the gates of a besieged town in olden days. The shock of the initial assault drove me back; enraged, Coeur-de-fer threatened me with harsher treatments were I to retreat from these; Dubois is instructed to redouble her efforts, one of the libertines grasps my shoulders and prevents me from staggering before the concussions: they become so fierce I am in blood and am able to avoid not a one.

'Indeed,' stammers Coeur-de-fer, 'in her place I'd prefer to open the doors rather than see them ruined this way, but she won't have it and we're not far from the capitulation . . . Vigorously . . . vigorously, Dubois . . .'

And the explosive eruption of this debauchee's flames, almost as violent as a stroke of lightning, flickers and dies upon ramparts ravaged without being breached.

The second had me kneel between his legs and while Dubois administered to him as she had to the other, two enterprises absorbed his entire attention: sometimes he slapped, powerfully but in a very nervous manner, either my cheeks or my breasts; sometimes his impure mouth fell to sucking mine. In an instant my face turned purple, my chest red . . . I was in pain, I begged him to spare me, tears leapt from my eyes; they roused him, he accelerated his activities; he bit my tongue, and the two strawberries on my breasts were so bruised that I slipped backward, but was kept from falling. They thrust me toward him, I was everywhere more furiously harassed, and his ecstasy supervened . . .

The third bade me mount upon and straddle two somewhat separated chairs and, seating himself betwixt them, excited by Dubois lying in his arms, he had me bend until his mouth was directly below the temple of Nature; never will you imagine,

Madame, what this obscene mortal took it into his head to do; willy-nilly, I was obliged to satisfy his every need . . . Just Heaven! what man, no matter how depraved, can taste an instant of pleasure in such things . . . I did what he wished, inundated him, and my complete submission procured this foul man an intoxication of which he was incapable without this infamy.

The fourth attached strings to all parts of me to which it was possible to tie them, he held the ends in his hand and sat down seven or eight feet from my body; Dubois' touches and kisses excited him prodigiously; I was standing erect: 'twas by sharp tugs now on this string, now on some other that the savage irritated his pleasures; I swayed, I lost balance again and again, he flew into an ecstasy each time I tottered; finally, he pulled all the cords at once I fell to the floor in front of him: such was his design: and my forehead, my breast, my cheeks received the proofs of a delirium he owed to none but this mania.

That is what I suffered, Madame, but at least my honour was respected even though my modesty assuredly was not.

ÉMILE ZOLA

from

Nana

Émile Zola's erotic novel 'Nana' was published in 1879, sending French critics and moralists into paroxysms of indignation. It tells the story of a young 'cocotte' in Paris of the Second Empire who becomes the mistress of rich and powerful men in a corrupt society.

TEN O'CLOCK struck, and suddenly it occurred to Muffat that it would be very easy to find out whether Nana were in her dressing-room or not. He went up the three steps, crossed the little yellow-painted lobby, and slipped into the court by a door which simply shut with a latch. At that hour of the night, the narrow damp well of a court, with its pestiferous water-closets, its fountain, its back view of the kitchen stove, and the collection of plants with which the portress used to litter the place, was drenched in dark mist; but the two walls, rising pierced with windows on either hand, were flaming with light, since the property room and the firemen's office were situated on the ground floor, with the managerial bureau on the left, and on the right and upstairs the dressing-rooms of the company. The mouths of furnaces seemed to be opening on the outer darkness from top to bottom of this well. The Count had at once marked the light in the windows of the dressing-room on the first floor; and, as a man who is comforted and happy, he forgot where he was, and stood gazing upward amid the foul mud and faint decaying smell peculiar to the premises of this antiquated Parisian building. Big drops were dripping from a broken water-spout, and a ray of gaslight slipped from Madame Bron's window, and cast a yellow glare over a patch of moss-clad pavement, over the base of a wall which had been rotted by water from a sink, over a whole corner-ful of nameless filth amid which old pails and broken crocks lay in fine confusion round the green of a weedy tree in a pot. A window-fastening creaked, and the Count fled.

Nana was certainly going to come down. He returned to his post in front of the reading-room; among its slumbering shadows, which seemed only broken by the glimmer of a night-light, the little old man still sat motionless, his side-face sharply outlined against his newspaper. Then Muffat walked again, and this time took a more prolonged turn, and, crossing the large gallery, followed the Galerie des Variétés as far as that of Feydeau. The last-mentioned was cold and deserted, and buried in melancholy shadow. He returned from it, passed by the theatre, turned the corner of the Galerie Saint-Marc, and ventured as far as the Galerie Montmartre, where a sugar-chopping machine in front of a grocer's interested him a while. But when he was taking his third turn, he was seized with such dread lest Nana should escape behind his back that he lost all self-respect. Thereupon he stationed himself beside the fair gentleman, in front of the very theatre. Both exchanged a glance of fraternal humility, with which was mingled a touch of distrust, for it was possible they might yet turn out to be rivals. Some scene-shifters, who came out smoking their pipes between the acts, brushed rudely against them, but neither one nor the other ventured to complain. Three big wenches with untidy hair and dirty gowns appeared on the doorstep. They were munching apples and spitting out the cores, but the two men bowed their heads, and patiently braved their impudent looks and rough speeches, though they were hustled, and as it were soiled, by these trollops, who amused themselves by pushing each other down upon them.

At that very moment Nana descended the three steps. She grew very pale when she noticed Muffat.

'Oh, it's you!' she stammered.

The sniggering extra ladies were quite frightened when they recognized her, and they formed in line, and stood up looking as stiff and serious as servants whom their mistress has caught behaving badly. The tall fair gentleman had moved away; he was at once reassured and sad at heart.

'Well, give me your arm,' Nana continued impatiently.

They walked quietly off. The Count had been getting ready to question her, and now found nothing to say.

It was she who in rapid tones told a story to the effect that she had been at her aunt's as late as eight o'clock, when, seeing Louiset very much better, she had conceived the idea of going down to the theatre for a few minutes.

'On some important business?' he queried.

'Yes, a new piece,' she replied, after some slight hesitation. 'They wanted my advice.'

He knew that she was not speaking the truth, but the warm touch of her arm, as it leant firmly on his own, left him powerless. He felt neither anger nor rancour after his long, long wait: his one thought was to keep her where she was now that he had got hold of her. Tomorrow, and not before, he would try and find out what she had come to her dressing-room after. But Nana still appeared to hesitate: she was manifestly a prey to the sort of secret anguish that besets people when they are trying to regain lost ground and to initiate a plan of action. Accordingly, as they turned the corner of the Galerie des Variétés, she stopped in front of the show in a fan-seller's window.

'I say, that's pretty,' she whispered; 'I mean that mother-of-pearl mount with the feathers.'

Then, indifferently,—

'So you're seeing me home?'

'Of course,' said he, with some surprise, 'since your child's better.'

She was sorry she had told him that story. Perhaps Louiset was passing through another crisis! She talked of returning to the Batignolles. But when he offered to accompany her she did not insist on going. For a second or two she was possessed with the kind of white-hot fury which a woman experiences when she feels herself entrapped and must nevertheless behave prettily. But in the end she grew resigned, and determined to gain time. If only she could get rid of the Count towards midnight, everything would happen as she wished.

'Yes, it's true, you're a bachelor tonight,' she murmured. 'Your wife doesn't return till tomorrow, eh?'

'No,' replied Muffat. It embarrassed him somewhat to hear her talking familiarly about the Countess.

But she pressed him further, asking at what time the train was due, and wanting to know whether he were going to the station to meet her. She had begun to walk more slowly than ever, as though the shops interested her very much.

'Now do look!' said she, pausing anew before a jeweller's window, 'what a funny bracelet!'

She adored the Passage des Panoramas. The tinsel of the *article de Paris*, the false jewellery, the gilded zinc, the cardboard made to look like leather, had been the passion of her early youth. It remained, and when she passed the shop windows she could not tear herself away from them. It was the same with her today as when she was a ragged, slouching child, who fell into reveries in front of the chocolate-maker's sweet-stuff shows, or stood listening to a musical box in a neighbouring shop, or fell into supreme ecstasies over cheap, vulgarly-designed knick-knacks, such as nut-shell work-boxes, rag-pickers' baskets for holding toothpicks, Vendôme Columns and Luxor Obelisks on which thermometers were mounted. But that evening she was too much agitated, and looked at things without seeing them. When all was said and done, it bored her to think she was not free. An obscure revolt raged within her, and amid it all she felt a wild desire to do something foolish. It was a great thing gained, forsooth, to be the mistress of men of position! She had been devouring the Prince's substance, and Steiner's too, with her childish caprices, and yet she had no notion where her money went. Even, at this time of day, her flat in the Boulevard Haussmann was not entirely furnished. The drawing-room alone was finished, and with its red satin upholsteries and excess of ornamentation and furniture it struck a decidedly false note. Her creditors, moreover, would now take to tormenting her more than ever before whenever she had no money in hand, a fact which caused her constant surprise, seeing that she was wont to quote herself as a model of economy. For a month past that thief Steiner had been scarcely able to pay up his thousand francs on the occasions when she threatened to kick him out of doors in case he failed to bring them. As to Muffat, he was an idiot: he had no notion as to what it was usual to give, and she could not therefore grow angry with him on the score of miserliness. Oh, how gladly she would have turned all these folks off, had she not repeated to herself, a score of times daily, a whole string of economical maxims!

One ought to be sensible, Zoé kept saying every morning, and Nana herself was constantly haunted by the queenly vision seen at Chamont. It had now become an almost religious memory with her, and through dint of being ceaselessly recalled it grew ever more grandiose. And for these reasons, though trembling with repressed indignation, she now hung submissively on the Count's arm as they went from window to window among the fast-diminishing crowd. The pavement was drying outside, and a cool wind blew along the gallery, swept the close hot air up beneath the glass that imprisoned it, and shook the coloured lanterns, and the lines of gas-jets, and the giant fan which was flaring away like a set piece in an illumination. At the door of the restaurant a waiter was putting out the gas, while the motionless attendants in the empty glaring shops looked as though they had dropped off to sleep with their eyes open.

'Oh, what a duck!' continued Nana, retracing her steps as far as the last of the shops in order to go into ecstasies over a porcelain greyhound, standing with raised forepaw in front of a nest hidden among roses.

At length they quitted the passage, but she refused the offer of a cab. It was very pleasant out she said; besides, they were in no hurry, and it would be charming to return home on foot. When they were in front of the Café Anglais she had a sudden longing to eat oysters. Indeed, she said that owing to Louiset's illness she had tasted nothing since morning. Muffat dared not oppose her. Yet, as he did not in those days wish to be seen about with her, he asked for a private supper-room, and hurried to it along the corridors. She followed him with the air of a woman familiar with the house, and they were on the point of entering a private room, the door of which a waiter held open, when from a neighbouring saloon, whence issued a perfect tempest of shouts and laughter, a man rapidly emerged. It was Daguenet.

'By Jove, it's Nana!' cried he.

The Count had briskly disappeared into the private room, leaving the door ajar behind him. But Daguenet winked behind his round shoulders, and added in chaffing tones,—

'The deuce, but you're doing nicely! You catch 'em in the Tuileries nowadays!'

Nana smiled and laid a finger on her lips to beg him to be silent. She could see he was in a very excited condition, and yet she was glad to have met him, for she still felt tenderly towards him, and that despite the nasty way he had cut her when in the company of fashionable ladies.

'What are you doing now?' she asked amicably.

'Becoming respectable. Yes, indeed, I'm thinking of getting married.'

She shrugged her shoulders with a pitying air. But he jokingly continued to the effect that to be only just gaining enough on 'Change to buy ladies bouquets could scarcely be called an income, if you wanted to look respectable too! His three hundred thousand francs had only lasted him eighteen months! He wanted to be practical, and he was going to marry a girl with a huge

dowry, and end off as a *préfet*, like his father before him! Nana still
smiled incredulously. She nodded in the direction of the saloon:

'Who are you with in there?'

'Oh! a whole gang,' said he, forgetting all about his projects
under the influence of returning intoxication. 'Just think! Léa is
telling us about her trip in Egypt. Oh, it's screaming! There's a
bathing story—'

And he told the story, while Nana lingered complaisantly. They
had ended by leaning up against the wall in the corridor, facing
one another. Gas-jets were flaring under the low ceiling, and a
vague smell of cookery hung about the folds of the hangings. Now
and again, in order to hear each other's voices, when the din in
the saloon became louder than ever, they had to lean well forward. Every few seconds, however, a waiter with an armful of
dishes found his passage barred, and disturbed them. But they did
not cease their talk for that; on the contrary, they stood close up to
the walls, and, amid the uproar of the supper-party and the
jostlings of the waiters, chatted as quietly as if they were by their
own firesides.

'Just look at that,' whispered the young man, pointing to the
door of the private room, through which Muffat had vanished.

Both looked. The door was quivering slightly; a breath of air
seemed to be disturbing it, and at last, very, very slowly, and
without the least sound, it was shut-to. They exchanged a silent
chuckle. The Count must be looking charmingly happy, all alone
in there!

'By-the-by,' she asked, 'have you read Fauchery's article about
me?'

'Yes, "The Golden Fly",' replied Daguenet; 'I didn't mention it
to you, as I was afraid of paining you.'

'Paining me—why? His article's a very long one.'

She was flattered to think that the *Figaro* should concern
itself about her person. But failing the explanations of her hairdresser Francis, who had brought her the paper, she would not
have understood that it was she who was in question. Daguenet

scrutinised her slyly, sneering in his chaffing way. Well, well, since she was pleased, everybody else ought to be.

'By your leave!' shouted a waiter, holding iced pudding in both hands, as he separated them.

Nana had stepped towards the little saloon, where Muffat was waiting.

'Well, goodbye!' continued Daguenet. 'Go and find your cuckold again.'

But she halted afresh.

'Why d'you call him cuckold?'

'Because he is a cuckold, by Jove!'

She came and leant against the wall again; she was profoundly interested.

'Ah!' said she, simply.

'What, d'you mean to say you didn't know that? Why, my dear girl, his wife is Fauchery's mistress. It probably began in the country. Some time ago, when I was coming here, Fauchery left me, and I suspect he's got an assignation with her at his place tonight. They've made up a story about a journey, I fancy.'

Overcome with surprise, Nana remained voiceless.

'I suspected it,' said she at last, slapping her leg. 'I guessed it by merely looking at her on the high road that day. To think of its being possible for an honest woman to deceive her husband, and with that blackguard Fauchery too! He'll teach her some pretty things!'

'Oh, it isn't her trial trip,' muttered Daguenet, wickedly. 'Perhaps she knows as much about it as he does.'

At this Nana gave vent to an indignant exclamation.

'Indeed she does! What a nice world! It's too foul!'

'By your leave!' shouted a waiter, laden with bottles, as he separated them.

Daguenet drew her forward again, and held her hand for a second or two. He adopted his crystalline tone of voice, the voice with notes as sweet as those of a harmonica, which had gained him his successes among the ladies of Nana's type.'

'Goodbye, darling! You know I love you always.'

She disengaged her hand from his, and while a thunder of shouts and bravos, which made the door in the saloon tremble again, almost drowned her words, she smilingly remarked,—

'It's over between us, stupid! But that doesn't matter. Do come up one of these days, and we'll have a chat.'

Then she became serious again, and in the outraged tones of a respectable woman,—

'So he's a cuckold, is he?' she cried. 'Well, that *is* a nuisance, dear boy. They've always sickened me, cuckolds.'

When at length she went into the private room she noticed that Muffat was sitting resignedly on a narrow divan with pale face and twitching hands. He did not reproach her at all, and she, greatly moved, was divided between feelings of pity and of contempt. The poor man! To think of his being so unworthily cheated by a vile wife! She had a good mind to throw her arms round his neck and comfort him. But it was only fair all the same! He was a fool with women, and this would teach him a lesson! Nevertheless, pity overcame her. She did not get rid of him as she had determined to do after the oysters had been discussed. They scarcely stayed a quarter of an hour in the Café Anglais, and together they went into the house in the Boulevard Haussmann. It was then eleven. Before midnight she would easily have discovered some means of getting rid of him kindly.

In the ante-room, however, she took the precaution of giving Zoé an order.

'You'll look out for him, and you'll tell him not to make a noise if the Count's still with me.'

'But where shall I put him, Madame?'

'Keep him in the kitchen. It's more safe.'

In the room inside, Muffat was already taking off his overcoat. A big fire was burning on the hearth. It was the same room as of old, with its rose-wood furniture and its hangings and chair coverings of figured damask with the large blue flowers on a grey background. On two occasions Nana had thought of having it re-done, the first in black velvet, the second in white satin, with rose-coloured bows; but directly Steiner consented, she demanded the money that these changes would cost simply with a view to pillaging him. She had, indeed, only indulged in a tiger-skin rug for the hearth and a cut-glass hanging-lamp.

'I'm not sleepy: I'm not going to bed,' said she, the moment they were shut in together.

The Count obeyed her submissively as became a man no longer afraid of being seen. His one care now was to avoid vexing her.

'As you will,' he murmured.

Nevertheless, he took his boots off, too, before seating himself in front of the fire. One of Nana's pleasures consisted in undressing herself in front of the mirror on her wardrobe door, which reflected her whole height. She would let everything slip off her in turn, and then would stand perfectly naked, and gaze and gaze at herself in complete oblivion of all around her. Passion for her own body, ecstasy over her satin skin and the supple contours of her shape, would keep her serious, attentive, and absorbed in the love of herself. The hairdresser frequently found her standing thus, and would enter without her once turning to look at him. Muffat used to grow angry then, but he only succeeded in astonishing her. What was coming over the man? She was doing it to please herself, not other people.

That particular evening she wanted to have a better view of herself, and she lit the six candles attached to the frame of the mirror. But while letting her shift slip down, she paused. She had been preoccupied for some moments past, and a question was on her lips.

'You haven't read the *Figaro* article, have you? The paper's on the table.'

Daguenet's laugh had recurred to her recollection, and she was harassed by a doubt. If that Fa* Faucherry had slandered her, she would be revenged.

'They say that it's about me,' she continued, affecting indifference. 'What's your notion, eh, darling?'

And letting go her shift, and waiting till Muffat should have done reading, she stood naked. Muffat was reading slowly. Fauchery's article, entitled "The Golden Fly", described the life of a harlot, descended from four or five generations of drunkards, and tainted in her blood by a cumulative inheritance of misery and drink, which in her case had taken the form of a nervous exaggeration of the sexual instinct. She had shot up to womanhood in the slums and on the pavements of Paris and tall, handsome, and as superbly grown as a dung-hill plant, she avenged the beggars and outcasts of whom she was the ultimate product. With her the rottenness that was allowed to ferment among the populace was carried upwards and rotted the aristocracy. She became a blind power of nature, a leaven of destruction, and unwittingly between her snow-white thighs she corrupted and brought all Paris to chaos just as every month women turn the milk. And it was at the end of this article that the comparison with a fly occurred, a fly of sunny hue, which had flown up out of the dung, a fly which sucked the carrion tolerated by the roadside, and then buzzing, dancing, and glittering like a precious stone, entered the windows of palaces and poisoned the men within by merely settling on them in her flight.

Muffat lifted his head; his eyes stared fixedly; he gazed at the fire. 'Well?' asked Nana.

But he did not answer. It seemed as though he wanted to read the article again. A cold shivering feeling was creeping from his scalp to his shoulders. This article had been written anyhow. The phrases were wildly extravagant, the unexpected epigrams and quaint collocations of words went beyond all bounds. Yet, notwithstanding this, he was struck by what he had read, for it had rudely awakened within him much that for months past he had not cared to think about.

He looked up. Nana had grown absorbed in her ecstatic contemplation. She was bending her neck and was looking attentively in the mirror at a little brown mark above her right haunch. She was touching it with the tip of her finger, and by dint of bending backward was making it stand out more clearly than ever. Situated where it was, it doubtless struck her as both quaint and pretty. After that she studied other parts of her body with an amused expression, and much of the vicious curiosity of a child. The sight of herself always astonished her, and she would look as surprised and ecstatic as a young girl who has discovered her puberty. Slowly, she spread out her arms to set off her figure, to bring out her plump Venus torso. She bent herself this way and that, and examined herself before and behind, stopping to look at the side-view of her bosom and at the sweeping contours of her thighs. And she ended with a strange amusement, which consisted of swinging to right and left, her knees apart, and her body swaying from the waist with the perpetual jogging, twitching movements peculiar to an Oriental dancer in the *danse du ventre*.

Muffat sat looking at her. She frightened him. The newspaper had dropped from his hand. For a moment he saw her as she was, and he despised himself. Yes, it was just that; she had corrupted his life, he already felt himself tainted to his very marrow by impurities hitherto undreamt of. Everything was now destined to rot within him, and in the twinkling of an eye he understood what this evil entailed. He saw the ruin brought about by this kind of 'leaven'—himself poisoned, his family destroyed, a bit of the social fabric cracking and crumbling. And, unable to take his eyes from the sight, he sat looking fixedly at her, striving to inspire himself with loathing for her nakedness.

Nana no longer moved. With an arm behind her neck, one hand clasped in the other, and her elbows far apart, she was throwing back her head, so that he could see a fore-shortened reflection of her half-closed eyes, her parted lips, her face clothed with amorous laughter. Her masses of yellow hair were unknotted behind, and they covered her back with the fell of a lioness.

Bending back thus so that her flanks stood out, she displayed her solid Amazonian waist and firm bosom, where strong muscles moved under the satin texture of the skin. A delicate line, to which the shoulder and the thigh added their slight undulations, ran from one of her elbows to her foot, and Muffat's eyes followed this tender profile, and marked how the outlines of the fair flesh vanished in golden gleams, and how its rounded contours shone like silk in the candlelight. He thought of his old dread of Woman, of the Beast of the Scriptures, at once lewd and wild. Nana was all covered with fine hair, a russet down made her body velvety; whilst the Beast was apparent in the almost equine development of her flanks, in the fleshly exuberances and deep hollows of her body, which lent her sex the mystery and suggestiveness lurking in their shadows. She was, indeed, that Golden Creature, blind as brute force, whose very odour ruined the world. Muffat gazed and gazed as a man possessed, till, at last, when he had shut his eyes in order to escape it, the Brute reappeared in the darkness of the brain, larger, more terrible more suggestive in its attitude. Now, he understood, it would remain before his eyes, in his very flesh, for ever.

But Nana was absorbed in herself. A little thrill of tenderness seemed to have traversed her members. Her eyes were moist; she tried, as it were, to make herself small, as though she could feel herself better thus. Then she unclasped her hands and slid them down her body as far as her breasts, and these she crushed in a passionate grasp. After which she threw her head and bosom back, and melting, as it were, in one great bodily caress, she rubbed her cheeks coaxingly first against one shoulder then against the other. Her lustful mouth breathed desire over her limbs. She put out her lips, kissed herself long and long in the neighbourhood of her armpit, and laughed at the other Nana who, also, was kissing herself in the mirror.

Then Muffat gave a long sigh. This solitary indulgence exasperated him. Suddenly all his resolutions were swept away as though by a mighty wind. In a fit of brutal passion he caught Nana to his breast and threw her down on the carpet.

'Leave me alone!' she cried. 'You're hurting me!'

He was conscious of his undoing; he recognized in her stupidity, vileness, and falsehood, and he longed to possess her, poisoned though she was.

'Oh, how stupid!' said she savagely, when he let her get up.

Nevertheless, she grew calm. He would go now. She slipped on a night-gown, trimmed with lace, and came and sat down on the floor in front of the fire. It was her favourite position. When she again questioned him about Fauchery's article, Muffat replied vaguely, for he wanted to avoid a scene. Besides, she declared that she had found a weak spot in Fauchery. And with that she relapsed into a long silence, and reflected on how to dismiss the Count. She would have liked to do it in an agreeable way, for she was still a good-natured girl, and it bored her to cause others pain, especially in the present instance where the man was a cuckold. The mere thought of his being that had ended by rousing her sympathies!

'So you expect your wife tomorrow morning?' said she at last.

Muffat had stretched himself in an arm-chair. He looked drowsy, and his limbs were tired. He gave a sign of assent. Nana sat gazing seriously at him, with a dull tumult in her brain. Propped on one leg, among her slightly rumpled laces, she was holding one of her bare feet between her hands, and was turning it mechanically about and about.

'Have you been married long?' she asked.

'Nineteen years,' replied the Count.

'Ah! And is your wife complaisant? Do you get on comfortably together?'

He was silent. Then, with some embarrassment,—

'You know I've begged you never to talk of those matters.'

'Dear me, why's that?' she cried, beginning to grow vexed directly. 'I'm sure I won't eat your wife if I *do* talk about her. Dear boy, why every woman has her price—'

But she stopped for fear of saying too much. She contented herself by assuming a superior expression, since she considered herself extremely kind. The poor fellow, he needed delicate handling! Besides, she had been struck by a laughable notion, and she smiled as she looked him carefully over.

'I say,' she continued, 'I haven't told you the story about you that

Fauchery's circulating. There's a viper, if you like! I don't bear him any ill-will, because his article may be all right, but he's a regular viper all the same.'

And laughing more gaily than ever, she let go her foot, and, crawling along the floor, came and propped her bosom against the Count's knees.

'Now just fancy, he swears you were still like that when you married your wife. You were still like that, eh? Is it true, eh?'

Her eyes pressed for an answer, and she raised her hands to his shoulders, and began shaking him in order to extract the desired confession.

'Without doubt,' he at last made answer gravely.

Thereupon she again sank down at his feet. She was shaking with uproarious laughter, and she stuttered, and dealt him little slaps.

'No, it's too funny! There's no one like you; you're a marvel. But, my poor pet, you must just have been stupid! When a man doesn't know, oh, it is so comical! Good heavens, I should have liked to have seen you! And it came off well, did it? Now tell me something about it! Oh, do, do tell me!'

She overwhelmed him with questions, forgetting nothing, and requiring the veriest details. And she laughed such sudden merry peals, which doubled her up with mirth, and her chemise slipped and got turned down to such an extent, and her skin looked so golden in the light of the big fire that, little by little, the Count described to her his bridal night. He no longer felt at all awkward. He himself began to be amused at last when he explained to her "the way he lost it", to quote the decent expression. Only he kept choosing his phrases, for he still had a certain sense of modesty. The young woman, now thoroughly interested, asked him about the Countess. According to his account she had a marvellous figure, but was a regular iceberg for all that.

'Oh! get along with you!' he muttered, indolently. 'You have no cause to be jealous.'

Nana had ceased laughing, and she now resumed her former

position, and, with her back to the fire, brought her knees up under her chin with her clasped hands. Then, in serious tone, she declared,—

'It doesn't pay, dear boy, to look like a ninny with one's wife the first night.'

'Why?' queried the astonished Count.

'Because,' she replied, slowly, assuming a doctorial expression.

And with that she looked as if she were delivering a lecture, and shook her head at him. In the end, however, she condescended to explain herself more lucidly.

'Well, look here! I know how it all happens. Yes, dearie, women don't like a man to be foolish. They don't say anything, because there's such a thing as modesty, you know, but you may be sure they think about it for a jolly long time to come. And sooner or later, when a man's been an ignoramus, they go and make other arrangements. That's it, my pet.'

He did not seem to understand. Whereupon she grew more definite still. She became maternal, and taught him his lesson out of sheer goodness of heart, as a friend might do. Since she had discovered him to be a cuckold, the information had weighed on her spirits; she was madly anxious to discuss his position with him.

'Good heavens! I'm talking of things that don't concern me. I've said what I have because everybody ought to be happy. We're having a chat, eh? Well then, you're to answer me as straight as you can.'

But she stopped to change her position, for she was burning herself.

'It's jolly hot, eh? My back's toasted. Wait a second, I'll cook my tummy a bit. That's what's good for the aches!'

And when she had turned round with her breast to the fire, and her feet tucked under her,—

'Let me see,' she said, 'you don't sleep with your wife any longer?'

'No, I swear to you I don't,' said Muffat, dreading a scene.

'And you believe she's really frigid?'

He bowed his head in the affirmative.

'And that's why you love me? Answer me! I shan't be angry.'

He repeated the same movement.

'Very well then;' she concluded. 'I suspected as much! Oh! the poor pet. Do you know my aunt Lerat? When she comes, get her to tell you the story about the fruiterer who lives opposite her. Just fancy that man—Damn it, how hot this fire is! I must turn round. I'm going to toast my left side now.'

And as she presented her side to the blaze, a droll idea struck her, and like a good-tempered thing, she made fun of herself, for she was delighted to see that she was looking so plump and pink in the light of the coal fire.

'I look like a goose, eh? Yes, that's it! I'm a goose on the spit, and I'm turning, turning, and cooking in my own juice, eh?'

And she was once more indulging in a merry fit of laughter, when a sound of voices and slamming doors became audible. Muffat was surprised, and questioned her with a look. She grew serious, and an anxious expression came over her face. It must be Zoé's cat, a cursed beast that broke everything. It was half-past twelve o'clock. How long was she going to bother herself in her cuckold's behalf? Now that the other man had come, she ought to get him out of the way, and that quickly.

'What were you saying?' asked the Count complaisantly, for he was charmed to see her so kind to him.

But in her desire to be rid of him, she suddenly changed her mood, became brutal, and did not take care what she was saying.

'Oh yes! the fruiterer and his wife. Well, my dear fellow, they never once touched one another! Not the least bit! She was very keen on it, you understand, but he, the ninny, didn't know it. He was so green that he thought her frigid, and so he went elsewhere, and took up with street-walkers, who treated him to all sorts of nastiness, whilst she, on her part, made up for it beautifully with fellows who were a lot slyer than her greenhorn of a husband. And things always turn out that way through people not understanding one another. I know it, I do!'

Muffat was growing pale. At last he was beginning to understand her allusions, and he wanted to make her keep silence. But
she was in full swing.

'No, hold your tongue, will you? If you weren't brutes you
would be as nice with your wives as you are with us, and if your
wives weren't geese they would take as much pains to keep you as
we do to get you. That's the way to behave. Yes, my duck, you can
put that in your pipe and smoke it.'

'Do not talk of honest women,' said he, in a hard voice. 'You do
not know them.'

At that Nana rose to her knees.

'I don't know them! Why, they aren't even clean, your honest
women aren't! They aren't even clean! I defy you to find me one
who would dare show herself as I am doing. Oh, you make me
laugh with your honest women! Don't drive me to it; don't oblige
me to tell you things I may regret afterwards.'

The Count, by way of answer, mumbled something insulting.
Nana became quite pale in her turn. For some seconds she looked
at him without speaking. Then, in her decisive way—

'What would you do if your wife were deceiving you?'

He made a threatening gesture.

'Well, then, if I were to?'

'Oh! you,' he muttered, with a shrug of his shoulders.

Nana was certainly not spiteful. Since the beginning of the conversation, she had been strongly tempted to throw his cuckold's
reputation in his teeth, but she had resisted. She would have liked
to confess him quietly on the subject, but he had begun to exas-
perate her at last. The matter ought to stop now.

'Well then, my dearie,' continued she, 'I don't know what you're
getting at with me. For two hours past you've been worrying my
life out. Now do just go and find your wife, for she's at it with
Fauchery. Yes, it's quite correct; they're in the Rue Taitbout, at the
corner of the Rue de Provence. You see, I'm giving you the address.'

Then, triumphantly, as she saw Muffat stagger to his feet like an
ox under the hammer,—

'If honest women must meddle in our affairs and take our sweethearts from us—! Oh, you bet they're a nice lot, those honest women!'

But she was unable to proceed. With a terrible push he had cast her full length on the floor, and lifting his heel he seemed on the point of crushing in her head in order to silence her. For the twinkling of an eye she felt sickening dread. Blinded with rage he had begun beating about the room like a maniac. Then his choking silence and the struggle with which he was shaken melted her to tears. She felt a mortal regret, and rolling herself up in front of the fire so as to roast her right side, she undertook the task of comforting him.

SIR RICHARD BURTON

from

The Perfumed Garden

Concerning Everything that is Favourable to the Act of Coition

'The Perfumed Garden' was completed in the sixteenth century by Shaykh Umar ibn Muhammed al-Nefzawi. This translation by the explorer and orientalist Richard Burton was published privately in 1886.

KNOW, O VIZIR (God be good to you!), if you would have pleasant coition, which ought to give an equal share of happiness to the two combatants and be satisfactory to both, you must first of all toy with the woman, excite her with kisses, by nibbling and sucking her lips, by caressing her neck and cheeks. Turn her over in the bed, now on her back, now on her stomach, till you see by her eyes that the time for pleasure is near, as I have mentioned in the preceding chapter, and certainly I have not been sparing with my observations thereupon.

Then when you observe the lips of the woman to tremble and get red, and her eyes become languishing, and her sighs to become quicker, know that she is hot for coition; then get between her thighs, so that your member can enter into her vagina. If you follow my advice, you will enjoy a pleasant embrace, which will give you the greatest satisfaction, and leave you with a delicious remembrance.

Someone has said:

If you desire coition, place the woman on the ground, cling closely to her bosom, with her lips close to yours; then clasp her to you, suck her breath, bite her; kiss her breasts, her stomach, her flanks, press her close in your arms, so as to make her faint with pleasure; when you see her so far gone, then push your member into her. If you have done as I said, the enjoyment will come to both of you simultaneously. This it is which makes the pleasure of the woman so sweet. But if you neglect my advice the woman will not be satisfied, and you will not have procured her any pleasure.

The coition being finished, do not get up at once, but come down softly on her right side, and if she has conceived, she will bear a male child, if it please God on high!

Sages and Savants (may God grant to all his forgiveness!) have said:

If anyone placing his hand upon the vulva of a woman that is with child pronounces the following words: 'In the name of God! may he grant salutation and mercy to his Prophet (salutation and mercy be with him). Oh! my God! I pray to thee in the name of the Prophet to let a boy issue from this conception,' it will come to pass by the will of God, and in consideration for our lord Mohammed (the salutation and grace of God be with him), the woman will be delivered of a boy.

Do not drink rain water directly after copulation, because this beverage weakens the kidneys.

If you want to repeat the coition, perfume yourself with sweet scents, then close with the woman, and you will arrive at a happy result.

Do not let the woman perform the act of coition mounted upon you, for fear that in that position some drops of her seminal fluid might enter the canal of your verge and cause a sharp urethritis.

Do not work hard directly after coition as this might affect your health adversely, but go to rest for some time.

Do not wash your verge directly after having withdrawn it from the vagina of the woman, until the irritation has gone down somewhat; then wash it and its opening carefully. Otherwise, do not wash your member frequently. Do not leave the vulva directly after the emission, as this may cause canker.

Sundry Positions for the Coitus

The ways of doing it to women are numerous and variable. And now is the time to make known to you the different positions which are usual.

God, the magnificent, has said: 'Women are your field. Go upon your field as you like.' According to your wish you can choose the position you like best, provided, of course, that coition takes place in the spot destined for it, that is, in the vulva.

Manner the first—Make the woman lie upon her back, with her thighs raised, then, getting between her legs, introduce your member into her. Pressing your toes to the ground, you can rummage her in a convenient, measured way. This is a good position for a man with a long verge.

Manner the second—If your member is a short one, let the woman lie on her back, lift her legs into the air, so that her right leg be near her right ear, and the left one near her left ear, and in this posture, with her buttocks lifted up, her vulva will project forward. Then put in your member.

Manner the third—Let the woman stretch herself upon the ground, and place yourself between her thighs; then putting one of her legs upon your shoulder, and the other under your arm, near the armpit, get into her.

Manner the fourth—Let her lie down, and put her legs on your shoulders; in this position your member will just face her vulva, which must not touch the ground. And then introduce your member.

Manner the fifth—Let her lie down on her side, then lie yourself down by her on your side, and getting between her thighs, put your member in her vagina. But sidelong coition predisposes for rheumatic pains and sciatica.

Manner the sixth—Make her get down on her knees and elbows, as if kneeling in prayer. In this position the vulva is projected backwards; you then attack her from that side, and put your member into her.

Manner the seventh—Place the woman on her side, and squat

between her thighs, with one of her legs on your shoulder and the other between your thighs, while she remains lying on her side. Then you enter her vagina, and make her move by drawing her towards your chest by means of your hands, with which you hold her embraced.

Manner the eighth—Let her stretch herself upon the ground on her back, with her legs crossed; then mount her like a cavalier on horseback, being on your knees, while her legs are placed under her thighs, and put your member into her vagina.

Manner the ninth—Place the woman so that she leans with her front, or, if you prefer it, her back upon a moderate elevation, with her feet set upon the ground. She thus offers her vulva to the introduction of your member.

Manner the tenth—Place the woman near to a low divan, the back of which she can take hold of with her hands; then, getting under her, lift her legs to the height of your navel, and let her clasp you with her legs on each side of your body; in this position plant your verge into her, seizing with your hands the back of the divan. When you begin the action your movements must respond to those of the woman.

Manner the eleventh—Let her lie upon her back on the ground with a cushion under her posterior; then getting between her legs, and letting her place the sole of her right foot against the sole of her left foot, introduce your member.

There are other positions besides the above named in use of the peoples of India. It is well for you to know that the inhabitants of those parts have multiplied the different ways to enjoy women, and they have advanced farther than we in the knowledge and investigation of coitus.

Amongst those manners are the following, called:

1. *El asemeud*, the stopperage.
2. *El modefedâ*, frog fashion.
3. *El mokefâ*, with the toes cramped.
4. *El mokeurmeutt*, with legs in the air.

5. *El setouri*, he-goat fashion.
6. *El loulabi*, the screw of Archimedes.
7. *El kelouci*, the somersault.
8. *Hachou en nekanok*, the tail of the ostrich.
9. *Lebeuss el djoureb*, fitting on of the sock.
10. *Kechef el astine*, reciprocal sight of the posteriors.
11. *Neza el kouss*, the rainbow arch.
12. *Nesedj el kheuzz*, alternative piercing.
13. *Dok el arz*, pounding on the spot.
14. *Nik el kohoul*, coition from the back.
15. *El keurchi*, belly to belly.
16. *El kebachi*, ram-fashion.
17. *Dok el outed*, driving the peg home.
18. *Sebek el heub*, love's fusion.
19. *Tred ech chate*, sheep-fashion.
20. *Kalen el miche*, interchange in coition.
21. *Rekeud el aïr*, the race of the member.
22. *El modakheli*, the fitter-in.
23. *El khouariki*, the one who stops in the house.
24. *Nik el haddadi*, the blacksmith's coition.
25. *El moheundi*, the seducer.

FIRST MANNER—*El asemeud* (the stopperage). Place the woman on her back, with a cushion under her buttocks, then get between her legs, resting the points of your feet against the ground; bend her two thighs against her chest as far as you can; place your hands under her arms so as to enfold her or cramp her shoulders. Then introduce your member, and at the moment of ejaculation draw her towards you. This position is painful for the woman, her thighs being bent upwards and her buttocks raised by the cushion, the walls of her vagina tighten, and the uterus tending forward there is not much room for movement, and scarcely space enough for the intruder; consequently the latter enters with difficulty and strikes against the uterus. This position should therefore not be adopted, unless the man's member is short or soft.

SECOND MANNER—*El modefedâ* (frog fashion). Place the woman on her back, and arrange her thighs so that they touch the heels, which latter are thus coming close to the buttocks; then down you sit in this kind of merry thought, facing the vulva, in which you insert your member; you then place her knees under your armpits; and taking firm hold of the upper part of her arms, you draw her towards you at the crisis.

THIRD MANNER—*El mokefâ* (with the toes cramped). Place the woman on her back, and squat on your knees, between her thighs, gripping the ground with your toes; raise her knees as high as your sides, in order that she may cross her legs over your back, and then pass her arms round your neck.

FOURTH MANNER—*El mokeurmeutt* (with legs in the air). The woman lying on her back, you put her thighs together and raise her legs up until the soles of her feet look at the ceiling; then enfolding her within your thighs you insert your member, holding her legs up with your hands.

FIFTH MANNER—*El setouri* (he-goat fashion). The woman being crouched on her side, you let her stretch out the leg on which she is resting, and squat down between her thighs with your calves bent under you. Then you lift her uppermost leg so that it rests on your back, and introduce your member. During the action you take hold of her shoulders, or, if you prefer it, by the arms.

SIXTH MANNER—*El loulabi* (the screw of Archimedes). The man being stretched on his back the woman sits on his member, facing him; she then places her hands upon the bed so that she can keep her stomach from touching the man's, and moves up and downwards, and if the man is supple he assists her from below. If in this position she wants to kiss him, she need only stretch her arms along the bed.

SEVENTH MANNER—*El kelouci* (the somersault). The woman must wear a pair of pantaloons, which she lets drop upon her heels; then she stoops, placing her head between her feet, so that her neck is in the opening of her pantaloons. At that moment, the man, seizing her legs, turns her upon her back, making her perform a somersault; then with her legs curved under him he brings his member right against her vulva, and, slipping it between her legs, inserts it.

It is alleged that there are women who, while lying on their back, can place their feet behind their head without the help of pantaloons or hands.

EIGHTH MANNER—*Hachou en nekanok* (the tail of the ostrich). The woman lying on her back along the bed, the man kneels in front of her, lifting up her legs until her head and shoulders only are resting on the bed; his member having penetrated into her vagina, he seizes and sets into motion the buttocks of the woman who, on her part, twines her legs around his neck.

NINTH MANNER—*Lebeuss el djoureb* (fitting on of the sock). The woman lies on her back. You sit down between her legs and place your member between the lips of her vulva, which you fit over it with your thumb and first finger; then you move so as to procure for your member, as far as it is in contact with the woman, a lively rubbing, which action you continue until her vulva gets moistened with the liquid emitted from your verge. When she is thus amply prepared for enjoyment by the alternate coming and going of your weapon in her scabbard, put it into her full length.

TENTH MANNER—*Kechef el astine* (reciprocal sight of the posteriors). The man lying stretched out on his back, the woman sits down upon his member with her back to the man's face, who presses her sides between his thighs and legs, whilst she places her hands upon the bed as a support for her movements, lowering her head, her eyes are turned towards the buttocks of the man.

ELEVENTH MANNER—*Neza el kouss* (the rainbow arch). The woman is lying on her side; the man also on his side, with his face towards her back, pushes in between her legs and introduces his member, with his hands lying on the upper part of her back. As to the woman, she then gets hold of the man's feet, which she lifts up as far as she can, drawing him close to her; thus she forms with the body of the man an arch, of which she is the rise.

TWELFTH MANNER—*Nesedj el kheuzz* (the alternate movement of piercing). The man in sitting attitude places the soles of his feet together, and lowering his thighs, draws his feet nearer to his member; the woman sits down upon his feet, which he takes care to keep firm together. In this position the two thighs of the woman are pressed against the man's flanks, and she puts her arms round his neck. Then the man clasps the woman's ankles, and drawing his feet nearer to his body, brings the woman, who is sitting on them, within range of his member, which then enters her vagina. By moving his feet he sends her back and brings her forward again, without ever withdrawing his member entirely.

The woman makes herself as light as possible, and assists as well as she can in this come-and-go movement; her co-operation is, in fact, indispensable for it. If the man apprehends that his member may come out entirely, he takes her round the waist, and she receives no other impulse than that which is imparted to her by the feet of the man upon which she is sitting.

THIRTEENTH MANNER—*Dok el arz* (pounding on the spot). The man sits down with his legs stretched out; the woman then places herself astride on his thighs, crossing her legs behind the back of the man, and places her vulva opposite his member, which latter she guides into her vagina; she then places her arms round his neck, and he embraces her sides and waist, and helps her to rise and descend upon his verge. She must assist in his work.

FOURTEENTH MANNER—*Nik el kohoul* (coitus from the back). The woman lies down on her stomach and raises her buttocks by help of a cushion; the man approaches from behind, stretches himself on her back and inserts his tool, while the woman twines her arms round the man's elbows. This is the easiest of all methods.

FIFTEENTH MANNER—*El keurchi* (belly to belly). The man and the woman are standing upright, face to face; she opens her thighs; the man then brings his feet forward between those of the woman, who advances hers a little. In this position the man must have one of his feet somewhat in advance of the other. Each of the two has the arms round the other's hips; the man introduces his verge, and the two move thus intertwined after a manner called *neza' el dela*, which I shall explain later, if it please God Almighty. (See FIRST MANNER.)

SIXTEENTH MANNER—*El kebachi* (after the fashion of the ram). The woman is on her knees, with her forearms on the ground; the man approaches from behind, kneels down, and lets his member penetrate into her vagina, which she presses out as much as possible; he will do well in placing his hands on the woman's shoulders.

SEVENTEENTH MANNER—*Dok el outed* (driving the peg home). The woman enlaces with her legs the waist of the man, who is standing, with her arms passed around his neck, steadying herself by leaning against the wall. Whilst she is thus suspended the man insinuates his pin into her vulva.

EIGHTEENTH MANNER—*Sebek el heub* (love's fusion). While the woman is lying on her right side, extend yourself on your left side; your left leg remains extended, and you raise your right one till it is up to her flank, when you lay her upper leg upon your side. Thus her uppermost leg serves the woman as a support for her back. After having introduced your member you move as you please, and she responds to your action as she pleases.

NINETEENTH MANNER—*Tred ech chate* (coitus of the sheep). The woman is on her hands and knees; the man, behind her, lifts her thighs till her vulva is on a level with his member, which he then inserts. In this position she ought to place her head between her arms.

TWENTIETH MANNER—*Kaleb el miche* (interchange in coition). The man lies on his back. The woman, gliding in between his legs, places herself upon him with her toe-nails against the ground; she lifts up the man's thighs, turning them against his own body, so that his virile member faces her vulva, into which she guides it; she then places her hands upon the bed by the sides of the man. It is, however, indispensable that the woman's feet rest upon a cushion to enable her to keep her vulva in concordance with his member.

In this position the parts are exchanged, the woman fulfilling that of the man, and vice-versa.

There is a variation to this manner. The man stretches himself out upon his back, while the woman kneels with her legs under her, but between his legs. The remainder conforms exactly to what has been said above.

TWENTY-FIRST MANNER—*Rekeud el aïr* (the race of the member). The man on his back, supports himself with a cushion under his shoulders, but his posterior must retain contact with the bed. Thus placed, he draws up his thighs until his knees are on a level with his face; then the woman sits down, impaling herself on his member; she must not lie down, but keep seated as if on horseback, the saddle being represented by the knees and the stomach of the man. In that position she can, by the play of her knees, work up and down and down and up. She can also place her knees on the bed, in which case the man accentuates the movement by plying his thighs, whilst she holds with her left hand on to his right shoulder.

TWENTY-SECOND MANNER—*El modakheli* (the fitter-in). The woman is seated on her coccyx, with only the points of her buttocks touching the ground; the man takes the same position, her vulva facing his member. Then the woman puts her right thigh over the left thigh of the man, whilst he on his part puts his right thigh over her left one.

The woman, seizing with her hands her partner's arms, gets his member into her vulva; and each of them leaning alternately a little back, and holding each other by the upper part of the arms, they initiate a swaying movement, moving with little concussions, and keeping their movements in exact rhythm by the assistance of their heels, which are resting on the ground.

TWENTY-THIRD MANNER—*El khouariki* (the one who stops at home). The woman being couched on her back, the man lies down upon her, with cushions held in his hands.

After his member is in, the woman raises her buttocks as high as she can off the bed, the man following her up with his member well inside; then the woman lowers herself again upon the bed, giving some short shocks, and although they do not embrace, the man must stick like glue to her. This movement they continue, but the man must make himself light and must not be ponderous, and the bed must be soft; in default of which the exercise cannot be kept up without break.

TWENTY-FOURTH MANNER—*Nik el haddadi* (the coition of the blacksmith). The woman lies on her back with a cushion under her buttocks, and her knees raised as far as possible towards her chest, so that her vulva stands out as a target; she then guides her partner's member in.

The man executes for some time the usual action of coition, then draws his tool out of the vulva, and glides it for a moment between the thighs of the woman, as the smith withdraws the glowing iron from the furnace in order to plunge it into cold water. This manner is called *sferdgeli*, position of the quince.

TWENTY-FIFTH MANNER—*El moheundi* (the seducer). The woman lying on her back, the man sits between her legs, with his croupe on his feet; then he raises and separates the woman's thighs, placing her legs under his arms, or over his shoulders; he then takes her round the waist, or seizes her shoulders.

The preceding descriptions furnish a large number of procedures, that cannot well be all put into proof; but with such a variety to choose from, the man who finds one of them difficult to practice, can easily find plenty of others more to his convenience.

I have not made mention of positions which it appeared to me impossible to realize, and if there be anybody who thinks that those which I have described are not exhaustive, he has only to look for new ones.

It cannot be gainsaid that the Indians have surmounted the greatest difficulties in respect of coition. As a grand exploit, originating with them, the following may be cited:

The woman being stretched out on her back, the man sits down on her chest, with his back to her face, his knees turned forward and his nails gripping the ground; he then raises her hips, arching her back until he has brought her vulva face to face with his member, which he then inserts, and thus gains his purpose.

This position, as you perceive, is very fatiguing and very difficult to attain. I even believe that the only realization of it consists in words and designs. With regard to the other methods described above, they can only be practised if both man and woman are free from physical defects, and of analogous construction; for instance, one or the other of them must not be humpbacked, or very little, or very tall, or too obese. And I repeat, that both must be in perfect health.

I shall now treat of coition between two persons of different conformation. I shall particularize the positions that will suit them in treating each of them severally.

I shall first discourse of the coition of a lean man and a corpulent woman, and the different postures they may assume for the act, assuming the woman to be lying down, and being turned successively over on her four sides.

If the man wants to work her sideways he takes the thigh of the woman which is uppermost, and raises it as high as possible on his flank, so that it rests over his waist; he employs her undermost arm as a pillow for the support of his head, and he takes care to place a stout cushion beneath his undermost hip, so as to elevate his member to the necessary height, which is indispensable on account of the thickness of the woman's thighs.

But if the woman has an enormous abdomen, projecting by reason of its obesity over her thighs and flanks, it will be best to lay her on her back, and to lift up her thighs towards her belly; the man kneels between them, having hold of her waist with his hands, and drawing her towards him; and if he cannot manage her in consequence of the obesity of her belly and thighs, he must with his two arms encircle her buttocks, but it is thus impossible for him to work her conveniently, owing to the want of mobility of her thighs, which are impeded by her belly. He may, however, support them with his hands, but let him take care not to place them over his own thighs, as, owing to their weight, he would not have the power nor the facility to move. As the poet has said:

> If you have to explore her, lift up her buttocks,
> In order to work like the rope thrown to a drowning man.
> You will then seem between her thighs
> Like a rower seated at the end of the boat.

The man can likewise couch the woman on her side, with the undermost leg in front; then he sits down on the thigh of that leg, his member being opposite her vulva, and lets her raise the upper leg, which she must bend at the knee. Then, with his hands seizing her legs and thighs, he introduces his member, with his body lying between her legs, his knees bent, and the points of his feet against the ground, so that he can elevate his posterior, and prevent her thighs from impeding the entrance. In this attitude they can enter into action.

If the woman's belly is enlarged by reason of her being with child, the man lets her lie down on one side; then placing one of her thighs over the other, he raises them both towards the stomach, without their touching the latter; he then lies down behind her on the same side, and can thus fit his member in. In this way he can thrust his tool in entirely, particularly by raising his foot, which is under the woman's leg, to the height of her thigh. The same may be done with a barren woman; but it is particularly to be recommended for the woman who is *enceinte*, as the above position offers the advantage of procuring her the pleasure she desires, without exposing her to any danger.

In the case of the man being obese, with a very pronounced rotundity of stomach, and the woman being thin, the best course to follow is to let the woman take the active part. To this end, the man lies down on his back with his thighs close together, and the woman lowers herself upon his member, astride of him; she rests her hands upon the bed, and he seizes her arms with his hands. If she knows how to move, she can thus, in turn, rise and sink upon his member; if she is not adroit enough for that movement, the man imparts a movement to her buttocks by the play of one of his thighs behind them. But if the man assumes this position, it may sometimes become prejudicial to him, inasmuch as some of the female sperm may penetrate into his urethra, and grave malady may ensue therefrom. It may also happen—and that is just as bad— that the man's sperm cannot pass out, and returns into the urethra.

If the man prefers that the woman should lie on her back, he places himself, with his legs folded under him, between her legs, which she parts only moderately. Thus, his buttocks are between the woman's legs, with his heels touching them. In performing this way he will, however, feel fatigue, owing to the position of his stomach resting upon the woman's and the inconvenience resulting therefrom; and, besides, he will not be able to get his whole member in the vulva.

It will be similar when both lie on their sides, as mentioned above in the case of the pregnant women.

When both man and woman are fat, and wish to unite in coition, they cannot contrive to do it without trouble, particularly when both have prominent stomachs. In these circumstances the best way to go about it is for the woman to be on her knees with her hands on the ground, so that her posterior is elevated; then the man separates her legs, leaving the points of the feet close together and the heels parted asunder; he then attacks her from behind, kneeling and holding up his stomach with his hand, and so introduces his member. Resting his stomach upon her buttocks during the act he holds the thighs or the waist of the woman with his hands. If her posterior is too low for his stomach to rest upon, he must place a cushion under her knees to remedy this.

I know of no other position so favourable as this for the coition of a fat man with a fat woman.

If, in fact, the man gets between the legs of a woman on her back under the above named circumstances, his stomach, encountering the woman's thighs, will not allow him to make free use of his tool. He cannot even see her vulva, or only in part; it may be almost said that it will be impossible for him to accomplish the act.

On the other hand, if the man makes the woman lie upon her side, and then places himself, with his legs bent behind her, pressing his stomach upon the upper part of her posterior, she must draw her legs and thighs up to her stomach, in order to lay bare her vagina and allow the introduction of his member; but if she cannot sufficiently bend her knees, the man can neither see her vulva, nor explore it.

If, however, the stomach of each person is not exaggeratedly large, they can manage very well all positions. Only they must not be too long in coming to the crisis, as they will soon feel fatigued and lose their breath.

In the case of a very big man and a very little woman, the difficulty to be solved is how to contrive that their organs of generation and their mouths can meet at the same time. To gain this end the woman had best lie on her back; the man places himself on his side near her, passes one of his hands under her neck, and with the other raises her thighs till he can put his member against her vulva from behind, the woman remaining still on her back. In this position he holds her up with his hands by the neck and the thighs. He can then enter her body, while the woman on her part puts her arms round his neck, and approaches her lips to his.

If the man wishes the woman to lie on her side, he gets between her legs, and, placing her thighs so that they are in contact with his sides, one above and one under, he glides in between them till his member is facing her vulva from behind; he then presses his thighs against her buttocks, which he seizes with one hand in order t o impart movement to them; the other hand he has round her neck. If the man then likes, he can get his thighs over those of the woman, and press her towards him; this will make it easier for him to move.

As regards the copulation of a very small man and a tall woman, the two actors cannot kiss each other while in action unless they take one of the three following positions, and even then they become fatigued.

FIRST POSITION—The woman lies on her back, with a thick cushion under her buttocks, and a similar one under her head; she then draws up her thighs as far as possible towards her chest. The man lies down upon her, introduces his member, and takes hold of her shoulders, drawing himself up towards them. The woman winds her arms and legs round his back, whilst he holds on to her shoulders, or, if he can, to her neck.

SECOND POSITION—Man and woman lie both on their side, face to face; the woman slips her undermost thigh under the man's flank, drawing it at the same time higher up; she does the like with her other thigh over his; then she arches her stomach out, while his member is penetrating into her. Both should have hold of the other's neck, and the woman, crossing her legs over his back, should draw the man towards her.

THIRD POSITION—The man lies on his back, with his legs stretched out; the woman sits on his member, and, stretching herself down over him, draws up her knees to the height of her stomach; then, laying her hands over his shoulders, she draws herself up, and presses her lips to his.

All these postures are more or less fatiguing for both; people can, however, choose any other position they like; but they must be able to kiss each other during the act.

I will now speak to you of those who are little, in consequence of being humpbacked. Of these there are several kinds.

First, there is the man who is crookbacked, but whose spine and neck are straight. For him, it is most convenient to unite himself with a little woman, but not otherwise than from behind. Placing himself behind her posterior, he thus introduces his member into her vulva. But if the woman is in a stooping attitude, on her hands and feet, he will do still better. If the woman be afflicted with a hump and the man is straight, the same position is suitable.

If both of them are crookbacked they can take what position they like for coition. They cannot, however, embrace; and if they lie on their side, face to face, there will be left an empty space between them. And if one or the other lies down on his back, a cushion must be placed under the head and the shoulder, to hold them up, and fill the place which is left vacant.

In the case of the man whose malformation affects only his neck, so as to press his chin towards his chest, but who is otherwise straight, he can take any position he likes for doing the business, and give himself up to any embraces and caresses, always excepting kisses on the mouth. If the woman is lying on her back, he will appear in action as if he were butting at her like a ram. If the woman has her neck deformed in similar manner, their coition will resemble the mutual attack of two horned beasts with their heads. The most convenient position for them will be that the woman should stoop down, and he attack her from behind. The man whose hump appears on his back in the shape of only the half of a jar is not so much disfigured as the one of whom the poet has said:

> Lying on his back he is a dish;
> Turn him over, and you have a dish-cover

In his case coition can take place as with any other man who is small in stature and straight; he cannot, however, easily lie on his back.

If a little woman is lying on her back, with a humpbacked man upon her belly, he will look like the cover over a vase. If, on the contrary, the woman is large-sized, he will have the appearance of a carpenter's plane in action. I have made the following verses on this subject:

> The humpback is vaulted like an arch;
> And seeing him you cry, 'Glory be to God!'
> You ask him how he manages in coitus?
> 'It is the retribution for my sins,' he says.
> The woman under him is like a board of deal;
> The humpback, who explores her, does the planning.

I have also said in verse:

> The humpback's dorsal cord is tied in knots,
> The Angels tire with writing all his sins;
> In trying for a wife of proper shape;
> And for her favours, she repulses him,
> And says, 'Who bears the wrongs we shall commit?'
> And he, 'I bear them well upon my hump!'
> And then she mocks him saying, 'Oh, you plane
> Destined for making shavings! take a deal board!'

If the woman has a hump as well as the man, they may take any of the various positions for coition, always observing that if one of them lies on the back, the hump must be environed with cushion, as with a turban, thus having a nest to lie in, which guards its top, which is very tender. In this way they can embrace closely.

If the man is humped both on back and chest he must renounce the embrace and the clinging, but can otherwise take any position he likes for coition. Yet generally speaking, the action must always be troublesome for himself and the woman. I have written on this subject;

> The humpback engaged in the act of coition
> Is like a vase provided with two handles.
> If he is burning for a woman, she will tell him,
> 'Your hump is in the way; you cannot do it;
> Your verge would find a place to rummage in
> But on your chest the hump, where would it be?'

If both the woman and the man have double humps, the best position they can assume for coitus is the following: Whilst the woman is lying on her side, the man introduces his member after the fashion described previously in respect to pregnant women. Thus the two humps do not encounter one another. Both are lying on their sides, and the man attacks from behind. Should the woman be on her back, her hump must be supported by a cushion, whilst the man kneels between her legs, she holding up her posterior. Thus placed, their two humps are not near each other, and all inconvenience is avoided.

The same is the case if the woman stoops down with her head,

with her croup in the air, after the manner of *El kouri*, which position will suit both of them, if they have the chest malformed, but
not the back. One of them then performs the action of come-and-
go.

But the most curious and amusing description which I have
ever met in this respect, is contained in these verses:

> Their two extremities are close together,
> And nature made a laughing stock of them;
> Foreshortened he appears as if cut off;
> He looks like someone bending to escape a blow,
> Or like a man who has received a blow
> And shrivels down so as to miss a second.

If a man's spine is curved about the hips and his back is straight,
so that he looks as though he was in prayer, half prostrated, coition
for him is very difficult; owing to the reciprocal positions of his
thighs and his stomach, he cannot possibly insert his member
entirely, as it lies so far back between his thighs. The best for him to
do is to stand up. The woman stoops down before him with her
hands to the ground and her posterior in the air; he can thus introduce his member as a pivot for the woman to move upon, for, be it
observed, he cannot well move himself. It is the manner *El kouri*,
with the difference, that it is the woman who moves.

A man may be attacked by the illness called *ikaad*, or *zomana*
(paralysis), which compels him to be constantly seated. If this
malady only affects his knees and legs, his thighs and spinal column
remaining sound, he can use all the sundry positions for coition,
except those where he would have to stand up. In the case of his
buttocks being affected, even if he is otherwise perfectly well, it is
the woman who will have to make all the movements.

Know that the most enjoyable coitus does not always exist in the
manners described here; I only give them, so as to render this
work as complete as possible. Sometimes most enjoyable coition
takes place between lovers, who, not quite perfect in their proportions, find their own means for their mutual gratification.

It is said that there are women of great experience who, lying with a man, elevate one of their feet vertically in the air, and upon that foot a lamp is set full of oil, and with the wick burning. While the man is ramming them, they keep the lamp steady and burning, and the oil is not spilled. Their coition is in no way impeded by this exhibition, but it must require great previous practice on the part of both.

Assuredly the Indian writers have in their works described a great many ways of making love, but the majority of them do not yield enjoyment, and give more pain than pleasure. That which is to be looked for in coition, the crowning point of it, is the enjoyment, the embrace, the kisses. This is the distinction between the coitus of men and that of animals. No one is indifferent to the enjoyment which proceeds from the difference between the sexes, and the man finds his highest felicity in it.

If the desire of love in man is aroused to its highest pitch, all the pleasure of coition becomes easy for him, and he satisfies his yearning in any way.

It is well for the lover of coition to put all these manners to the proof, so as to ascertain which is the position that gives the greatest pleasure to both combatants. Then he will know which to choose for the tryst, and in satisfying his desires retain the woman's affection.

Many people have essayed all the positions I have described, but none has been as much approved as the *Dok el arz*.

A story is told on this subject of a man who had a wife of incomparable beauty, graceful and accomplished. He used to explore her in the ordinary manner, never having recourse to any other. The woman experienced none of the pleasure which ought to accompany the act, and was consequently generally very moody after the coition was over.

The man complained about this to an old dame, who told him, 'Try different ways in uniting yourself to her, until you find the one which best satisfies her. Then work her in this fashion only, and her affection for you will know no limit.'

He then tried upon his wife various manners of coition, and when he came to the one called *Dok el arz* he saw her overcome by violent transports of love, and at the crisis of pleasure he felt her womb grasp his verge energetically; and she said to him, biting his lips. 'This is the veritable manner of making love!'

These demonstrations proved to the lover, in fact, that his mistress felt in that position the most lively pleasure, and he always thenceforward worked with her in that way. Thus he attained his end, and caused the woman to love him to folly.

Therefore try different manners; for every woman likes one in preference to all other for her pleasure. The majority of them have, however, a predilection for the *Dok el arz*, as, in the application of the same, belly is pressed to belly, mouth glued to mouth, and the action of the womb is rarely absent.

I have now only to mention the various movements practised during coitus, and shall describe some of them.

FIRST MOVEMENT—*Neza el dela* (the bucket in the well). The man and woman join in close embrace after the introduction. Then he gives a push, and withdraws a little; the woman follows him with a push, and also retires. So they continue their alternate movement, keeping proper time. Placing foot against foot, and hand against hand, they keep up the motion of a bucket in a well.

SECOND MOVEMENT—*El netahi* (the mutual shock). After the introduction, they each draw back, but without dislodging the member completely. Then they both push tightly together, and thus go on keeping time.

THIRD MOVEMENT—*El motadani* (the approach). The man moves as usual, and then stops. Then the woman, with the member in her receptacle, begins to move like the man, and then stops. And they continue this way until the ejaculation comes.

FOURTH MOVEMENT—*Khiate el heub* (Love's tailor). The man, with his member being only partially inserted in the vulva, keeps up a sort of quick friction with the part that is in, and then suddenly plunges his whole member in up to its root. This is the movement of the needle in the hands of the tailor, of which the man and woman must take cognisance.

Such a movement only suits those men and women who can at will retard the crisis. With those who are otherwise constituted it would act too quickly.

FIFTH MOVEMENT—*Souak el feurdj* (the toothpick in the vulva). The man introduces his member between the walls of the vulva, and then drives it up and down, and right and left. Only a man with a very vigorous member can execute this movement.

SIXTH MOVEMENT—*Tâchik el heub* (the boxing up of love). The man introduces his member entirely into the vagina, so closely that his hairs are completely mixed up with the woman's. In that position he must now move forcibly, without withdrawing his tool in the least.

This is the best of all the movements, and is particularly well adapted to the position *Dok el arz*. Women prefer it to any other kind, as it procures them the extreme pleasure of seizing the member with their womb; and appeases their lust most completely.

Those women called *tribades* always use this movement in their mutual caresses. And it provokes prompt ejaculation both with man and woman.

FRANK HARRIS

from

My Life and Loves

Frank Harris's candid autobiography 'My Life and Loves' was published in 1922. It led to his becoming a social outcast. He died in 1931.

ONE memorable afternoon I came upon the gardener, whom I had taken into my service, reading Dante, if you please, in the garden. I had a talk with him and found that he knew not only Dante, but Ariosto, and Leopardi, and Carducci, and was a real student of Italian literature. I passed a great afternoon with him, and resolved whenever I was tired in the future to come out and talk with him.

Two or three days afterwards I was overworked again, and I went out to him and he said: 'You know, when I saw you at first, I thought we should have a great time together here; that you would love life and love; and here you are writing, writing, writing, morning, noon and night—wearing yourself out without any care for beauty or for pleasure.'

'I like both,' I said, 'but I came here to work; still, I shouldn't mind having some distractions if they were possible; but what is possible here?'

'Everything,' he replied. 'I have been putting myself in your place: if I were rich, wouldn't I enjoy myself in this villa!'

'What would you do?' I asked.

'Well,' he said, 'I would give prizes for the prettiest girls, say one hundred francs for the first; fifty francs for the second; and twenty-five as consolation prizes if five or six girls came.'

'What good would that do?' I asked. 'You wouldn't get young girls that way, and you certainly wouldn't get their love.'

'Wouldn't I!' he cried. 'First of all, in order to see who was the prettiest, they would have to strip, wouldn't they? And the girl who is once naked before you is not apt to refuse you anything.'

I had come to a sort of impasse in my work; I saw that the whole assumption that Shakespeare had been a boy lover, drawn from the sonnets, was probably false, but since Hallam it was held by everyone in England, and everyone, too, in Germany, so prone are men always to believe the worst, especially of their betters— the great leaders of humanity.

Heinemann, the publisher, had asked me for my book on Shakespeare before I left England, but as soon as I wrote him that I was going to disprove Shakespeare's abnormal tastes, he told me that he had found every authority in England was against me and therefore he dared not publish my book. Just when I was making up my mind to set forth my conviction, came this proposal of my gardener. I had worked very hard for years on the *Saturday Review* and in South Africa, and I thought I deserved a little recreation; so I said to the gardener, 'Go to it. I don't want any scandal, but if you can get the girls through the prizes, I will put up the money cheerfully and will invite you to play master of ceremonies.'

'This is Tuesday,' he said. 'I think next Sunday would be about the best day.'

'As you please,' I replied.

On Sunday, having given a *congé* to my cook and waiting-maid, I walked about to await my new guests, the cook having laid out a good *déjeuner* with champagne on the table in the dining-room. About eleven o'clock a couple of girls fluttered in, and my gardener conducted them into two bedrooms and told them to make themselves pretty and we would all lunch at half-past twelve. In half an hour five girls were assembled. He put them all into different rooms and went from room to room, telling them that they must undress and get ready for inspection. There was much giggling and some exclamations, but apparently no revolt. In ten minutes he came to me and asked me, was I ready for inspection?

'Certainly,' I said; and we went to the first room. A girl's head looked out from under the clothes: she had got into bed. But my gardener knew better than to humour her: he went over and threw down the bed clothes, and there she was completely nude. 'Stand up, stand up,' he said, 'you are worth looking at!'

And indeed she was. Nothing loath, she stood on the bed as directed and lent herself to the examination. She was a very pretty girl of twenty or twenty-one; and at length, to encourage her, he took her in his arms and kissed her. I followed suit and found her flesh perfectly firm and everything all right, except that her feet were rather dirty; whereupon my gardener said, 'That's easily remedied.' We promised her a prize and told her that we would return when she had washed and put on her clothes and made herself as pretty as possible; and he led me into the next room.

The girl in this one was sitting on the bed, half-undressed but she was very slight and much younger, and evidently very much excited, because she glowered at us as if she hated us. The moment we came into the room she went for the gardener, telling him that if she had known it was required to be naked, she wouldn't have come near us. The gardener kissed her at once and told her not to be frightened, that she was pretty sure of winning a prize, and she need not undress. And we went on to the third room.

There I had one of the surprises of my life: a girl stood on the rug near the bed with the colour coming and going in her cheeks; she was in her shirt, but with her dress held round her hips. She, too, said she didn't want to strip—she would rather go home.

'But nothing has happened to you,' said the gardener. 'Surely a couple of men to admire you isn't going to make you angry; and that frown doesn't suit your loveliness at all.'

In two or three minutes the wily Italian had dissipated her anger and she began to smile, and suddenly, shrugging her shoulders, she put down the dress and then at once stood up at his request, trying to laugh. She had one of the loveliest figures and faces that I ever saw in my life. Her breasts were small, but beautifully rounded and strangely firm; her hips, too, and bottom were as firm as marble, but a little slight. Her face was lit up with a pair of great hazel eyes and her mouth, though a little large, was perfectly formed: her smile won me. I told the gardener that I didn't want to see any more girls, that I was quite content, and he encouraged me to kiss and talk to her while he went into the next room to see the next applicant.

As soon as the gardener left the room, my beauty, whose name was Flora, began questioning me: 'Why do you choose me? You are the owner, aren't you?'

I could only nod. I had sense enough to say, 'Partly for your beauty, but also because I like you, your ways, your courage.'

'But,' she went on, 'real liking does not grow as quickly as that, or just by the view of a body and legs.'

'Pardon me,' I rejoined, 'but passion, desire in a man comes first: it's for the woman to transform it into enduring affection. You like me a little because I admire and desire you; it's for me by kindness and sympathy to turn that liking into love; so kiss me and don't let us waste time arguing. Can you kiss?'

'Of course I can,' she said, 'everyone can!'

'That's not true,' I retorted. 'The majority of virgins can't kiss at all, and I believe you're a virgin.'

'I am,' she replied; 'but you'll not find many in this crowd.'

'Kiss me,' I went on, taking her in my arms and kissing her till I found response in hot lips. As she used her tongue, she asked roguishly, 'Well, Sir, can I kiss?'

'Yes,' I replied, 'and now I'll kiss you,' and I laid her on the bed and buried my face between her legs.

She was a virgin, I discovered, and yet peculiarly quick to respond to passion: an astonishing mistress! She didn't hide from me the fact that, like most school-girls in Italy, as in France, she had been accustomed to provoke her own sensuality by listening to naughty stories and by touching herself ever since puberty. But what kept her from giving herself freely was her fear of the possible consequences. My assurances seemed to have convinced her, for suddenly she started up and danced round me in her fascinating nudity. 'Shall I have a prize?'

'The first,' I cried.

'*Carissimo mio*,' and she kissed me a dozen times. 'I'll be whatever you want and cover you with love.'

Our talk had gone on for perhaps half an hour, when a knock came at the door, and the gardener came in to find us both quite happy and, I think, intimately pleased with each other. He said, 'The other two you had better see or they will be disappointed, but I think you have picked the prettiest.'

'I am quite content,' I replied, 'to rest on your approval of them.'

But my self-willed beauty said, 'Let us go and see them; I will go with you,' and we went into the next room, said a few flattering things, and went on to the fifth room, where there was a girl who said she wouldn't undress.

'At any rate,' said the gardener, 'the matter is settled; we can all go in and have lunch, and then my master will give the prizes.'

We had a great lunch, all helping each other and ourselves, and when the champagne was opened, every one seemed to enjoy the feast infinitely. But when the prize giving came, I was ashamed, hating to give one less than the other, so I called the gardener to one side and told him my reluctance. 'Nothing easier,' he said. 'I have made you out to be a great English lord. Go into that bedroom on the right and I will send them in one by one. If I were you, I would give the two first prizes and I will give the consolation stakes.'

'Splendid,' I said, 'but give me a reasonable half-hour before sending in the second one.' Flora came in and got her first prize, kissed me, and offered herself to my desire by opening the bed. Then for some reason or other a good idea came into my head.

I put up my hands. 'That's for later, I hope,' I exclaimed. 'It means affection, and you don't care for me yet; perhaps you will with time, and if you don't, I'll forgive you. There's no compulsion here.'

'How good of you,' she exclaimed. 'Just for saying that I want to kiss you, *caro mio* (you dear),' and she threw her arms round my neck and gave me a long kiss.

Naturally, I improved the occasion, and turned the kiss into an embrace by putting my hands up her dress on her sex. After I had touched her for a minute or so, she trembled and came, and as I put my arms round her and kissed her, she kissed me passionately in return. '*Carissimo mio*,' she murmured, and hid her glowing cheek on my neck. While she was putting her dress in order before the glass, she began talking quickly: 'You know, I hope this isn't the only time. I want to come back without any prize, for I like you and you have been kind to me. I was frightened at first—you must forget all that; you will, won't you? *Cuore mio*; I'll find new love names for you,' and she did.

'But why did you want to see us all naked,' she went on, 'we're all alike, aren't we?'

'No, indeed,' I cried, 'you are all different.'

'But you can't love one because her breasts are smaller than another's. No woman would care for such a thing. I love your voice and what you say and your eyes, but not your legs: fancy!' and she laughed aloud.

Finally she said, 'When may I come again? soon, please!'

'Surely,' I replied, 'when will you come? I want your photograph.'

'Any day you like,' Flora said. And we fixed the meeting for Tuesday. She went off delighted.

The next girl who came in was the young girl, the second we saw, who had not undressed and who had declared that she wouldn't have come if she had known the conditions. At once she said to me: 'I don't mind undressing for you: I know you now,' and in a trice she had pulled her things off: she was very pretty. I afterwards photographed her in the swing in the garden. But she was nothing astonishing, just a very pretty and well-made girl of sixteen. Her name, she told me, was Yolande; she lived with an aunt. I may have more to tell of her later, though her quick temper made me avoid her.

When I gave her the second prize of seventy-five francs, she said, 'You are giving me the second prize; if I had been nicer you perhaps would have given me the first.'

Her frankness amused me. 'Does it make much difference to you the difference between seventy-five and one hundred francs.?'

She nodded her head: 'It will make a difference to my dress,' she said. 'I want pretty underthings'—and she curled up her nose.

'Well,' I replied, 'say nothing about it, and take another twenty-five francs.' At once she threw her arms around my neck and kissed me, and then, 'May I come back?'

'Sure, sure,' I replied.

'May I bring someone else?'

'Anyone you please,' I said.

That is about all I remember of the first séance, except that the beauty, Flora, whom I have tried to describe, did not leave the villa till long after dinner.

When I talked with my gardener of the event afterwards, he told me that he had preferred the youngest of all, whom I had not seen. 'Clara,' he said, 'was the prettiest of the lot.' As I told him I thought her too thin for beauty and too young to be mentally attractive, he promised to show me her nudity the next Sunday. I wanted to know about the next Sunday. 'Will you be able to get three or four new girls?'

'Good God,' he exclaimed, 'twenty, if you like! These girls will whisper it all about and you may be sure you will have an ever-increasing number. This villa is going to get a good name if you continue!'

'I will continue weekly,' I said, 'but if there are likely to be more girls, I might bring a friend over from Monte Carlo, who happens to be there and who is really an English lord.'

'By all means,' he said; 'the more, the merrier.'

Accordingly, I sent a telegram to my friend, Ernest—asking him to come and spend a happy weekend with me. In due time he came. And it was well that he did come, for the second week showed me that the gardener was wiser and knew his country people better than I did: at least twenty girls came to win prizes, girls of all ages from fifteen to thirty. My gardener proposed that he should weed them out to six or seven, giving them consolation prizes without stripping them. Both Ernest and I were quite content, but we wanted to see his choice, and we were astonished by the ability with which he made his selection: practically, we had to agree with him. Twelve or fourteen girls were sent home with twenty-five francs each, without any further attempt at discrimination; and our inspection began without making me waver in my allegiance to Flora.

It was in these first weeks at San Remo that I began to discover that the body was not so important in love or in passion as the mind and character. I had no slightest desire to leave my beauty for any of the newer queens; and I didn't want her to strip, even for Ernest's inspection, although she was willing to. But I had become her lover now, and love desires exclusive possession.

The third meeting had a new termination. Another young Englishman, named George—a friend of Ernest, had fallen in love with one the week before. We had the three queens as we called them, to dinner, as well as to lunch. After dinner the gardener appeared with one, and declared that if our girls would strip, he would show that his was the prettiest of the lot. None of the three girls minded: they were all willing, so we had another contest; but we resolved to give the winner of this contest two hundred francs. I don't believe that the famous choice of Paris, with the three queens of Heaven before him, ever showed such beauties. I must try to describe them. Of two of them I have photographs, which I must not reproduce; and the third, my queen, I have already described. It is for my readers to use their imaginations. And I cannot even give the photo of the gardener's choice, for she wasn't a bit more than fourteen years of age. When we made fun of him about this, he said philosophically, 'I am older than you men, and

I have noticed that the older we get the younger we like the girls.'
On this we all burst out laughing. My readers may compare the
four beauties for themselves.

This was the first time in my life that I ever studied the sex of
women; and it was the gardener who brought it about. We had
decided that all our three beauties were lovelier than his, when he
challenged us to a new test. 'What do we desire most in a girl?' he
asked: 'surely a small and well-made sex. Well, I'll bet Clara has the
smallest and best sex of the lot.'

Ernest at once declared that the gardener was right; so we asked
our beauties to submit to his examination. They laughed at us but
yielded to the general wish. Clara won, as the gardener predicted;
my Flora was second; Ernest's beauty, third; and George's fourth.
But all had to admit that from the outside Flora's sex was the most
perfectly formed.

We found that the chief centre of pleasure, as a rule, was the
clitoris and that almost in proportion to its size; sometimes it was
not distinguishable, but in the three beauties it was normal, whereas in Clara it was abnormally developed—fully an inch long. The
inner lips too, in her case, were very heavy; and when the gardener told us that he had brought her twice to fainting, we had to
agree with him that she felt more acutely than any of the rest.

Flora, however, disdained the test and said that she felt more at
something said, at a beautiful thought or fine deed than she ever
felt by mere sexual excitement.

One day Ernest and George went to Monte Carlo and brought
over two more friends. The gardener was overjoyed, for as the girls
increased, so his tips increased, and his amusement, too, I think.
But from now on, our Sundays occasionally developed into orgies;
that is, we wandered about, selecting now this and that girl, instead
of remaining faithful to the queens; but usually, as soon as the newcomers went away, we returned to our old allegiances. But from
the outset I limited my time for amusement to two days a week:
Wednesdays and Sundays; all the other days I spent working.

I shall never forget one occasion when we all went down

bathing in a state of nature—half a dozen girls and four men. After the bath, we all came up and lay about on the grass and soon the lovely girlforms seduced the men, and the scene turned to embracing, which the beauty and abandon of the girls made memorable.

This life continued for five or six weeks, till one Thursday I was interrupted by the gardener, who came and asked me to come down to see a cousin of Clara's, Adriana. I found a very lovely girl with reddish fair hair and grey eyes: quite different in looks from the ordinary Italian. I could reproduce the likeness of her that a painter-friend, Rousselet, developed later from a photograph. But she was certainly one of the most beautiful beings I have ever seen in my life, and curiously enough, she seemed at first as sweet and sympathetic and passionate as she was lovely. I took to her at once and, strange to say, even Flora liked her. She told us she was an orphan and seemed always grateful for any kindness: when Flora told her she liked her and was not jealous, 'How could you be jealous?' said Adriana. 'You are too lovely to know what envy means.'

Flora kissed her, saying: 'My dear, I don't know whether it is wisdom in you or goodness, but you are certainly wonderful.'

We had been at these games more than half the summer when Ernest proposed we should vary the procedure by letting the girls select their favourites. No sooner proposed than done. We gave them prizes and asked them to apportion them: at once they established one purse and gave us all an equal prize; but they determined, too, who was the first favourite and who the second, and so on.

I had no reason to complain of the result; but I was at a loss to know why I was chosen so frequently: was it due to a hint of the gardener, or simply to the fact that I was known to be the owner of the villa? I never could quite determine, but I was chosen so often that the game became monotonous; and when I was left out, Ernest was the winner, though George was far better looking than either of us, and at least ten years younger.

At length we hit on a new game: one Sunday about fifty girls had come, so Ernest proposed that our four beauties should select the prettiest four of the newcomers, while we men stood round and studied their feminine choice. We soon found it was impossible to know why this or that girl was chosen, but assuredly the prettiest were seldom, if ever, successful; nevertheless, the four selected were soon initiated.

One day there came a new development: three mothers had brought their girls, and George proposed we should get the mothers to select the most beautiful four to throne it at our lunch. To my delight, Flora was selected, and an excellent selection made from the others.

Every week, I had almost said, every Wednesday and every Sunday, there was something new: we constantly drove in George's carriage, or Ernest's, or both, either into the mountains or along the coast. George had discovered a wonderful lonely, little bay for bathing, almost uninhabited, and we used to go there frequently, and half a dozen of us would bathe together; then the meals, especially the dinners, were always feasts which often ended in some droll invention.

The curious part of my personal adventure was the changes in the character of Adriana. It was almost indescribable; from being all sympathy and sweetness, she began, I think, through jealousy, to become more and more imperious.

'You know,' she began one day, when she had come of her own accord to see me, 'your Flora is engaged to be married; as soon as I saw her, I knew she wouldn't go begging long; she's pretty, though you must know her legs are thin. But perhaps you like thin legs?'

'You are the best made of them all,' I began, 'please let me see you, and don't bother about anyone else.'

'If I'm the only one,' she replied, pouting; 'I can't bear to be second—'

'Make yourself the first,' I said; 'it's up to you: be sweeter than Flora, more passionate than Clara, and you'll win—'

'Clara,' she cried, 'is nothing but a little prostitute, like her mother before her; she's quite common—'

I couldn't help provoking her. 'The gardener swears,' I said, 'that she has the smallest sex in the whole country and is besides the most passionate of all of you—'

'I hate these comparisons,' cried Adriana. 'They degrade one to the level of the mere animal; surely there's more to me than round limbs and a small sex? I'd give anything, everything to love, but to mere desire—nothing—'

'Desire,' I remarked, 'is the door to love and the guide; physical beauty can be seen and measured, so to speak, whereas affection and devotion need time to be appreciated. Do you know,' I added warningly, 'jealousy is no proof of affection; on the contrary, I think jealous people are usually hard-hearted: pride is their master passion, not affection.'

'Oh; I'm proud,' she cried, 'I admit it, but I think if you cared for me and me alone, I would do anything for you, whatever you wished.'

I turned the talk by admiring her arms and bust, for I didn't wish to change Flora; and lovely though Adriana was, I resented her imperiousness; but her body was too perfect and I ended by making her feel and enjoy herself.'

'Did I please you?' she asked afterwards.'

'More than ever,' I said.'

'You see,' she cried; 'may I come tomorrow?'

'Oh, you know,' I said, 'I have to work; I would like you to come, but not before Saturday.'

'Then you will have Flora on Wednesday,' she said pouting.

'No,' I replied, to get rid of her, 'I promise I'll have no one until you come again.'

She kissed me, and there the matter ended for the time. But she soon made herself impossible by her exactions.

It was the advent into our company of one Frenchman, whom I shall call by his Christian name, Jean, who brought us to an acquaintance with new sensualities. He chose again a girl, Rosa, and declared that by whipping her bottom he could bring her to a passion of desire and soon the whippings, just to redden the skin, became more or less general among us: from time to time we all tried it; and strange to say the girls were most partial to it —the sufferers, so to speak, though the suffering plainly was very slight and soon lost in pleasure. On more than one occasion the whippings became general, and nothing prettier could be imagined than three or four girls being excited in this way. Generally it was one of the girls who did the whipping; it was curious how much rougher they were than the men; it showed us all very plainly that women think less of small pains than men do.

Another thing Jean did was to send to Paris and get half a dozen instruments resembling the sex of men in stiff Indian rubber; and these, too we found could be used to excite our beauties to a hitherto unknown extent.

We all agreed finally that the sensuality of women lasted much longer than that of men, and women needed much more exciting. But Jean's greatest achievement was altogether new to most of us. He heard the gardener one day bragging of his mistress because she had the smallest sex.

'Of course,' said Jean, 'you know that you can make any girl's sex as small as you like.'

We showed astonishment and he went on: 'There are three or four injections which will contract the sex as much as you please, contract it so that you cannot enter easily the sex of a woman who has had a child: it's ridiculous to talk of a small sex as a beauty when anyone can have it.'

In the next week or ten days we had all tried his injections of alum water and found that his remedy was in every case infallible; but still we preferred those who were naturally small.

Ernest told us that he had had a similar experience in the East, I think in Java, and I had to admit that I had learned about it in India.

Jean, too, would not be fettered for a moment to any girl, but every Wednesday and every Sunday chose a new partner; and he used to amuse us all infinitely with his stories of how he treated them and how he enjoyed them. One day when Jean had been bragging of his performances, one of his mistresses suddenly interrupted him by saying, 'The only way one can ever get you to go twice is by whipping you,' and we all laughed, for Jean was distinctly younger than any of us except George, and we hitherto had taken his bragging, more or less, to be the truth.

Looking back over that wonderful summer, I consider my most valuable experiences to be the stories the girls told of themselves: the sex experiences in girlhood of Flora and Adriana taught me a great deal, for they both were normal. I am sure Flora's confessions were perfectly truthful and, though Adriana concealed a good deal usually, she now and then revealed herself very completely. This is what Flora told me: but I'll keep these revelations for another chapter.

*   *   *

The Girl's Confessions
Flora

'YOU ASKED ME to strip my mind; well I'll try,' Flora began 'and if I omit anything, you must just question me, for I want to please you, you dear!

'Ever since I can remember, I have revelled in certain kinds of—may I call them, naked thoughts. Even as young as seven I must have been lewd—this is stripping myself with a vengeance. I remember I had measles at school, and a doctor whose pet I was attended me. He was very good-looking. I suppose he was a hero to me—anyway, I distinctly remember the sensation he caused me by undressing and touching me. That may be ordinary enough, but I used to dream about it, think about it, delight in it. Is that natural? I've never told anyone—they wouldn't understand—so I don't know whether it is usual or not.

'And later at nine years of age or so, a girl much older than myself made me much worse. Of course, she used to gratify her sensations, but it was very bad for me. She put my hand on her and told me to rub. I think I must have been really depraved, for later two other girls got very intimate with me, but this time I was the ring-leader. I can hardly say what we didn't do—you will understand. This at the age of nine and ten, and they say boys are more depraved than girls! I don't believe it. From that you can have some idea what I am like now.

'My dreams lead to sensations. I just revel in passions that have no outlet whatever, unless I satisfy them myself. And often I do that. That's one side of me.

'I wish to God those of my sex weren't such hypocrites. Even my best friend, with whom I discuss all sorts of things, chiefly men and women, often seems thoroughly disgusted and tells me seriously I'm getting very immoral. She was saying the other day that she had dreamt she was walking naked and alone down the main street, and she thought everyone had had that dream more or less frequently. I said I had never dreamt I was naked and *alone* anywhere! That it was wasting a splendid sensation. She was really annoyed.

'Then there were two other girls; they were about the same age as myself, thirteen and fourteen. They were sisters and very wild; I mean undisciplined. I didn't like them at all, they were too rude and bold and very mean. Still they served a purpose. They used to strip and put me in bed and one of them rubbed vaseline or some sort of grease between my legs, and the other looked on till her turn came. The sensation of being looked at was almost as good as the one of being rubbed. I must have been a cunning little devil, because I certainly wasn't able to analyze the why and the wherefore of it at all; I just knew I liked it.

'And then came older girls; when I was about fifteen, a girl took me up to her room and locked the door; it was a sort of wardrobe room—small and pitch dark. I was old enough to realize then just what I was doing. She put my hand on her sex and I touched her as well as I could. I know I liked doing it. Naturally she was fully developed and somehow that was an added enjoyment for me. It did me harm in that I used to brood over it, gloat over it, enjoy my lewd thoughts—well, fifteen is too young for that, especially as I didn't need encouraging.'

'But why shouldn't you be encouraged?' I couldn't help asking.

'I was already too much inclined that way,' she replied

'So much the better,' I went on; 'I can't understand the implied condemnation.'

'Nor can I,' she rejoined. 'It's merely habit, the customary way of thinking and speaking.

'You want to know everything: are girls' desires as vagrant as those of men? Yes, and quite as strong, I think; when as a young girl, a man attracted me, a complete stranger—or showed me he wanted me, in the tram or anywhere, I used to cross my legs and press my thighs together and squeeze my sex till I came just as if I had used my hand; often I was all wet. There, you have the truth!

'Why did I come here? Naturally, I hoped to win a first prize, but really that was not my chief motive. The gardener said there was a young good-looking Englishman in the villa who would be very nice to me; the money was only the hope we all used to excuse ourselves. We pretended to be seeking the money, but in truth we were seeking lover and love—new emotions.

'When the gardener left me in the bedroom that first morning, I noticed how fine the sheets were and the pretty pictures in the room: 'When will he come?' I asked myself; 'What will he do?' And my heart was in my mouth.

'Before you came in that first time to see me, the hope of you set all my pulses throbbing. I threw myself on the bed and thought about it, and thinking gradually brought about the feeling that demands satisfaction, so I satisfied it by touching myself—waiting for you: you dear, you!

'I've told you nothing about men, you say; but really, I had no experiences to speak of till I came here. My mother was always warning me of the consequences and the risk of having a child was always present.

'I often saw men in the town I could have liked, but we lived right out in the country, and till your gardener came and talked to me and assured me there was no risk and a great deal of fun, I never gave myself to any man: you are the first, and you know it, don't you, dear?

'One young fellow used to come out last summer from the town and we used to take long walks, and he said he loved me and was always touching my breasts and trying to excite me in fifty ways; but when I mentioned marriage, he sheered off. Men want pleasure and no ties and I don't blame them. If I were a man, I'd do the same: it's we women run the risk; but not with you, dear.

'Oh, now, often I can feel those slow long kisses of yours on my breasts and—I close my eyes and give myself to you: love is the best thing in the world, but how am I to love when you go away and the great days are ended? Oh, I wish my life could end with them: I have had the best of life.'

'Don't say that,' I cried. 'The best of your life is still to come, and I shall not be gone forever.'

And then the love play began again and went on till we were called out to lunch, and we found a feast that deserves to be described at length, but I am afraid of tiring my readers.

Though I liked Flora immensely, I often made fun of her coldness. She used to resent this, saying: 'You do not know me!'

One day she found me with Adriana, and that evening she asked me: 'Do you go with her because she's passionate?'

I nodded my head: it's useless to try to explain to a woman the attraction of novelty.

The next day, to my astonishment, Flora surpassed herself: she really used her sex as an instrument and gave me intense thrills.

As I cried out, 'Enough, dear!' she triumphed.

'Am I better than your Adriana?'

'Much better,' I replied, 'but why don't you act like that always?'

'I don't know!' she replied. 'It's due to a sort of reserve I can't explain, but you mustn't believe with the gardener that Clara or Adriana or any of them feel more than I do. A man may be proud of liking the act; a woman is always ashamed to confess it or show it!'

The year after I had left San Remo, Flora wrote to me at the Hotel de Paris at Monte Carlo. She told me that all her life since I had gone away was stale and flat. If I didn't want her any more, she would prefer to kill herself: she could not endure her dull, uneventful existence. The letter was some months old, but I raced over to San Remo at once to make things right if possible. Naturally, I first sought out my gardener. He was astonished. 'She has just been married,' he cried, when I showed him the letter, 'and well married, he's rich. I'll tell you all about it to-morrow.'

It turned out to be as he had said: my Flora had married, and married exceedingly well, and when I sought her out, she didn't hesitate to tell me that half her success had come from the apprenticeship she had gone through with us Englishmen. 'You taught me to love, Sir,' she said, 'and it was your teaching mainly that made it easy for me later to excite love without feeling it much. Yet my husband is a dear fellow and I think I shall be happy with him: you don't mind?' she asked, smiling archly the while.

'Mind! Of course not!' And I said to myself, 'Another ship come safely to port.'

Adriana

Adriana's account was very like that of Flora's in the early years, but at first she was more outspoken.

'Passion—I'm made of it, a colt—wild, crazy, untamed colt—quick, rashly impulsive, savage—and yet I've emotion enough in me—high poetry; the violin, "flame in the skies of sunset"—all bring tears to my eyes: the rippling of a stream, the green foliage of trees, books and pictures—a deep sweet world.

'Of course, it was an older girl who first taught me sensuality; I don't really think she ever touched me. It was quite a one-sided affair, but what I did to her gave me quite a little pleasure of my own. Of course, I didn't know what she did it for. I liked it and that was all that mattered to me.

'I had a governess just before I went to school. I can't remember, but, anyway, she's the only female, barring the first I mentioned, who made me aware of her passion. She would insist on bathing me. I knew that was funny, as none of the others had wished to. But she banged on the door the first night, and when I admitted her, she came over to me and slowly took away the towel covering me. I felt ashamed—her eyes made me feel so—her look made me blush—it also began to make me feel strangely pleased, with that feeling of pleasure we all experience, I think, when we are looked at. Well, every week she bathed me and I became fully aware of her feelings towards me once behind the bathroom door. And I loved it. She would lift me out of the bath and lay me across her knees and the delightful sensation of being devoured by her greedy eyes made me open my legs—for her to rub me.

'From twelve to fourteen I was at school and developed a passion for one of the seniors. And while I would have been thrilled at a single touch of her fingers even on my hand, she never took even the very slightest notice of me. The sight of her thrilled me, and if she passed me and I felt her brush against me, it set my heart beating. But that sort of hero worship is very common at school.

'Another girl of my own age one night surprised me by asking me to accompany her into the bathroom. I went along wondering. She locked the door and then in a somewhat shamefaced fashion, asked me to touch her. I did, and she touched me. Both of us were highly excited, but we were interrupted, and somehow we never tried anything further afterwards.

'You ask me about exciting myself. I was doing it constantly from ten or eleven on. About thirteen I got quite thin and pale, and my mother told me one evening how a young girl friend of hers had ruined her health by touching her sex and so warned me. After that, I used to do it every Saturday night. Then I had an orgy, once a week; it was splendid. I used to think of some man who had attracted me or shown that he wanted me and I'd begin.

'One day in the tram a common man came in and threw

himself down opposite me. Of a sudden I noticed that his trousers
were unbuttoned and I saw his sex: it made me angry at first; he
was so dirty and common. But as I stole glances at it, it excited me
fearfully; I crossed my legs and squeezed my sex and at once I
came. I could not help it: when I got out I was all streaming—wet
to my knees.

'You ask me about my feelings. I have only to wait a very short
time before I come, usually. But it all depends on the state of my
mind. If there is not a good (I should say bad) atmosphere, it takes
long, but if I feel really passionate—almost lewd—a minute will do
it. And I can do it again perhaps three times but that's the limit. My
legs give way under me after that—so I judge I've had the best of
myself; anyway I couldn't do more than that consecutively.

'No one thrill is ever exactly like the last; you soon learn to
differentiate. Of course, they all recur, but never one after the
other—and sometimes my favourite thrill comes most seldom; it is
when all my muscles stiffen and grow rigid; it may not occur for
days, even weeks.'

Naturally, I went to work at once to bring on the rigid paroxysm in Adriana and I found no difficulty. 'You could not do it
again,' she said, but in ten minutes I proved that I could bring
about the rigid orgasm as often as I liked. In fact, once after bringing on the paroxysm three or four times, she burst out crying and
laughing in a sort of wild hysteria that took me hours to quiet.

'I love you,' she said to me, 'and that's why I can't control
myself. But why do you want anyone else? I'll give you all myself,
more than anyone else can, you dear! But you must be faithful!'

'When are you most passionate?' I asked, and she replied:

'I have not noticed that I am more passionate at certain times—
at least orthodox times—than others. I know it is so, or should be
so, but everything to me depends on my mind and emotion.

'Did I tell you of any man having me? She wouldn't, I'm sure,
your Flora, but I will. I was only sixteen and my folks got me work
in the office of a hotel. He was the manager and married: I knew
his wife, and his eldest daughter was older than I was. He was very

kind to me from the beginning. I saw he desired me, of course.

'One fête day, three years ago, everyone was in the street; but he had given me some work and I didn't like to leave it. In the middle of the procession he came to the door and sent me to fetch his fountain pen from his bedroom on the fourth floor. Of course I went, and while I was searching for his pen, he came into the room and had locked the door before I knew or guessed anything. He took me almost by force; he put his hands up my clothes and lifted me on to the bed; and while I was saying I'd cry out, he hurt me so that I shrieked; but he went on. Afterwards he kissed me and told me all sorts of sweet things, but I never put myself in his power again. I had a terrible dread for two weeks and then I feared the pain for years more. One day a girl told me I'd not suffer again.

'Then a boy came. I was tempted by his virginity, but I didn't yield; then last year a young visitor at the hotel made love to me— he didn't hurt, and I enjoyed it ecstatically, for I really liked him, and he had such dear pleasing ways: he was always bringing me flowers, and he would kiss my hands and was always telling me how pretty I was and how much he loved my eyes; he was a dear!

'But now I've fallen in love with you with my whole soul and body passionately; and that's what makes me wild with jealousy. Flora is always boasting that you like her best, and I can't believe it, but I hate to hear her. I could strike the slut. But you do go with her, and I go home and cry half the night. Why can't you love me alone or love me best? Then I wouldn't care. But always to be second, to find that Flora is preferred to me: it's driving me crazy.'

Of course I kissed her, smiling, and she said: 'Promise you'll only go with me for this next week, and I'll give my very soul to you; promise! You'll see how sweet I can be—promise! I'll say all the naughty words and do all the naughty things: I want to! There! Do you hear that; I'll do more than you imagine, you dear, you!'

I promised and kept my word, but after that week Adriana never came back again, and so we lost the loveliest figure of all. In her, jealousy was stronger than passion, as it is in many, many women.

Clara

It was the gardener again who brought me to the chief discovery. He told me that Clara had no reticences and would tell me anything, so one day I got him to bring her and questioned her. She said:

'What is there to tell? It's the same thing over and over again, only it gets better and better all the time, different to (sic) most things in life. I don't know when I began. I don't think it was more than seven, but almost immediately I noticed that I didn't care for girls touching me; I only wanted boys, and I was very curious about them, though I pretended not to be.

'One boy, five or six years older than I was, when I was about ten, told me all about it and suited the action to the word. He hurt me a little, but the pleasure, even at the beginning, was greater than the pain, and so I went on with anyone I liked; and I liked a good many.

'I got very careful about thirteen because I knew what the consequences might be, and I made up my mind only to go with a man I really cared for. I don't know why I fell in love, but I did when I was about fifteen, with a gentleman who was good-looking and had charming manners. He spoke to me in the street, took me for a drive, kissed me and put his hand all over me. I didn't mind. He really was charming but when he took me up to his bedroom in his hotel, I told him I was frightened; but he assured me that I'd run no risk with him, and he kept his word. Yet, that sort of half-pleasure didn't content me, so I was very glad, indeed, when your gardener came; and since then I have been as happy as a bird!

'You want to know whether I have touched myself. Sure; all girls have. If they say they haven't, they lie; the silly fools. Why shouldn't we have pleasure when it's so easy?

'I remember my father took me once to the picture gallery in Genoa. I loved the pictures; but one had a young man in it who looked right at me. I got off next morning and went back to the gallery to my pictured lover. I could not help it! I sat down on

the bench opposite to him and crossed my legs and squeezed my
sex till I was wet. And when I went to bed that night I thought of
him, and his lovely limbs and his great eyes, and I touched myself
with my hand pretending it was him till I came again and again,
and at last got so wild I just had to stop or I'd have screamed—but
lots of girls are like that.

'I think I was one of the few who let a boy have me time and
again. I could not resist: the truth is, I wanted him as much as he
wanted me, and when an older man came after me, it was worse:
I could not refuse him, and I felt more with him than with any
boy, till I came here, and the great games began. Oh, I love them
all; and I've always been taken with you since you gave me the first
prize when I had only won the second. You great sweet!'

Naturally, after this we had a long kissing match that ended in a
new rendezvous, which was repeated frequently, for I found Clara
in many respects the most delightful of all the girls. She had really
no reticences, and loved to show her sex and to talk about her
intense sensations in the crudest terms; but she never invented or
beautified anything, and this simplicity of truth in her was most
attractive. When, for example, she said, 'When you have me I
feel the thrills running all down my thighs to the knees,' she was
plainly describing an immediate personal experience, and when
she told me that merely hearing my voice in the villa made her sex
open and shut, I could be sure it was the truth. And bit by bit this
truth of reciprocated sensation grew on me, till I, too, was won by
the novelty of the emotion. Clara was the most wonderful mistress
of them all; though the youngest.

D. H. LAWRENCE

from

Lady Chatterley's Lover

D. H. Lawrence's 'Lady Chatterley's Lover' was first printed in 1928 but the unexpurgated edition was only published in Britain in 1960 after a famous trial for obscenity.

SHE had only one desire now, to go to the clearing in the wood. The rest was a kind of painful dream. But sometimes she was kept all day at Wragby, by her duties as hostess. And then she felt as if she too were going blank, just blank and insane

One evening, guests or no guests, she escaped after tea. It was late, and she fled across the park like one who fears to be called back. The sun was setting rosy as she entered the wood, but she pressed on among the flowers. The light would last long overhead.

She arrived at the clearing flushed and semi-conscious. The keeper was there, in his shirt-sleeves, just closing up the coops for the night, so the little occupants would be safe. But still one little trio was pattering about on tiny feet, alert drab mites, under the straw shelter, refusing to be called in by the anxious mother.

'I had to come and see the chickens!' she said, panting, glancing shyly at the keeper, almost unaware of him. 'Are there any more?'

'Thurty-six so far!' he said. 'Not bad!'

He too took a curious pleasure in watching the young things come out.

Connie crouched in front of the last coop. The three chicks had run in. But still their cheeky heads came poking sharply through the yellow feathers, then withdrawing, then only one beady little head eyeing forth from the vast mother-body.

'I'd love to touch them,' she said, putting her fingers gingerly through the bars of the coop. But the mother-hen pecked at her hand fiercely, and Connie drew back startled and frightened.

'How she pecks at me! She hates, me!' she said in a wondering voice. 'But I wouldn't hurt them!'

The man standing above her laughed, and crouched down beside her, knees apart, and put his hand with quiet confidence slowly into the coop. The old hen pecked at him, but not so savagely. And slowly, softly, with sure gentle fingers, he felt among the old bird's feathers and drew out a faintly peeping chick in his closed hand.

'There!' he said, holding out his hand to her. She took the little drab thing between her hands, and there it stood, on its impossible little stalks of legs, its atom of balancing life trembling through its almost weightless feet into Connie's hands. But it lifted its handsome, clean-shaped little head boldly, and looked sharply round, and gave a little 'peep'. 'So adorable! So cheeky!' she said softly.

The keeper, squatting beside her, was also watching with an amused face the bold little bird in her hands. Suddenly he saw a tear fall on to her wrist.

And he stood up, and stood away, moving to the other coop. For suddenly he was aware of the old flame shooting and leaping up in his loins, that he had hoped was quiescent for ever. He fought against it, turning his back to her. But it leapt, and leapt downwards, circling in his knees.

He turned again to look at her. She was kneeling and holding her two hands slowly forward, blindly, so that the chicken should run in to the mother-hen again. And there was something so mute and forlorn in her, compassion flamed in his bowels for her.

Without knowing, he came quickly towards her and crouched beside her again, taking the chick from her hands, because she was afraid of the hen, and putting it back in the coop. At the back of his loins the fire suddenly darted stronger.

He glanced apprehensively at her. Her face was averted, and she was crying blindly, in all the anguish of her generation's forlorn-ness. His heart melted suddenly, like a drop of fire, and he put out his hand and laid his fingers on her knee.

'You shouldn't cry,' he said softly.

But then she put her hands over her face and felt that really her heart was broken and nothing mattered any more.

He laid his hand on her shoulder, and softly, gently, it began to travel down the curve of her back, blindly, with a blind stroking motion, to the curve of her crouching loins. And there his hand softly, softly, stroked the curve of her flank, in the blind instinctive caress.

She had found her scrap of handkerchief and was blindly trying to dry her face.

'Shall you come to the hut?' he said, in a quiet, neutral voice.

And closing his hand softly on her upper arm, he drew her up and led her slowly to the hut, not letting go of her till she was inside. Then he cleared aside the chair and table, and took a brown, soldier's blanket from the tool chest, spreading it slowly. She glanced at his face, as she stood motionless.

His face was pale and without expression, like that of a man sub-mitting to fate.

'You lie there,' he said softly, and he shut the door, so that it was dark, quite dark.

With a queer obedience, she lay down on the blanket. Then she felt the soft, groping, helplessly desirous hand touching her body, feeling for her face. The hand stroked her face softly, softly, with infinite soothing and assurance, and at last there was the soft touch of a kiss on her cheek.

She lay quite still, in a sort of sleep, in a sort of dream. Then she quivered as she felt his hand groping softly, yet with queer thwart-ed clumsiness, among her clothing. Yet the hand knew, too, how to unclothe her where it wanted. He drew down the thin silk sheath, slowly, carefully, right down and over her feet. Then with a quiver of exquisite pleasure he touched the warm soft body, and touched her navel for a moment in a kiss. And he had to come in to her at once, to enter the peace on earth of her soft, quiescent body. It was the moment of pure peace for him, the entry into the body of the woman.

She lay still, in a kind of sleep, always in a kind of sleep. The activity, the orgasm, was his, all his; she could strive for herself no more. Even the tightness of his arms round her, even the intense movement of his body, and the springing of his seed in her, was a kind of sleep, from which she did not begin to rouse till he had finished and lay softly panting against her breast.

Then she wondered, just dimly wondered, why? Why was this necessary? Why had it lifted a great cloud from her and given her peace? Was it real? Was it real?

Her tormented modern-woman's brain still had no rest. Was it real? And she knew, if she gave herself to the man, it was real. But if she kept herself for herself, it was nothing. She was old; millions of years old, she felt. And at last, she could bear the burden of herself no more. She was to be had for the taking. To be had for the taking.

The man lay in a mysterious stillness. What was he feeling? What was he thinking? She did not know. He was a strange man to her, she did not know him. She must only wait, for she did not dare to break his mysterious stillness. He lay there with his arms round her, his body on hers, his wet body touching hers, so close. And completely unknown. Yet not unpeaceful. His very stillness was peaceful.

She knew that, when at last he roused and drew away from her. It was like an abandonment. He drew her dress in the darkness down over her knees and stood a few moments apparently adjusting his own clothing. Then he quietly opened the door and went out.

She saw a very brilliant little moon shining above the afterglow over the oaks. Quickly she got up and arranged herself; she was tidy. Then she went to the door of the hut.

All the lower wood was in shadow, almost darkness. Yet the sky overhead was crystal. But it shed hardly any light. He came through the lower shadow towards her, his face lifted like a pale blotch.

'Shall we go then ?' he said.

'Where?'

'I'll go with you to the gate.'

He arranged things his own way. He locked the door of the hut and came after her.

'You aren't sorry, are you ?' he asked, as he went at her side.

'No! No! Are you?' she said.

'For that! No!' he said. Then after a while he added: 'But there's the rest of things.'

'What rest of things?' she said.

'Sir Clifford. Other folks. All the complications.'

'Why complications?' she said, disappointed.

'It's always so. For you as well as for me. There's always complications.' He walked on steadily in the dark.

'And are you sorry?' she said.

'In a way!' he replied, looking up at the sky. 'I thought I'd done with it all. Now I've begun again.'

'Begun what?'

'Life.'

'Life!' she re-echoed, with a queer thrill.

'It's life,' he said. 'There's no keeping clear. And if you do keep clear you might almost as well die. So if I've got to be broken open again, I have.'

She did not quite see it that way, but still . . .

'It's just love,' she said cheerfully.

'Whatever that may be,' he replied.

They went on through the darkening wood in silence, till they were almost at the gate.

'But you don't hate me, do you?' she said wistfully.

'Nay, nay,' he replied. And suddenly he held her fast against his breast again, with the old connecting passion. 'Nay, for me it was good, it was good. Was it for you?'

'Yes, for me too,' she answered, a little untruthfully, for she had not been conscious of much.

He kissed her softly, softly, with the kisses of warmth.

'If only there weren't so many other people in the world,' he said lugubriously.

She laughed. They were at the gate to the park. He opened it for her.

'I won't come any further,' he said.

'No!' And she held out her hand, as if to shake hands. But he took it in both his.

'Shall I come again?' she asked wistfully.

'Yes! Yes!'

She left him and went across the park.

He stood back and watched her going into the dark, against the pallor of the horizon. Almost with bitterness he watched her go. She had connected him up again, when he had wanted to be alone. She had cost him that bitter privacy of a man who at last wants only to be alone.

He turned into the dark of the wood. All was still, the moon had set. But he was aware of the noises of the night, the engines at Stacks Gate, the traffic on the main road. Slowly he climbed the denuded knoll. And from the top he could see the country, bright rows of lights at Stacks Gate, smaller lights at Tevershall pit, the yellow lights of Tevershall and lights everywhere, here and there, on the dark country, with the distant blush of furnaces, faint and rosy, since the night was clear, the rosiness of the outpouring of white-hot metal. Sharp, wicked electric lights at Stacks Gate! An undefinable quick of evil in them! And all the unease, the ever-shifting dread of the industrial night in the Midlands. He could hear the winding-engines at Stacks Gate turning down the seven-o'clock miners. The pit worked three shifts.

He went down again into the darkness and seclusion of the wood. But he knew that the seclusion of the wood was illusory. The industrial noises broke the solitude, the sharp lights, though unseen, mocked it. A man could no longer be private and withdrawn. The world allows no hermits. And now he had taken the woman, and brought on himself a new cycle of pain and doom. For he knew by experience what it meant.

It was not woman's fault, nor even love's fault, nor the fault of sex. The fault lay there, out there, in those evil electric lights and diabolical rattlings of engines. There, in the world of the mechanical greedy, greedy mechanism and mechanized greed, sparkling with lights and gushing hot metal and roaring with traffic, there lay the vast evil thing, ready to destroy whatever did not conform. Soon it would destroy the wood, and the bluebells would spring no more. All vulnerable things must perish under the rolling and running of iron.

He thought with infinite tenderness of the woman. Poor forlorn thing, she was nicer than she knew, and oh! so much too nice for the tough lot she was in contact with. Poor thing, she too had some of the vulnerability of the wild hyacinths, she wasn't all tough rubber-goods and platinum, like the modern girl. And they would do her in! As sure as life, they would do her in, as they do in all naturally tender life. Tender! Somewhere she was tender, tender with a tenderness of the growing hyacinths, something that has gone out of the celluloid woman of today. But he would protect her with his heart for a little while. For a little while, before the insentient iron world and the Mammon of mechanized greed did them both in, her as well as him.

He went home with his gun and his dog, to the dark cottage, lit the lamp, started the fire, and ate his supper of bread and cheese, young onions and beer. He was alone, in a silence he loved. His room was clean and tidy, but rather stark. Yet the fire was bright, the hearth white, the petroleum lamp hung bright over the table, with its white oil-cloth. He tried to read a book about India, but tonight he could not read. He sat by the fire in his shirt-sleeves, not smoking, but with a mug of beer in reach. And he thought about Connie.

To tell the truth, he was sorry for what had happened, perhaps most for her sake. He had a sense of foreboding. No sense of wrong or sin; he was troubled by no conscience in that respect. He knew that conscience was chiefly fear of society, or fear of oneself. He was not afraid of himself. But he was quite consciously afraid of society, which he knew by instinct to be a malevolent, partly-insane beast.

The woman! If she could be there with him, and there were nobody else in the world! The desire rose again, his penis began to stir like a live bird. At the same time an oppression, a dread of exposing himself and her to that outside Thing that sparkled viciously in the electric lights, weighted down his shoulders. She, poor young thing, was just a young female creature to him; but a young female creature whom he had gone into and whom he desired again.

Stretching with the curious yawn of desire, for he had been alone and apart from man or woman for four years, he rose and took his coat again, and his gun, lowered the lamp and went out into the starry night, with the dog. Driven by desire and by dread of the malevolent Thing outside, he made his round in the wood, slowly, softly. He loved the darkness and folded himself into it. It fitted the turgidity of his desire, which, in spite of all, was like a riches; the stirring restlessness of his penis, the stirring fire in his loins! Oh, if only there were other men to be with, to fight that sparkling electric Thing outside there, to preserve the tenderness of life, the tenderness of women, and the natural riches of desire. If only there were men to fight side by side with! But the men were all outside there, glorying in the Thing, triumphing or being trodden down in the rush of mechanized greed or of greedy mechanism.

Constance, for her part, had hurried across the park, home, almost without thinking. As yet she had no afterthought. She would be in time for dinner.

She was annoyed to find the doors fastened, however, so that she had to ring. Mrs Bolton opened.

'Why there you are, your Ladyship! I was beginning to wonder if you'd gone lost!' she said a little roguishly. 'Sir Clifford hasn't asked for you, though! he's got Mr Linley in with him, talking over something. It looks as if he'd stay to dinner, doesn't it, my Lady?'

'It does rather,' said Connie.

'Shall I put dinner back a quarter of an hour? That would give you time to dress in comfort.'

'Perhaps you'd better.'

Mr Linley was the general manager of the collieries, an elderly man from the north, with not quite enough punch to suit Clifford; not up to post-war conditions, nor post-war colliers either, with their 'ca' canny' creed. But Connie liked Mr Linley, though she was glad to be spared the toadying of his wife.

Linley stayed to dinner, and Connie was the hostess men liked so much, so modest, yet so attentive and aware, with big, wide blue eyes and a soft repose that sufficiently hid what she was really thinking. Connie had played this woman so much, it was almost second nature to her; but still, decidedly second. Yet it was curious how everything disappeared from her consciousness while she played it.

She waited patiently till she could go upstairs and think her own thoughts. She was always waiting, it seemed to be her *forte*.

Once in her room, however, she felt still vague and confused. She didn't know what to think. What sort of a man was he, really? Did he really like her? Not much, she felt. Yet he was kind. There was something, a sort of warm naïve kindness, curious and sudden, that almost opened her womb to him. But she felt he might be kind like that to any woman. Though even so, it was curiously soothing, comforting. And he was a passionate man, wholesome and passionate. But perhaps he wasn't quite individual enough; he might be the same with any woman as he had been with her. It really wasn't personal. She was only really a female to him.

But perhaps that was better. And after all, he was kind to the female in her, which no man had ever been. Men were very kind to the *person* she was, but rather cruel to the female, despising her or ignoring her altogether. Men were awfully kind to Constance Reid or to Lady Chatterley; but not to her womb they weren't kind. And he took no notice of Constance or of Lady Chatterley; he just softly stroked her loins or her breasts.

She went to the wood next day. It was a grey, still afternoon, with the dark-green dogs'-mercury spreading under the hazel copse, and all the trees making a silent effort to open their buds. Today she could almost feel it in her own body, the huge heave of the sap in the massive trees, upwards, up, up to the bud-tips, there to push into little flamey oak-leaves, bronze as blood. It was like a tide running turgid upward, and spreading on the sky.

She came to the clearing, but he was not there. She had only half expected him. The pheasant chicks were running lightly abroad, light as insects, from the coops where the fellow hens clucked anxiously. Connie sat and watched them, and waited. She only waited. Even the chicks she hardly saw. She waited.

The time passed with dream-like slowness, and he did not come. She had only half expected him. He never came in the afternoon. She must go home to tea. But she had to force herself to leave.

As she went home, a fine drizzle of rain fell.

'Is it raining again?' said Clifford, seeing her shake her hat.

'Just drizzle.'

She poured tea in silence, absorbed in a sort of obstinacy. She did want to see the keeper today, to see if it were really real. If it were really real.

'Shall I read a little to you afterwards?' said Clifford.

She looked at him. Had he sensed something?

'The spring makes me feel queer—I thought I might rest a little,' she said.

'Just as you like. Not feeling really unwell, are you?'

'No! Only rather tired—with the spring. Will you have Mrs Bolton to play something with you?'

'No! I think I'll listen in.'

She heard the curious satisfaction in his voice. She went upstairs to her bedroom. Then she heard the loudspeaker begin to bellow, in an idiotically velveteen-genteel sort of voice, something about a

series of street-cries, the very cream of genteel affectation imitat-
ing old criers. She pulled on her old violet-coloured mackintosh,
and slipped out of the house at the side door.

The drizzle of rain was like a veil over the world, mysterious,
hushed, not cold. She got very warm as she hurried across the
park. She had to open her light waterproof.

The wood was silent, still and secret in the evening drizzle of
rain, full of the mystery of eggs and half-open buds, half-
unsheathed flowers. In the dimness of it all trees glistened naked
and dark as if they had unclothed themselves, and the green things
on earth seemed to hum with greenness.

There was still no one at the clearing. The chicks had nearly all
gone under the mother-hens, only one or two last adventurous
ones still dibbed about in the dryness under the straw roof-shelter.
And they were doubtful of themselves.

So! He still had not been. He was staying away on purpose. Or
perhaps something was wrong. Perhaps she should go to the
cottage and see.

But she was born to wait. She opened the hut with her key. It
was all tidy, the corn put in the bin, the blankets folded on the
shelf, the straw neat in a corner; a new bundle of straw. The hurricane lamp hung on a nail. The table and chair had been put back
where she had lain.

She sat down on a stool in the doorway. How still everything
was! The fine rain blew very softly, filmily, but the wind made no
noise. Nothing made any sound. The trees stood like powerful
beings, dim, twilit, silent, and alive. How alive everything was!

Night was drawing near again; she would have to go. He was
avoiding her.

But suddenly he came striding into the clearing, in his black,
oilskin jacket like a chauffeur, shining with wet. He glanced
quickly at the hut, half-saluted, then veered aside and went on to
the coops. There he crouched in silence, looking carefully at
everything, then carefully shutting the hens and chicks up safe
against the night.

At last he came slowly towards her. She still sat on her stool. He stood before her under the porch.

'You come then,' he said, using the intonation of the dialect.

'Yes,' she said, looking up at him. 'You're late!'

'Ay!' he replied, looking away into the wood.

She rose slowly, drawing aside her stool.

'Did you want to come in?' she asked.

He looked down at her shrewdly.

'Won't folks be thinkin' somethink, you comin' here every night?' he said.

'Why?' She looked up at him, at a loss. 'I said I'd come. Nobody knows.'

'They soon will, though,' he replied. 'An' what then?'

She was at a loss for an answer.

'Why should they know?' she said.

'Folks always does,' he said fatally.

Her lip quivered a little.

'Well, I can't help it,' she faltered.

'Nay,' he said. 'You can help it by not comin'—if yer want to,' he added, in a lower tone.

'But I don't want to,' she murmured.

He looked away into the wood, and was silent.

'But what when folks finds out?' he asked at last. 'Think about it! Think how lowered you'll feel, one of your husband's servants.'

She looked up at his averted face.

'Is it,' she stammered, 'is it that you don't want me?'

'Think!' he said. 'Think what if folks finds out—Sir Clifford an' a'—an' everybody talkin'—'

'Well, I can go away.'

'Where to?'

'Anywhere! I've got money of my own. My mother left me twenty thousand pounds in trust, and I know Clifford can't touch it. I can go away.'

'But 'appen you don't want to go away.'

'Yes, yes! I don't care what happens to me.'

'Ay, you think that! But you'll care! You'll have to care, every-body has. You've got to remember your Ladyship is carrying on with a game-keeper. It's not as if I was a gentleman. Yes, you'd care. You'd care.'

'I shouldn't. What do I care about my ladyship! I hate it really. I feel people are jeering every time they say it. And they are, they are! Even you jeer when you say it.'

'Me!'

For the first time he looked straight at her, and into her eyes. 'I don't jeer at you,' he said.

As he looked into her eyes she saw his own eyes go dark, quite dark, the pupils dilating.

'Don't you care about a' the risk?' he asked in a husky voice. 'You should care. Don't care when it's too late!'

There was a curious warning pleading in his voice.

'But I've nothing to lose,' she said fretfully. 'If you knew what it is, you'd think I'd be glad to lose it. But are you afraid for your-self?'

'Ay!' he said briefly. 'I am. I'm afraid. I'm afraid. I'm afraid o' things.'

'What things?' she asked.

He gave a curious backward jerk of his head, indicating the outer world.

'Things! Everybody! The lot of 'em.'

Then he bent down and suddenly kissed her unhappy face.

'Nay, I don't care,' he said. 'Let's have it, an' damn the rest. But if you was to feel sorry you'd ever done it—'

'Don't put me off,' she pleaded.

He put his fingers to her cheek and kissed her again suddenly.

'Let me come in then,' he said softly. 'An' take off your mackin-tosh.'

He hung up his gun, slipped out of his wet leather jacket, and reached for the blankets.

'I brought another blanket,' he said, 'so we can put one over us if you like.'

'I can't stay long,' she said. 'Dinner is half past seven.'

He looked at her swiftly, then at his watch.

'All right,' he said.

He shut the door, and lit a tiny light in the hanging hurricane lamp.

'One time we'll have a long time,' he said.

He put the blankets down carefully, one folded for her head. Then he sat down a moment on the stool, and drew her to him, holding her close with one arm, feeling for her body with his free hand. She heard the catch of his intaken breath as he found her. Under her frail petticoat she was naked.

'Eh! what it is to touch thee!' he said, as his finger caressed the delicate, warm, secret skin of her waist and hips. He put his face down and rubbed his cheek against her belly and against her thighs again and again. And again she wondered a little over the sort of rapture it was to him. She did not understand the beauty he found in her, through touch upon her living secret body, almost the ecstasy of beauty. For passion alone is awake to it. And when passion is dead, or absent, then the magnificent throb of beauty is incomprehensible and even a little despicable; warm, live beauty of contact, so much deeper than the beauty of vision. She felt the glide of his cheek on her thighs and belly and buttocks, and the close brushing of his moustache and his soft thick hair, and her knees began to quiver. Far down in her she felt a new stirring, a new nakedness emerging. And she was half afraid. Half she wished he would not caress her so. He was encompassing her somehow. Yet she was waiting, waiting.

And when he came into her, with an intensification of relief and consummation that was pure peace to him, still she was waiting. She felt herself a little left out. And she knew, partly it was her own fault. She willed herself into the separateness. Now perhaps she was condemned to it. She lay still, feeling his motion within her, his deep-sunk intentness, the sudden quiver of him at the springing of his seed, then the slow subsiding thrust. That thrust of the buttocks, surely it was a little ridiculous. If you were a woman,

and a part in all the business, surely that thrusting of the man's buttocks was supremely ridiculous. Surely the man was intensely
ridiculous in this posture and this act!

But she lay still, without recoil. Even when he had finished. She
did not rouse herself to get a grip on her own satisfaction, as she
had done with Michaelis; she lay still, and the tears slowly filled
and ran from her eyes.

He, lay still, too. But he held her close and tried to cover her
poor naked legs with his legs, to keep them warm. He lay on her
with a close, undoubting warmth.

'Are yer cold?' he asked, in a soft, small voice, as if she were
close, so close. Whereas she was left out, distant.

'No ! But I must go,' she said gently.

He sighed, held her close, then relaxed to rest again.

He had not guessed her tears. He thought she was there with him.

'I must go,' she repeated.

He lifted himself, kneeled beside her a moment, kissed the
inner side of her thighs, then drew down her skirts, buttoning his
own clothes unthinking, not even turning aside, in the faint, faint
light from the lantern.

'Tha mun com ter th' cottage one time,' he said, looking down
at her with a warm, sure, easy face.

But she lay there inert, and was gazing up at him thinking:
Stranger! Stranger! She even resented him a little.

He put on his coat and looked for his hat, which had fallen,
then he slung on his gun.

'Come then!' he said, looking down at her with those warm,
peaceful sort of eyes.

She rose slowly. She didn't want to go. She also rather resented
staying. He helped her with her thin waterproof, and saw she was
tidy.

Then he opened the door. The outside was quite dark. The faithful dog under the porch stood up with pleasure seeing him. The
drizzle of rain drifted greyly past upon the darkness. It was quite dark.

'Ah mun ta'e th' lantern,' he said. 'The'll be nob'dy.'

He walked just before her in the narrow path, swinging the hurricane lamp low, revealing the wet grass, the black shiny tree-roots like snakes, wan flowers. For the rest, all was grey rain-mist and complete darkness.

'Tha mun come to the cottage one time,' he said, 'shall ta? We might as well be hung for a sheep as for a lamb.'

It puzzled her, his queer, persistent wanting her, when there was nothing between them, when he never really spoke to her, and in spite of herself she resented the dialect. His 'tha mun come' seemed not addressed to her, but some common woman. She recognized the foxglove leaves of the riding and knew, more or less, where they were.

'It's quarter past seven,' he said, 'you'll do it.' He had changed his voice, seemed to feel her distance. As they turned the last bend in the riding towards the hazel wall and the gate, he blew out the light. 'We'll see from here,' he said, taking her gently by the arm.

But it was difficult, the earth under their feet was a mystery, but he felt his way by tread: he was used to it. At the gate he gave her his electric torch. 'It's a bit lighter in the park,' he said; 'but take it for fear you get off th' path.'

It was true, there seemed a ghost-glimmer of greyness in the open space of the park. He suddenly drew her to him and whipped his hand under her dress again, feeling her warm body with his wet chill hand.

'I could die for the touch of a woman like thee,' he said in his throat. 'If tha' would stop another minute.'

She felt the sudden force of his wanting her again.

'No, I must run,' she said, a little wildly.

'Ay,' he replied, suddenly changed, letting her go.

She turned away, and on the instant she turned back to him saying: 'Kiss me.'

He bent over her indistinguishable and kissed her on the left eye. She held her mouth and he softly kissed it, but at once drew away. He hated mouth kisses.

'I'll come tomorrow,' she said, drawing away; 'if I can,' she added.

'Ay! not so late,' he replied out of the darkness. Already she could not see him at all.

'Goodnight,' she said.

'Goodnight, your Ladyship,' his voice.

She stopped and looked back into the wet dark. She could just see the bulk of him. 'Why did you say that?' she said.

'Nay,' he replied. 'Goodnight then, run!'

She plunged on in the dark-grey tangible light. She found the side door open, and slipped into her room unseen. As she closed the door, the gong sounded, but she would take her bath all the same—she must take her bath. 'But I won't be late any more,' she said to herself; 'it's too annoying.'

The next day she did not go to the wood. She went instead with Clifford to Uthwaite. He could occasionally go out now in the car, and had got a strong young man as chauffeur, who could help him out of the car if need be. He particularly wanted to see his god-father, Leslie Winter, who lived at Shipley Hall, not far from Uthwaite. Winter was an elderly gentleman now, wealthy, one of the wealthy coal-owners who had had their heyday in King Edward's time. King Edward had stayed more than once at Shipley, for the shooting. It was a handsome old stucco hall, very elegantly appointed, for Winter was a bachelor and prided himself on his style: but the place was beset by collieries. Leslie Winter was attached to Clifford, but personally did not entertain a great respect for him, because of the photographs in illustrated papers and the literature. The old man was a buck of the King Edward school, who thought life was life and the scribbling fellows were something else. Towards Connie the Squire was always rather gallant; he thought her an attractive demure maiden and rather wasted on Clifford, and it was a thousand pities she stood no chance of bringing forth an heir to Wragby. He himself had no heir.

Connie wondered what he would say if he knew that Clifford's game-keeper had been having intercourse with her, and saying to her 'tha mun come to th' cottage one time.' He would detest and despise her, for he had come almost to hate the shoving forward of the working classes. A man of her own class he would not mind, for Connie was gifted from nature with this appearance of demure, submissive maidenliness, and perhaps it was part of her nature. Winter called her 'dear child' and gave her a rather lovely miniature of an eighteenth-century lady, rather against her will.

But Connie was preoccupied with her affair with the keeper.

After all, Mr Winter, who was really a gentleman and a man of the world, treated her as a person and a discriminating individual; he did not lump her together with all the rest of his female womanhood in his 'thee' and 'tha'.

She did not go to the wood that day nor the next, nor the day following. She did not go so long as she felt, or imagined she felt, the man waiting for her, wanting her. But the fourth day she was terribly unsettled and uneasy. She still refused to go to the wood and open her thighs once more to the man. She thought of all the things she might do—drive to Sheffield, pay visits, and the thought of all these things was repellent. At last she decided to take a walk, not towards the wood, but in the opposite direction; she would go to Marehay, through the little iron gate in the other side of the park fence. It was a quiet grey day of spring, almost warm. She walked on unheeding, absorbed in thoughts she was not even conscious of. She was not really aware of anything outside her, till she was startled by the loud barking of the dog at Marehay Farm. Marehay Farm! Its pastures ran up to Wragby park fence, so they were neighbours, but it was some time since Connie had called.

'Bell!' she said to the big white bull-terrier. 'Bell! have you forgotten me? Don't you know me?' She was afraid of dogs, and Bell stood back and bellowed, and she wanted to pass through the farmyard on to the warren path.

Mrs Flint appeared. She was a woman of Constance's own age, had been a school-teacher, but Connie suspected her of being rather a false little thing.

'Why, it's Lady Chatterley! Why!' And Mrs Flint's eyes glowed again, and she flushed like a young girl. 'Bell, Bell. Why! barking at Lady Chatterley! Bell! Be quiet!' She darted forward and slashed at the dog with a white cloth she held in her hand, then came forward to Connie.

'She used to know me,' said Connie, shaking hands. The Flints were Chatterley tenants.

'Of course she knows your Ladyship! She's just showing off,' said Mrs Flint, glowing and looking up with a sort of flushed confusion, 'but it's so long since she's seen you. I do hope you are better.'

'Yes thanks, I'm all right.'

'We've hardly seen you all winter. Will you come in and look at the baby?'

'Well!' Connie hesitated. 'Just for a minute.'

Mrs Flint flew wildly in to tidy up, and Connie came slowly after her, hesitating in the rather dark kitchen, where the kettle was boiling by the fire. Back came Mrs Flint.

'I do hope you'll excuse me,' she said. 'Will you come in here?'

They went into the living-room, where a baby was sitting on the rag hearthrug, and the table was roughly set for tea. A young servant-girl backed down the passage, shy and awkward.

The baby was a perky little thing of about a year, with red hair like its father, and cheeky pale-blue eyes. It was a girl, and not to be daunted. It sat among cushions and was surrounded with rag dolls and other toys in modern excess.

'Why, what a dear she is!' said Connie, 'and how she's grown! A big girl! A big girl!'

She had given it a shawl when it was born, and celluloid ducks for Christmas.

'There, Josephine! Who's that come to see you? Who's this Josephine? Lady Chatterley—you know Lady Chatterley, don't you?'

The queer pert little mite gazed cheekily at Connie. Ladyships were still all the same to her.

'Come! Will you come to me?' said Connie to the baby.

The baby didn't care one way or another, so Connie picked her up and held her in her lap. How warm and lovely it was to hold a child in one's lap, and the soft little arms, the unconscious cheeky little legs.

'I was just having a rough cup of tea all by myself. Luke's gone to market, so I can have it when I like. Would you care for a cup, Lady Chatterley? I don't suppose it's what you're used to, but if you would . . .'

Connie would, though she didn't want to be reminded of what she was used to. There was a great re-laying of the table, and the best cups brought and the best tea-pot.

'If only you wouldn't take any trouble,' said Connie.

But if Mrs Flint took no trouble, where was the fun! So Connie played with the child and was amused by its little female dauntless-ness, and got a deep voluptuous pleasure out of its soft young warmth. Young life! And so fearless! So fearless, because so defenceless. All the other people, so narrow with fear!

She had a cup of tea, which was rather strong, and very good bread and butter, and bottled damsons. Mrs Flint flushed and glowed and bridled with excitement, as if Connie were some gal-lant knight. And they had a real female chat, and both of them enjoyed it.

'It's a poor little tea, though,' said Mrs Flint.

'It's much nicer than at home,' said Connie truthfully.

'Oh-h!' said Mrs Flint, not believing, of course.

But at last Connie rose.

'I must go,' she said. 'My husband has no idea where I am. He'll be wondering all kinds of things.'

'He'll never think you're here,' laughed Mrs Flint excitedly. 'He'll be sending the crier round.'

'Goodbye, Josephine,' said Connie, kissing the baby and ruffling its red, wispy hair.

Mrs Flint insisted on opening the locked and barred front door. Connie emerged in the farm's little front garden, shut in by a priv-et hedge. There were two rows of auriculas by the path, very vel-vety and rich.

'Lovely auriculas,' said Connie.

'Recklesses, as Luke calls them,' laughed Mrs Flint. 'Have some.'
And eagerly she picked the velvet and primrose flowers.

'Enough! Enough!' said Connie.

They came to the little garden gate.

'Which way were you going?' asked Mrs Flint.

'By the warren.'

'Let me see! Oh yes, the cows are in the gin close. But they're
not up yet. But the gate's locked, you'll have to climb.'

'I can climb,' said Connie.

'Perhaps I can just go down the close with you.'

'They went down the poor, rabbit-bitten pasture. Birds were
whistling in wild evening triumph in the wood. A man was calling
up the last cows, which trailed slowly over the path-worn pasture.

'They're late, milking, tonight,' said Mrs Flint severely. 'They
know Luke won't be back till after dark.'

They came to the fence, beyond which the young fir-wood
bristled dense. There was a little gate, but it was locked. In the
grass on the inside stood a bottle, empty.

'There's the keeper's empty bottle for his milk,' explained Mrs
Flint. 'We bring it as far as here for him, and then he fetches it
himself.'

'When?' said Connie.

'Oh, any time he's around. Often in the morning. Well, goodbye,
Lady Chatterley! And do come again. It was so lovely having you.'

Connie climbed the fence into the narrow path between the
dense, bristling young firs. Mrs Flint went running back across the
pasture, in a sun-bonnet, because she was really a school-teacher.
Constance didn't like this dense new part of the wood; it seemed
gruesome and choking. She hurried on with her head down,
thinking of the Flints' baby. It was a dear little thing, but it would
be a bit bow-legged like its father. It showed already, but perhaps
it would grow out of it. How warm and fulfilling somehow to
have a baby, and how Mrs Flint had showed it off! She had something anyhow that Connie hadn't got, and apparently couldn't

have. Yes, Mrs Flint had flaunted her motherhood. And Connie had been just a bit, just a little bit jealous. She couldn't help it.

She started out of her muse, and gave a little cry of fear. A man was there.

It was the keeper. He stood in the path like Balaam's ass, barring her way.

'How's this?' he said in surprise.

'How did you come?' she panted.

'How did you? Have you been to the hut?'

'No! No! I went to Marehay.'

He looked at her curiously, searchingly, and she hung her head a little guiltily.

'And were you going to the hut now?' he asked rather sternly.

'No! I mustn't. I stayed at Marehay. No one knows where I am. I'm late. I've got to run.'

'Giving me the slip, like?' he said, with a faint ironic smile.

'No! No. Not that. Only—'

'Why, what else?' he said. And he stepped up to her and put his arms around her. She felt the front of his body terribly near to her, and alive.

'Oh, not now, not now,' she cried, trying to push him away.'

'Why not? It's only six o'clock. You've got half an hour. Nay! Nay! I want you.'

He held her fast and she felt his urgency. Her old instinct was to fight for her freedom. But something else in her was strange and inert and heavy. His body was urgent against her, and she hadn't the heart any more to fight.

He looked around.

'Come—come here! Through here,' he said, looking penetratingly into the dense fir-trees, that were young and not more than half-grown.

He looked back at her. She saw his eyes, tense and brilliant, fierce, not loving. But her will had left her. A strange weight was on her limbs. She was giving way. She was giving up.

He led her through the wall of prickly trees, that were difficult

to come through, to a place where was a little space and a pile of
dead boughs. He threw one or two dry ones down, put his coat
and waistcoat over them, and she had to lie down there under the
boughs of the tree, like an animal, while he waited, standing there
in his shirt and breeches, watching her with haunted eyes. But still
he was provident—he made her lie properly, properly. Yet he
broke the band of her underclothes, for she did not help him, only
lay inert.

He too had bared the front part of his body and she felt his
naked flesh against her as he came into her. For a moment he was
still inside her, turgid there and quivering. Then as he began to
move, in the sudden helpless orgasm, there awoke in her strange
thrills rippling inside her. Rippling, rippling, rippling, like a flapping overlapping of soft flames, soft as feathers, running to points
of brilliance, exquisite, exquisite and melting her all molten inside.
It was like bells rippling up and up to a culmination. She lay
unconscious of the wild little cries she uttered to the last. But it
was over too soon, too soon, and she could no longer force her
own conclusion with her own activity. This was different,
different. She could do nothing. She could no longer harden and
grip for her own satisfaction upon him. She could only wait, wait
and moan in spirit as she felt him withdrawing, withdrawing and
contracting, coming to the terrible moment when he would slip
out of her and be gone. Whilst all her womb was open and soft,
and softly clamouring, like a sea-anemone under the tide, clamouring for him to come in again and make a fulfilment for her. She
clung to him unconscious in passion, and he never quite slipped
from her, and she felt the soft bud of him within her stirring, and
strange rhythms flushing up into her with a strange rhythmic
growing motion, swelling and swelling till it filled all her cleaving
consciousness, and then began again the unspeakable motion that
was not really motion, but pure deepening whirlpools of sensation
swirling deeper and deeper through all her tissue and consciousness, till she was one perfect concentric fluid of feeling, and she lay
there crying in unconscious inarticulate cries. The voice out of the

uttermost night, the life! The man heard it beneath him with a kind of awe, as his life sprang out into her. And as it subsided, he subsided too and lay utterly still, unknowing, while her grip on him slowly relaxed, and she lay inert. And they lay and knew nothing not even of each other, both lost. Till at last he began to rouse and become aware of his defenceless nakedness, and she was aware that his body was loosening its clasp on her. He was coming apart; but in her breast she felt she could not bear him to leave her uncovered. He must cover her now for ever.

But he drew away at last, and kissed her and covered her over, and began to cover himself. She lay looking up to the boughs of the tree, unable as yet to move. He stood and fastened up his breeches, looking round. All was dense and silent, save for the awed dog with its paws against its nose. He sat down again on the brushwood and took Connie's hand in silence.

She turned and looked at him. 'We came off together that time,' he said.

MARY McCARTHY

from

The Group

Mary McCarthy published 'The Group' in 1954. It is regarded as a classic account of girls growing up in the America of the thirties and, amongst other things, discovering about sex.

JUST at first, in the dark hallway, it had given Dottie rather a funny feeling to be tiptoeing up the stairs only two nights after Kay's wedding to a room right across from Harald's old room, where the same thing had happened to Kay. An awesome feeling, really, like when the group all got the curse at the same time; it filled you with strange ideas about being a woman, with the moon compelling you like the tides. All sorts of weird, irrelevant ideas floated through Dottie's head as the key turned in the lock and she found herself, for the first time, alone with a man in his flat. Tonight was midsummer's night, the summer solstice, when maids had given up their treasure to fructify the crops; she had that in background reading for *A Midsummer Night's Dream*. Her Shakespeare teacher had been awfully keen on anthropology and had had them study in Frazer about the ancient fertility rites and how the peasants in Europe, till quite recent times, had lit big bon-fires in honour of the Corn Maiden and then lain together in the fields. College, reflected Dottie as the lamp clicked on, had been almost *too* rich an experience. She felt stuffed with interesting thoughts that she could only confide in Mother, not in a man, certainly, who would probably suppose you were barmy if you started telling him about the Corn Maiden when you were just about to lose your virginity. Even the group would laugh if Dottie confessed that she was exactly in the mood for a long, comfy discussion with Dick, who was so frightfully attractive and unhappy and had so much to give.

But the group would never believe, never in a million years, that Dottie Renfrew would come here, to this attic room that smelled of cooking-fat, with a man she hardly knew, who made no secret of his intentions, who had been drinking heavily, and who was evidently not in love with her. When she put it that way, crudely, she could scarcely believe it herself, and the side of her that wanted to talk was still hoping, probably, to gain a little time, the way, she had noticed, she always started a discussion of current events with the dentist to keep him from turning on the drill. Dottie's dimple twinkled. What an odd comparison! If the group could hear that!

And yet when It happened, it was not at all what the group or even Mother would have imagined, not a bit sordid or messy, in spite of Dick's being tight. He had been most considerate, undressing her slowly, in a matter-of-fact way, as if he were helping her off with her outdoor things. He took her hat and furs and put them in the closet and then unfastened her dress, bending over the snaps with a funny, concentrated scowl, rather like Daddy's when he was hooking Mother up for a party. Lifting the dress carefully off her, he had glanced at the label and then back at Dottie, as though to match the two, before he carried it, walking very steadily, to the closet and arranged it on a wooden hanger. After that, he folded each garment as he removed it and set it ceremoniously on the armchair, looking each time at the label with a frown between his brows. When her dress was gone, she felt rather faint for a minute, but he left her in her slip, just as they did in the doctor's office, while he took off her shoes and stockings and undid her brassière and girdle and step-ins, so that finally, when he drew her slip over her head, with great pains so as not to muss her hairdo, she was

hardly trembling when she stood there in front of him with nothing on but her pearls. Perhaps it was going to the doctor so much
or perhaps it was Dick himself, so detached and impersonal, the
way they were supposed to be in art class with the model, that made
Dottie brave. He had not touched her once, all the time he was
undressing her, except by accident, grazing her skin. Then he
pinched each of her full breasts lightly and told her to relax, in just
the tone Dr Perry used when he was going to give her a treatment
for her sciatica.

He handed her a book of drawings to look at, while he went
into the closet, and Dottie sat there in the armchair, trying not to
listen. With the book on her lap, she studied the room conscien-
tiously, in order to know Dick better. Rooms told a lot about a
person. It had a skylight and a big north window and was surprisingly neat for a man; there was a drawing-board with some work
on it which she longed to peek at, a long plain table, like an
ironing-table, monk's-cloth curtains, and a monk's-cloth spread on
the single bed. On the chest of drawers was a framed photograph
of a blonde woman, very striking, with a short, severe haircut; that
must be 'Betty', the wife. Tacked up on the wall there was a snap-
shot that looked like her in a bathing-suit and a number of
sketches from the nude, and Dottie had the sinking feeling that
they might be of Betty too. She had been doing her very best not
to let herself think about love or let her emotions get entangled,
for she knew that Dick would not like it. It was just a physical
attraction, she had been telling herself over and over, while trying
to remain cool and collected despite the pounding of her blood,
but now, suddenly, when it was too late to retreat, she had lost her
sang-froid and was jealous. Worse than that, even, the idea came to
her that Dick was, well, *peculiar*. She opened the book of drawings
on her lap and found more nudes, signed by some modern artist
she had never heard of! She did not know, a second later, just what
she had been expecting, but Dick's return was, by contrast, less
bad.

He came in wearing a pair of white shorts and carrying a

towel, with a hotel's name on it, which he stretched out on the
bed, having turned back the covers. He took the book away from
her and put it on a table. Then he made Dottie lie down on the
towel, telling her to relax again, in a friendly, instructive voice;
while he stood for a minute, looking down at her and smiling,
with his hands on his hips, she tried to breathe naturally, reminding herself that she had a good figure, and forced a wan, answering
smile to her lips. 'Nothing will happen unless you want it, baby.' The
words, lightly stressed, told her how scared and mistrustful she
must be looking. 'I know, Dick,' she answered, in a small, weak,
grateful voice, making herself use his name aloud for the first time.
'Would you like a cigarette?' Dottie shook her head and let it drop
back on the pillow. 'All right, then?' 'All right.' As he moved to
turn out the light, she felt a sudden harsh thump of excitement,
right in *there*, like what had happened to her in the Italian
restaurant when he said 'Do you want to come home with me?'
and fastened his deep, shadowed eyes on her. Now he turned and
looked at her steadily again, his hand on the bridge lamp; her own
eyes, widening with amazement at the funny feeling she noticed,
as if she were on fire, in the place her thighs were shielding, stared
at him, seeking confirmation; she swallowed. In reply, he switched
off the lamp and came towards her in the dark, unbuttoning his
shorts.

This shift gave her an instant in which to be afraid. She had
never seen *that* part of a man, except in statuary and once, at the
age of six, when she had interrupted Daddy in his bath, but she
had a suspicion that it would be something ugly and darkly
inflamed, surrounded by coarse hair. Hence, she had been very
grateful for being spared the sight of it, which she did not think
she could have borne, and she held her breath as the strange body
climbed on hers, shrinking. 'Open your legs,' he commanded, and
her legs obediently fell apart. His hand squeezed her down there,
rubbing and stroking; her legs fell farther apart, and she started to
make weak, moaning noises, almost as if she wanted him to stop.
He took his hand away, thank heaven, and fumbled for a second;

then she felt it, the thing she feared, being guided into her as she braced herself and stiffened. 'Relax,' he whispered. 'You're ready.' It was surprisingly warm and smooth, but it hurt terribly, pushing and stabbing. 'Damn it,' he said. 'Relax. You're making it harder.' Just then, Dottie screamed faintly; it had gone all the way in. He put his hand over her mouth and then settled her legs around him and commenced to move it back and forth inside her. At first, it hurt so that she flinched at each stroke and tried to pull back, but this only seemed to make him more determined. Then, while she was still praying for it to be over, surprise of surprises, she started to like it a little. She got the idea, and her body began to move too in answer, as he pressed *that* home in her slowly, over and over, and slowly drew it back, as if repeating a question. Her breath came quicker. Each lingering stroke, like a violin bow, made her palpitate for the next. Then, all of a sudden, she seemed to explode in a series of long, uncontrollable contractions that embarrassed her, like the hiccups, the moment they were over, for it was as if she had forgotten Dick as a person; and he, as if he sensed this, pulled quickly away from her and thrust that part of himself onto her stomach, where it pushed and pounded at her flesh. Then he too jerked and moaned, and Dottie felt something damp and sticky running down the hill of her belly.

Minutes passed; the room was absolutely still; through the skylight Dottie could see the moon. She lay there, with Dick's weight still on her, suspecting that something had gone wrong—probably her fault. His face was turned sideward so that she could not look into it, and his chest was squashing her breasts so that she could hardly breathe. Both their bodies were wet, and the cold perspiration from him ran down her face and matted her side hair and made a little rivulet between her breasts; on her lips it had a salty sting that reminded her forlornly of tears. She was ashamed of the happiness she had felt. Evidently, he had not found her satisfactory as a partner or else he would say something. Perhaps the woman was not supposed to move? 'Damn it,' he had said to her, when he was hurting her, in such a testy voice, like a man saying

'Damn it, why can't we have dinner on time?' or something unromantic like that. Was it her screaming out that had spoiled everything? Or had she made a *faux pas* at the end, somehow? She wished that books were a little more explicit; Krafft-Ebing, which Kay and Helena had found at a secondhand bookstore and kept reading aloud from, as if it were very funny, mostly described nasty things like men making love to hens, and even then did not explain how it was done. The thought of the blonde on the bureau filled her with hopeless envy; probably Dick at this moment was making bitter comparisons. She could feel his breathing and smell the stale alcohol that came from him in gusts. In the bed, there was a peculiar pungent odour, and she feared that it might come from her.

The horrible idea occurred to her that he had fallen asleep, and she made a few gentle movements to try to extricate herself from under him. Their damp skins, stuck together, made a little sucking noise when she pulled away, but she could not roll his weight off her. Then she knew that he was asleep. Probably he was tired, she said to herself forgivingly; he had those dark rings under his eyes. But down in her heart she knew that he ought not to have gone to sleep like a ton of bricks on top of her; it was the final proof, if she still needed one, that she meant nothing to him. When he woke up tomorrow morning and found her gone, he would probably be glad. Or perhaps he would not even remember who had been there with him; she could not guess how much he had had to drink before he met her for dinner. What had happened, she feared, was that he had simply passed out. She saw that her only hope of saving her own dignity was to dress in the dark and steal away. But she would have to find the bathroom somewhere outside in that unlit hall. Dick began to snore. The sticky liquid had dried and was crusting on her stomach; she felt she could not go back to the Vassar Club without washing it off. Then the worst thought, almost, of all struck her. Supposing he had started to have an emission while he was still inside her? Or if he had used one of the rubber things and it had broken when she had jerked like that

and that was why he had pulled so sharply away? She had heard of
the rubber things breaking or leaking and how a woman could get
pregnant from just a single drop. Full of determination, Dottie
heaved and squirmed to free herself, until Dick raised his head in
the moonlight and stared at her, without recognition. It was all
true then, Dottie thought miserably; he had just gone to sleep and
forgotten her. She tried to slide out of the bed.

Dick sat up and rubbed his eyes. 'Oh, it's you, Boston,' he muttered, putting an arm around her waist. 'Forgive me for dropping
off.' He got up and turned on the bridge lamp. Dottie hurriedly
covered herself with the sheet and averted her face; she was still
timorous of seeing him in the altogether. 'I must go home, Dick,'
she said soberly, stealing a sideward look at her clothes folded on
the armchair. '*Must* you?' he inquired in a mocking tone; she
could imagine his reddish eyebrows shooting up. 'You needn't
trouble to dress and see me downstairs,' she went on quickly and
firmly, her eyes fixed on the rug where his bare handsome feet
were planted. He stooped and picked up his shorts; she watched
his feet clamber into them. Then her eyes slowly rose and met his
searching gaze. 'What's the matter, Boston?' he said kindly. 'Girls
don't run home, you know, on their first night. Did it hurt you
much?' Dottie shook her head. 'Are you bleeding?' he demanded.
'Come on, let me look.' He lifted her up and moved her down on
the bed, the sheet trailing along with her; there was a small blood-
stain on the towel. 'The very bluest,' he said, 'but only a minute
quantity. Betty bled like a pig.' Dottie said nothing. 'Out with it,
Boston,' he said brusquely, jerking a thumb towards the framed
photograph. 'Does *she* put your nose out of joint?' Dottie made a
brave negative sign. There was one thing she had to say. 'Dick,' and
she shut her eyes in shame, 'do you think I should take a douche?'
'A douche?' he repeated in a mystified tone. 'Why? What for?'
'Well, in case . . . *you* know . . . birth control,' murmured Dottie.
Dick stared at her and suddenly burst out laughing; he dropped
onto a straight chair and threw his handsome head back. 'My dear
girl,' he said, 'we just employed the most ancient form of birth

control. *Coitus interruptus*, the old Romans called it, and a horrid nuisance it is.' 'I thought perhaps . . .?' said Dottie. 'Don't think. What did you think? I promise you, there isn't a single sperm swimming up to fertilize your irreproachable ovum. Like the man in the Bible, I spilled my seed on the ground, or, rather, on your very fine belly.' With a swift motion, he pulled the sheet back before she could stop him. 'Now,' he said, 'lay bare your thoughts.' Dottie shook her head and blushed. Wild horses could not make her, for the words embarrassed her frightfully; she had nearly choked on 'douche' and 'birth control', as it was. 'We must get you cleaned up,' he decreed after a moment's silence. He put on a robe and slippers and disappeared to the bathroom. It seemed a long time before he came back, bringing a dampened towel, with which he swabbed off her stomach. Then he dried her, rubbing hard with the dry end of it, sitting down beside her on the bed. He himself appeared much fresher, as though he had washed, and he smelled of mouthwash and tooth powder. He lit two cigarettes and gave her one and settled an ashtray between them.

'You *came*, Boston,' he remarked, with the air of a satisfied instructor. Dottie glanced uncertainly at him; could he mean that thing he had done that she did not like to think about? 'I beg your pardon,' she murmured. 'I mean you had an orgasm.' Dottie made a vague, still-inquiring noise in her throat; she was pretty sure, now, she understood, but the new word discombobulated her. 'A climax,' he added, more sharply. 'Do they teach that word at Vassar?' 'Oh,' said Dottie, almost disappointed that that was all there was to it. 'Was that . . .?' She could not finish the question. 'That was it,' he nodded. 'That is, if I am a judge.' 'It's normal then?' she wanted to know, beginning to feel better. Dick shrugged. 'Not for girls of your upbringing. Not the first time, usually. Appearances to the contrary, you're probably highly sexed.'

Dottie turned even redder. According to Kay, a climax was something very unusual, something the husband brought about by carefully studying his wife's desires and by patient manual stimulation. The terms made Dottie shudder, even in memory; there was a horrid bit, all in Latin, in Krafft-Ebing, about the Empress Maria Theresa and what the court doctor told her consort to do that Dottie had glanced at quickly and then tried to forget. Yet even Mother hinted that satisfaction was something that came after a good deal of time and experience and that love made a big difference. But when Mother talked about satisfaction, it was not clear exactly what she meant, and Kay was not clear either, except when she quoted from books. Polly Andrews once asked her whether it was the same as feeling passionate when you were necking (that was when Polly was engaged), and Kay said yes, pretty much, but Dottie now thought that Kay had been mistaken or else trying to hide the truth from Polly for some reason. Dottie had felt passionate, quite a few times, when she was dancing with someone terribly attractive, but that was quite different from the thing Dick meant. You would almost think that Kay did not know what she was talking about. Or else that Kay and Mother meant something else altogether and this thing with Dick was abnormal. And yet he seemed so pleased, sitting there, blowing out smoke rings; probably, having lived abroad, he knew more than Mother and Kay.

'What are you frowning over now, Boston?' Dottie gave a start. 'To be highly sexed,' he said gently, 'is an excellent thing in a woman. You mustn't be ashamed.' He took her cigarette and put it out and laid his hands on her shoulders. 'Buck up,' he said. 'What you're feeling is natural. '*Post coitum, omne animal triste est*,' as the Roman poet said.' He slipped his hand down the slope of her shoulder and lightly touched her nipple. 'Your body surprised you tonight. You must learn to know it.' Dottie nodded. 'Soft,' he murmured, pressing the nipple between his thumb and forefinger. 'Detumescence, that's what you're experiencing.' Dottie drew a quick breath, fascinated; her doubts slid away. As he continued to squeeze it, her nipple stood up. 'Erectile tissue,' he said informatively and touched the other breast. 'See,' he said, and they both looked downward. The two nipples were hard and full, with a pink aureole of goose pimples around them; on her breasts were a few dark hairs. Dottie waited tensely. A great relief had surged through her; these were the very terms Kay cited from the marriage handbooks. Down there, she felt a quick new tremor. Her lips parted. Dick smiled. 'You feel something?' he said. Dottie nodded. 'You'd like it again?' he said, assaying her with his hand. Dottie stiffened; she pressed her thighs together. She was ashamed of the violent sensation his exploring fingers had discovered. But he held his hand there, between her clasped thighs, and grasped her right hand in his other, guiding it downward to the opening of his robe and pressed it over that part of himself, which was soft and limp, rather sweet, really, all curled up on itself like a fat worm. Sitting beside her, he looked into her face as he stroked her down there and tightened her hand on him 'There's a little ridge there,' he whispered. 'Run your fingers up and down it.' Dottie obeyed, wonderingly; she felt his organ stiffen a little, which gave her a strange sense of power. She struggled against the excitement his tickling thumb was producing in her own external part; but as she felt him watching her, her eyes closed and her thighs spread open. He disengaged her hand, and she fell back on the bed, gasping. His thumb continued its play and she let herself yield to what it was doing, her whole attention concentrated on a tense pinpoint of sensation, which suddenly discharged itself in a nervous, fluttering spasm; her body arched and heaved and then lay still. When his hand returned to touch her, she struck it feebly away. 'Don't,' she moaned, rolling over on her stomach. This second climax, which she now recognized from the first one, though it was different, left her jumpy and disconcerted; it was something less thrilling and more like being tickled relentlessly or having to go to the bathroom. 'Didn't you like that?' he demanded, turning her head over on the pillow, so that she could not hide herself from him. She hated to think of his having watched her while he brought *that* about. Slowly, Dottie opened her eyes and resolved to tell the truth. 'Not quite so much as the other, Dick.' Dick laughed. 'A nice normal girl. Some of your sex prefer that.' Dottie shivered; she could not deny that it had been exciting but it seemed to her

almost perverted. He appeared to read her thoughts. 'Have you
ever done it with a girl, Boston?' He tilted her face so that he
could scan it. Dottie reddened. 'Heavens, no.' 'You come like a
house afire. How do you account for that?' Dottie shook her head
violently; the suggestion wounded her. 'In your dreams?' Dottie
reluctantly nodded. 'A little. Not the whole thing.' 'Rich erotic
fantasies of a Chestnut Street virgin,' remarked Dick, stretching.
He got up and went to the chest of drawers and took out two pairs
of pyjamas and tossed one of them to Dottie. 'Put them on now
and go to the bathroom. Tonight's lesson is concluded.'

PAULINE RÉAGE

from

The Story of O

'The story of O', one of the most famous erotic novels of all time, was written by Pauline Réage. It was published in Paris in 1954 though not in England until 1970.

Sir Stephen

THE Ile Saint-Louis apartment O lived in was in the attic storey of an old building on a southern quay by the Seine. The rooms were mansarded, spacious and low, and the two of them that were on the façade side each opened out upon a balcony inset between sloping sections of roof. One of these last was O's bedroom; the other—where, on one wall, full-length bookcases framed the fire-place—served as a living-room, as a study and could, if need be, function temporarily as a bedroom: there was a broad divan before the two windows, and a large antique table in front of the fireplace. Were her dinner guests too numerous, they would eat here instead of in the small dining-room, hung in dark green serge, which faced in upon the court. Another room, also on the court, was René's, where he kept his clothes and would dress in the morning. They shared the yellow bathroom and the tiny yellow kitchen. O had a cleaning woman in every day. The rooms overlooking the court were tiled in red—the tiles were the old six-sided sort one still finds on stair-treads and landings from the third floor up in old

Paris hotels. Seeing them again caused O's heart to beat faster: they were the same as the tiles in the Roissy hallways. Her bedroom was small, the pink and black chintz curtains were drawn, the fire glistened behind the screen, the bed was made, the covers turned down.

'You didn't have a nylon blouse,' said René, 'so I bought you one.' True enough: there, unfolded on the side of the bed where O slept was a white nylon blouse, pleated, tailored, fine, like one of the garments that appear on Egyptian figurines, and nearly transparent. O tried it on: round her waist she put a thin belt to conceal the series of elastics inside, and the blouse was so sheer that the tips of her breasts turned it pink.

Everything, except for the curtains and the headboard panel overlaid with the same material and the two little armchairs upholstered in the same chintz, everything in this room was white: the walls were white, the fringe round the mahogany four-poster bed was white, so was the bearskin rug on the floor. Wearing her new white blouse, O sat down by the fire to listen to her lover. He told her that, to begin with, she mustn't think of herself as free. From now on, that is to say, she was not free; or rather she was free in one sense, only in one: to stop loving him and to leave him immediately. But if she did love him, if she were going to, then she wasn't free at all. She listened to him without saying a word, calling it fortune, calling herself happy that he wanted to prove to himself, no matter how, that she belonged to him, but thinking also that there was a naïveté in his failing to realize that the degree to which he possessed her lay beyond the scope of any proof. Perhaps, though, he did realize it, and wished only to stress it? Perhaps it gave him pleasure to stress it to her? She gazed at the fire while he talked; but he, unwilling, not daring to meet her gaze, he was looking elsewhere. He was on his feet. He was pacing to and fro, staring at the floor. He suddenly said that, before anything else, in order that she hear what he was saying he wanted her, right away, to unlock her knees and unfold her arms—for she was sitting with her knees locked together and her arms folded. So she drew up her skirt and, kneeling, but sitting back on her heels, in the posture the Carmelites or the Japanese women adopt, she waited. Except that, her knees being spread, between her parted thighs she felt the faint needling of the white bearskin's fur; no, that wouldn't do, he insisted, she wasn't opening her legs wide enough. The word *open* and the expression *open your legs*, when uttered by her lover, would acquire in her mind such overtones of restiveness and of force that she never heard them without a kind of inward prostration, of sacred submission, as if they had emanated from a god, not from him. And so she remained perfectly still, her hands, palms turned upward, resting on either side of her knees, and her pleated skirt lay in a quiet circle around her. What her lover wanted of her was simple: that she be constantly and immediately accessible. It wasn't enough for him to know that she was: to her accessibility every obstacle had to be eliminated, and by her carriage and manner, in the first place, and in the second place by the clothing she wore, she would, as it were, signify her accessibility to those who knew what these signs implied. That he continued, involved doing two things. The first of them she already knew: for on the evening of her arrival at the château it had been made clear to her that she was never to cross her legs and was to keep her lips open at all times. All this, she probably thought, meant very little (she did in fact think exactly that), but she was wrong: to the contrary, she would discover that conformance to this discipline would require a continual effort of attention which would continually remind her, when they two and perhaps certain others were together even though in the midst of the most everyday occupations and while amongst those who did not share the secret, of what in reality her condition was. As for her clothing, it was up to her to choose it and, if need be, to devise a costume which would render unnecessary that half-undressing he had submitted her to in the car while taking her to Roissy: tomorrow she would go through her clothes-closets and bureau drawers and sort out every last garter-belt and pair of panties, which she would hand over to him; he would likewise take all the brassieres, like the one whose

shoulder-straps he'd had to cut in order to get it off her, all the slips
she had whose upper part covered her breasts, all her blouses and
dresses which didn't open in front, any of her skirts which were
too narrow to be raised instantly, with a single quick motion. She'd
have other brassieres, other blouses and other dresses made.
Between now and then was she to go to her corset-maker with her
breasts naked under her blouse or sweater? Yes, he replied, that was
how she would go to her corset-maker, her breasts naked under
her blouse or sweater. And if anyone were to notice and comment,
she'd make whatever explanations she liked, or would make none;
either way, that was her own affair and no concern of his. Now as
to the rest of what he had to tell her, he preferred to wait a few
days and when the next time she sat down to listen to him, he
wanted her to be dressed in the way she should be. In the little
drawer of her writing-desk she'd find all the money she'd need.
When he had finished speaking, she murmured: 'I love you'—
pronounced those words without stirring an eyelash. It was he
who added wood to the fire, lit the pink opaline lamp by the bed.
Then he told O to get into bed and to wait for him, as he was
going to sleep with her. When he returned, O put out her hand to
turn off the light: it was her left hand and before darkness engulfed
everything the last thing she saw was her ring. Propped on one
elbow, lying on one hip, she saw the dull glint of iron, then
touched the switch; and at that same instant her lover's low voice
summoned her by her name, she went to him, he laid his whole
hand upon her womb and drew her the rest of the way.

   The next morning, O was in the dining room, in her dressing-
gown, having just finished breakfast and alone—René had gone
early and wasn't to be back until evening to take her to dinner—
when the telephone rang. The phone was in her room, on the
bedside table by the lamp. O sat on the floor and picked up the
receiver. It was René. The cleaning-woman, he asked, had she
left? Yes, she'd gone just a moment ago, after serving breakfast, and
she wasn't due back until the following day.

   'Have you started to go through your things?' René asked.

'I was about to,' she replied, 'but I got up very late, didn't finish my bath till noon—'

'Are you dressed?'

'No, I'm in my nightgown and bathrobe.'

'Set the receiver down—no, don't hang up, set it on the bed. Take off your nightgown and your bathrobe.'

O obeyed, a little hastily, for the receiver slipped off the bed and fell onto the white rug; still more hastily, fearing the connection had been broken, she snatched it up, said: 'Hello.'

No, it wasn't broken.

'Are you naked?' René asked.

'Yes,' she said. 'Where are you calling from?'

He didn't reply to her question. 'You've still got your ring on?'

She had it on. Then he told her to stay as she was until he returned and, staying that way, to put the things she was discarding into a suitcase; and he hung up.

It was past one o'clock, the weather was clear. A patch of sunlight fell on the rug where, after taking them off, she had let fall the white nightgown and the velvet corduroy bathrobe, pale green in colour, like the hulls of fresh almonds. She collected them and started towards the bathroom to hang them up in a closet; on the way she encountered a three-sided mirror formed by a glass mounted on a door and two others, one straight ahead and one on the right, in a bend in the hall: she encountered her reflection: she was naked save for the green leather clogs of the same green as her bathrobe and not much darker than the clogs she had worn at Roissy, and the ring. She was no longer wearing collar or leather wristbands, and she was alone, sole spectator to herself. Be that as it may, she had never felt so utterly subject to a foreign will, never so utterly a slave nor so happy to be one. When she bent to open a drawer, she saw her breasts sway softly. She was almost two hours at laying out on the bed the clothes she was supposed next to put in the suitcase. First of all, the panties; well, there was no problem here, they all went into a pile by the bedpost. The brassieres? The same thing, they all had to go: for they all crossed behind and hooked at the side. But she did see that the same model could perfectly well do if the catch were brought round to the front, just under the hollow between her breasts. Out went the garter-belts too, but she hesitated getting rid of the rose satin corset which laced up the back and which so closely resembled the bodice she'd worn at Roissy. So she set it aside, on the dressing-table. René'd decide. He'd also decide about the sweaters which, without exception, were the slipover sort and tight around the neck, hence unopenable. But they could, why not? they could be pulled up from the waist by anyone wanting to get at her breasts. Well, she'd wait and see. On the other hand, there was no doubt about the full-length slips: they were in a heap on the bed. In the bureau drawer remained one half-slip, black crêpe hemmed with fine lace at the bottom; she used to wear it beneath a pleated circular sun's-ray skirt in loose-woven wool, light enough to be transparent. She'd have to have other half-slips, light-coloured and short. She also realized that she'd have to give up wearing slipover dresses, but that she might be able to get the same effect from a dress which buttoned all the way down in front and it might be possible to have a built-in slip made which would unbutton at the same time the dress was unbuttoned. In connection with the half-skirts there wasn't likely to be any trouble, nor with the dresses, but what in the world would her dressmaker say about these underthings? She'd tell her she wanted a removable lining because she was sensitive to the cold. Come to think of it, she *was* sensitive to the cold and she suddenly wondered how, with the light clothing she usually wore, she ever managed out-of-doors in the winter. Finally, when she'd finished the job, and from her wardrobe salvaged only those of the blouses which buttoned in front, her black pleated half-slip, her coats of course, and the suit she'd worn back from Roissy, she went to make some tea. She moved up the thermostat in the kitchen; the woman hadn't remembered to fill the living-room firewood basket and O knew that her lover would be delighted to find her in the living-room by the fire when he came home that evening. Out in the corridor there was a big wood-box; she filled the basket, carried it into the living-room, and got a fire going. Thus did she wait, curled up in a big chair, the tea-tray next to her, thus did she await his return; but this time, as he had ordered, she awaited him naked.

The first difficulty O met with was at work. Difficulty? Not quite; rather, she met with astonishment. O worked in the fashion branch of a photograph agency. Which meant that, in the studio where they posed hour after hour, she took the pictures of the strangest—and prettiest-looking—girls whom *couturiers* had selected to model their gowns. They were astonished, or at least surprised, that O had extended her vacation so far into the autumn and, in so doing, had absented herself at the very period when professional activity was at its height, when new styles were about to be released. That surprised them. But they were truly astonished at the change that had taken place in her. At first glance, you couldn't tell in just what way, but you sensed there'd been some sort of a change, and the more you looked at her, the surer of it you were. She stood straighter, her gaze was clearer, sharper, but what was downright striking was this faultless immobility when she was still and, when she moved, the measure, the sureness in her movements. Previously, she'd always dressed soberly, as working girls do when their work resembles men's work, but so cleverly that sobriety seemed quite right for her; and owing to the fact that the other girls, who constituted the very object of her work, had clothing and adornments by way of occupation and vocation, they were quick to detect what other eyes might not have seen. Sweaters worn next to the skin and which so softly outlined her breasts—René had ended up permitting sweaters— pleated skirts which, when she turned, swirled so readily, these took on the quality of a discreet uniform, so regularly was O seen wearing them. 'Very little-girl,' and that in a teasing manner, from a blond green-eyed mannequin with high Slavic cheek-bones and the Slavic olive tint, 'but you're wrong about the garterbelt, you're not going to do your legs any good wearing elastic-bands all the time'—for O, in front of her and without paying attention, had sat down a little too quickly and at an angle upon the arm of a heavy leather-upholstered chair and her skirt had, for a moment, flown up. The tall girl had caught a flash of naked thigh above the rolled-down stocking stopping just above the knee. O had seen her smile, smile so curiously that, at that very instant, she'd wondered what the girl had supposed or perhaps understood. She pulled her stockings up tight, first one stocking, then the other (it wasn't as easy keeping them tight that way as when they mounted to mid-thigh and when garters held them in place), and replied, as if to justify herself: 'It's practical.'

'Practical for what?' Jacqueline said.

'I don't like garter-belts,' O answered. But Jacqueline wasn't listening to her; her eyes fixed on the iron ring.

During the next few days O made some fifty photographs of Jacqueline. They were like none she had ever taken before. Perhaps she had never had such a model before. In any case, she had never been able to extract anything quite like this impassioned meaningfulness from a face or a body. Yet she had undertaken no more than to highlight the silks, the furs, the laces, with the fairy-tale loveliness, the suddenly awakened Sleeping Beauty surprise which swept over Jacqueline no matter what she was wearing, the simplest blouse or the most elegant mink. Her hair was cut short, it was thick and blonde, faintly waved, and, as they were readying the shot, she'd bend her head ever so slightly towards her left shoulder, leaning her cheek against the upturned collar of her fur, if she was wearing a fur. O caught her once that way, smiling and sweet, her hair faintly lifted as though by some gentle breeze, and her soft but hard cheek grazing silver-fox, as grey and delicate as fresh firewood ash. Her lips were parted, her eyes half-closed. Under the cool brilliance of glossy paper one would have thought this the picture of some blessed victim of a drowning; pale, so very pale. From the negative O had made a high-key print all in soft greys. She had taken another photograph of Jacqueline, even more stunning than the first: this one was side-lit, her shoulders bare, her delicately-shaped head and delicately-featured face too enveloped

in a large-mesh black veil, that surmounted by absurd-looking
egret feathers wafting upward in a crown of mist or smoke; she was
wearing an immense gown of heavy silk and brocade, red, like
what brides wore in the Middle Ages, going to within a few
inches of the floor, flaring at the hips, tight at the waist, and whose
armature sketched her breasts. Nobody ever wore such dresses
anymore, it was what the *couturiers* called a show-gown. The very
high-heeled sandals were also of red silk. And all the while
Jacqueline was there before O in this dress and in those sandals and
that veil, which was like a suggestion of mask, in mind O completed the image, modified it according to a prototype she had: just
a shade of this, a shade of that—the waist constricted a little more
tightly, the breasts a little more sharply uplifted—and it was the
Roissy dress, the same dress Jeanne had been wearing, the same
heavy silk, shining, smooth, cascading, the silk one seizes in great
handfuls and raises when one's told to . . . And, yes, Jacqueline had
hold of handfuls of it and was lifting it as she stepped down from
the platform where she had been posing for a quarter of an hour.
It was the same rustling, the same dry-leaves crackling. Nobody
ever wears such dresses anymore? Oh, but there are still some who
wear them. Round her neck, Jacqueline also was wearing a
golden choker, two golden bracelets on her wrists. O caught herself in the midst of imagining that she'd be lovelier with a collar
and with bracelets of leather. And now, doing something she'd
never done before, she followed Jacqueline out into the large
dressing-room, adjacent to the studio, where the models dressed
and made up and where they left their clothes and make-up when
they left. She leaned against the doorjamb, her eyes riveted upon
the hairdresser's mirror before which Jacqueline still wearing her
dress, had sat down. The mirror was so tall—it reflected the
entirety of the room, and the dressing-table was an ordinary table
surfaced with black glass—that O could see both Jacqueline's and
her own image, and the image also of the dressing-assistant who
was detaching the egret plumes and removing the tulle veil.
Jacqueline herself undid her choker, her naked arms lifted like two

swans' necks; a trace of sweat glistened under her armpits, which were shaven (why shaven? What a pity, thought O, she is so fair), and O could smell the keen, pungent odour, somewhat vegetable and wondered what perfume Jacqueline ought to be wearing— what perfume they'd give Jacqueline to wear. Then Jacqueline undid her bracelets, posed them on the glass table-top where, for a fleet instant, they made a clicking like chains clicking. She was so fair-haired that her skin was of a darker hue than her hair, bistre, beige, like fine sand just after the tide has retreated. On the photo, the red silk would come out black. At that same moment, the thick eye-lashes Jacqueline painted only to satisfy the requirements of her job and reluctantly, lifted, and in the mirror O caught a glance so keen, so steady, that, the while unable to remove her own she sensed a warmth flow into her cheeks. That was all, just one glance.

'I beg your pardon, I must undress.'

'Excuse me,' O murmured, and closed the door.

The next day she took home the prints made the day before, not knowing whether she did or didn't desire to show them to her lover; with him she was dining out that evening. While making up before the dressing-table in her room, she gazed at them and would now and then interrupt what she was doing to touch her finger to the photo and trace the line of an eyebrow, the contour of a smile. But when she heard the sound of a key in the front-door lock, she slipped the prints away into the drawer.

For two whole weeks O had been entirely taken up with work, and wasn't getting used to it, and then, coming home one evening from the studio, she found a note from her lover asking her to be ready at eight to join him and a friend for dinner. A car would be sent to fetch her, the chauffeur would come to the door. In a postscript he asked her to wear her fur jacket, dress entirely in black (*entirely* was underlined), and take care to make up and perfume herself in exactly the way she had at Roissy. It was already six. Entirely in black, and for dinner—and it was mid-December, cold outside, that meant black silk stockings, black gloves, pleated skirt, her thick knitted sweater or the crêpe page-boy jacket. She thought it had better be the page-boy jacket. It was padded and quilted in large squares, reinforced and stiff from collar down to waist, like the narrow coats men wore in the sixteenth century, and the reason why it moulded her bust so perfectly was because the soutien-gorge was fitted inside. It was lined with the same faille, and the basques, split, reached down to her hips. It was black everywhere except for the large golden hooks, which looked like the hooks on children's snow-boots, opening and closing with a scraping noise made by the large flat clasps. After she had laid her costume out on the bed and at the foot of the bed set her black suede shoes with platform soles and needle-heels, O thought it the strangest thing in the world to find herself in her own bathroom, free and alone after her bath, and now meticulously making up and perfuming herself, as at Roissy. Her cosmetics weren't the same which were used there, however. In the drawer of her dressing-table she found some cake-rouge which she'd never used before but which managed to accentuate the halo round her nipples. It was one of those rouges one barely sees when applying it, but whose colour deepens later on. At first she thought she'd applied too much, wiped off a little with alcohol—it didn't wipe off easily or well—and began again: she achieved a dark peony-red: two flowers blossomed at the tips of her breasts. In vain she sought to rouge the lips the fleece of her belly hid, the cake-rouge refused to take on them. Amongst the various lipsticks she had in the same drawer she finally located one of those kiss-proof rouges which she didn't like to use because they were too dry and remained too long on the lips. But for present purposes the kissproof variety worked well. She did her hair, finished her face, then perfumed herself. In an atomizer which expelled a thick spray was a perfume whose name she didn't know, but which had a dry-wood or poignant, somewhat wild-plant odour. The mist melted upon her skin, flowed over the hair under her arms and at her belly, hanging in tiny droplets. At Roissy O had learned not to be in a hurry: she perfumed herself three times, each time letting the perfume dry on her body. First she put on her stockings, then her high-heeled shoes, then the half-slip and the skirt, then the jacket. She put on her gloves, took her bag. In her bag were her compact, her lipsticks, a comb, her key, one thousand francs. Gloves on her hands, she took her fur wrap from the armoire, checked the time by her bedside clock: it was a quarter before eight. She sat down on the edge of the bed and, her eyes fixed on the dial of the little clock, in perfect stillness awaited the sound of the doorbell. When she heard it and rose to leave, before turning out the light, she glanced at the dressing-table mirror and saw her reflected gaze: bold, mild, and docile.

Upon opening the door to the little Italian restaurant before which the car had stopped, the first person she saw was René, at the bar. He smiled tenderly, took her hand, and turning toward a sort of grey-haired athlete, introduced her, in English to Sir Stephen H. O was offered a stool between the two men and as she was about to seat herself, René whispered to her to be careful not to wrinkle her dress. He helped her slide her skirt over the edge of the stool, and she felt the cold leather against her skin, the cold metal rim against the lower part of her womb itself, for she dared not sit all the way down at first, dreading lest if, she did, she yield to the temptation to cross one leg over the other. Her skirt hung down all the way around her. Her right heel was hooked on one of the rungs of the stool, the tip of her left foot touched the floor. The expressionless Englishman, who without saying a word had simply made an imperceptible bow, had not taken his eyes off her; she noticed him study first her knees, her hands next, finally her lips—but study them so tranquilly, and with an attention so precise and so sure of itself, that O felt herself being weighed and hefted for the instrument she very well knew she was, and it was as though under the pressure of his gaze and so to speak in spite of herself that she removed her gloves: she knew that he would speak as soon as her hands were bare —because her hands were unusual, resembling those of a youth rather than those of a woman, and

because, on the third finger of her left hand, she wore the iron ring
with the triple golden spiral. But no. He didn't say anything, he
smiled: he'd seen the ring. René was drinking his second Martini
and O the grapefruit juice René had ordered for her; as he set
down his glass he said that unless O were otherwise disposed, she
would do him the kindness of concurring in their view that it
might be better to go downstairs to eat, for the dining-room below
was smaller and sure to be quieter than this one which, on the
ground floor, was hardly separated from the bar.

'Certainly,' said O who had already picked her bag and gloves up
from where she had laid them on the bar.

Sir Stephen, helping her down from the stool, offered her
his right hand in which she laid hers, and finally addressing her
directly, did so to observe that such hands were made for irons, so
admirably did iron become her. But as he said it in English there
was a faint ambiguity in the terms, and one might be in doubt
whether to understand if he was alluding only to the metal or if
not also, and above all, to chains.

The downstairs was a simple *cave*, whitewashed but airy and gay,
with, it turned out, only four tables, one of which was occupied
by people who were finishing their meal. On the walls they had
fresco-like representations of *l'Italie gastronomique* done in soft ice-
cream colours: vanilla, raspberry, pistachio; looking about her, O
decided to ask for an ice-cream dessert, with pralines and
whipped-cream. For she felt in a happy, light-hearted mood,
under the table René's knee touched hers, and when he spoke, she
knew he was talking on her behalf. He too was gazing at her lips.
Her request for ice-cream was granted but to coffee they said no.
Sir Stephen proposed that O and René join him for coffee at his
home. All three had dined lightly, almost sparingly, and O
remarked to herself that, if the men had drunk exceedingly little,
she'd been allowed to drink even less: half a flask of chianti had
sufficed for the three of them. And they had eaten quickly too: it
was only a few minutes after nine.

'I dismissed the chauffeur,' said Sir Stephen. 'René, will you drive? I think the simplest thing would be to go straight to my place.'

René took the wheel, O sat next to him, Sir Stephen next to her. The automobile was a large Buick, providing ample space for three in the front seat.

After the Alma circle; the Cours de la Reine was clearly visible through the leafless branches of the trees; and the Place de la Concorde was scintillating and dry, overhung by those dark clouds promising snow which can't make up its mind to fall. O heard a click and felt warm air climb up along her legs: Sir Stephen had switched on the heater. René followed the Right Bank a little while longer, then took the Pont Royal to the Left Bank: between the bridges' stone arches the Seine looked as immobile as stone, and black. When she'd been fifteen, her best friend, who'd been thirty and with whom she'd been in love, had worn a ring with a huge hematite set in a cluster of diamonds. O had always wanted a necklace of those black stones, but without diamonds, a tight-fitting necklace, a choker, who knows? a very tight-fitting choker, perhaps that's what she'd always wanted. But the collars they gave her now—no they didn't give them—would she have exchanged them for the hematite necklace, the choker, the one she'd cherished in her adolescent's dreams? Once again she saw the mean, shoddy room Marion had taken her to, behind the Turbigo intersection, and visualized how she, O, not Marion, had undone her two large schoolgirl's braids after Marion had undressed her and had her lie down on the iron bedstead. When caressed Marion was beautiful and it's perfectly true that eyes can look like stars; hers had resembled trembling blue stars. René parked the car. O didn't recognize this little street, one of those running between the rue de l'Université and the rue de Lille.

Sir Stephen's apartment was at the far end of a court-yard in a wing of an old *hôtel*, and the rooms were laid out in a line, one opening into the next. The furthest from the entry was the largest and the most restful, furnished in dark English mahogany and pale silks, striped yellow and grey.

'I shan't ask you to tend the fire,' Sir Stephen said to O, 'but this couch is for you. Sit down, would you please, René will see to the coffee, I should like you simply to listen to me.'

The broad damascus-covered couch was set perpendicular to the fireplace, opposite windows overlooking a garden and facing away from other windows, on the other side of the room, which overlooked the courtyard. O removed her wrap and hung it over the back of the couch. When she turned, she saw that her lover and Sir Stephen, both standing, were waiting for her to comply with Sir Stephen's invitation. She laid her bag near the fur wrap, removed her gloves. When, oh when she wondered, when ever would she find the one rapid and furtive and unobtrusive gesture whereby she would be able to lift her skirts at the same moment she sat down so as to prevent anyone from noticing, no one would notice, the gesture which would allow her to forget her nakedness, to take it and her submission for granted? It would not at any rate be so long as René and this stranger stared at her in silence, as they were doing. She finally yielded. Sir Stephen placed fuel on the fire, René suddenly passed behind the couch and, seizing O's neck and hair, drew her head against the back of the couch and kissed her mouth, kissed her for so long and so profoundly that she lost her breath, gasped, and felt something melt in her belly, and burn. When he released her it was to say that he loved her; so saying, he took hold of her again, immediately. O's hands, idle, empty, the palms helplessly turned upward, lay on the black dress spread like a corolla around her; Sir Stephen had approached and when René finally let her go and she opened her eyes, it was the keen grey gaze of the Englishman they encountered. Bewildered as she still was, and dizzy from joy, she was nevertheless very able to see that he was looking at her admiringly, and that he desired her. Who could have resisted her moist, half-opened mouth, her swollen lips, her white neck flung back against the black collar of her page-boy jacket, her wide-open and bright eyes, her steady, unfugitive eyes? But Sir Stephen's single gesture was to caress her eyebrows and then her lips, softly with the tip of his finger. Then he took a place opposite her, on the other side of the fireplace, and when René had also seated himself in an armchair, he began to speak.

'I don't believe René has ever spoken to you of his family. You may perhaps know, however, that, before wedding his father, René's mother was married to an Englishman who had a son by a first marriage. I am that son, I was brought up by René's mother until the day she left my father. Thus, strictly speaking, I am in no way related to René, and yet we are brothers, after a fashion. René loves you, I know it. I would have known it even had he not told me so, even if he had not stirred: it's quite enough to see the way he looks at you. I also know that you are one of those who have been at Roissy, and I dare say you will be going back there. Theoretically, I have the right to do as I like with you, the ring you are wearing gives it to me as to anyone else who, seeing it, knows what it signifies; but the simple exercise of my right is one thing, what we want from you is quite another and more serious. I say 'we' because, as you observe, René isn't saying anything: he wishes me to address you in both his behalf and mine. If we are brothers, I am the elder, he being ten years younger than I. Between the two of us there also exists a freedom of such long standing and of such an absolute character that what belongs to me has always been his, and contrariwise. Will you consent to common ownership? I do very much hope that you will, and I am posing the question because your acquiescence will require much more on your part than did passive endurance of an imposed condition. We should like to move beyond that stage, you see. Before replying, consider that I am merely and cannot be other than another form of your lover: thus, you will always have a single master. A somewhat more redoubtable master, I rather expect, than the men to whom you were surrendered at Roissy; for I'll constantly be there. And besides,' Sir Stephen concluded, couching this final phrase in English, 'I have a fondness for habits and ritual.'

His calm, even voice pierced an absolute silence. Even the flames in the fireplace danced soundlessly. O was as though riveted to the couch, like a butterfly impaled by a pin, a long pin of words and glances which penetrated the middle of her body and nailed her naked and attentive loins to the warm silk. She no longer seemed mistress of her breasts, nor of the nape of her neck, nor of her hands; but of one thing she was certain: the object of those habits and that ritual was going to be the possession of, amongst other parts of her body, the long thighs that were hidden under her black skirt and that, already, beforehand, were open. The two men were facing her. René was smoking, but had lit one of those lamps which counteract smoke, and the air in the room, purified by the wood fire, had the cool smell of night-time.

'Will you answer me now?' Sir Stephen enquired. 'Or would you like me to tell you a little more?'

'If you give your consent,' René put in, 'I myself will explain Sir Stephen's preferences to you—'

'My expectations rather,' Sir Stephen corrected him.

Consent, O was telling herself, consent wasn't the difficult part, and it was then she realized that neither of the men had for one instant anticipated the possibility of her not consenting; neither had she. Speaking, saying anything—that was the difficult part. Her lips were afire, her mouth was dry, the saliva wasn't there anymore, an anguish composed of fear and desire had her by the throat, and the hands she had recovered control of were cold and clammy. If she could have but closed her eyes, at least. But no, two gazes pursued hers, stalked hers; she could not elude the hunter, nor did she wish to. They drew her back towards what she thought she had left for a long time and perhaps forever at Roissy. For since her return, René had always taken her by means of caresses, caressingly, and the symbol declaring that she belonged to whomsoever knew its secret had simply not happened to produce any consequences: either, she had not encountered anyone who knew it, or else, if she had, those who knew the secret had not betrayed the fact—the one person she could possibly suspect was Jacqueline (and if Jacqueline had been at Roissy, why didn't she too have a ring on her finger? And, furthermore, if Jacqueline did know the secret, what rights over O did knowing it confer upon her?) Did she have to move in order to speak? But she couldn't move of her own accord—an order would probably have brought her to her feet in an instant, but this time what they wanted from her was not obedience to an order, it was that, voluntarily, she come forward and acknowledge herself a slave and surrender herself as such. That's what they called her avowal of consent. She recalled that she had never said anything to René except 'I love you' and 'I am yours.' It seemed as if they wanted to have her talk today, and in so many plain words accept what up until now only her silence had accepted. In the end she straightened her back and, as if what she had to say was smothering her, unfastened the upper clasps on her tunic, baring herself down to the cleft between her breasts. Then she stood up, all the way up. Her knees and hands were trembling. 'I am yours,' she told René at last, 'I'll be what you want me to be.'

'No,' said he, 'you're to be ours. Repeat it after me: 'I belong to both of you, I will be what both of you want me to be." '

HENRY MILLER

from

Sexus

Henry Miller, though American, wrote most of his novels in Paris. 'Tropic of Cancer' (1936) and 'Tropic of Capricorn' (1939) were both condemned as obscene as was 'Sexus', written in 1949 though not published in English, unexpurgated, until the 1960s.

'I'M awfully glad to see you,' she said. 'Dolores and I are always talking about you . . . Don't you want to drop up for a minute? Dolores will be delighted to see you. We have an apartment together. It's right near here. Do come up . . . I'd love to talk to you a while. It must be over a year since I saw you last. You had just left your wife, you remember? And now you're living with Arthur— that's strange. How is he getting on? Is he doing well? I hear he has a beautiful wife.'

It didn't require much coaxing to persuade me to run up and have a quiet drink with them. Irma seemed to be bubbling over with joy. She had always been very friendly with me, but never this effusive. I wondered what had come over her.

When we got upstairs the place was dark. 'That's funny,' said Irma. 'She said she would be home early this evening. Oh well, she'll be along in a few minutes, no doubt. Take your things off . . . sit down . . . I'll get you a drink in a minute.'

I sat down, feeling somewhat dazed. Years ago, when I first knew Arthur Raymond, I had been rather fond of Irma. When they

separated she had fallen in love with my friend O'Mara, and he had
made her just as miserable as Arthur had. He complained that she
was cold—not frigid, but selfish. I hadn't given much attention to
her then because I was interested in Dolores. Only once had there
even been anything approaching intimacy between us. That had
been a pure accident and neither of us had made anything of it. We
had met on the street in front of a cheap cinema one afternoon and
after a few words, both of us being rather listless and weary, we had
gone inside. The picture was unbearably dull, the theatre almost
empty. We had thrown our overcoats over our laps and then, more
out of boredom and the need of some human contact, our hands
met and we sat thus for a while staring vacantly at the screen. After
a time I slung my arm around her and drew her to me. In a few
moments she let go my hand and placed her own on my prick. I
did nothing, curious to see what she would make of the situation.
I remembered O'Mara saying that she was cold and indifferent. So
I sat still and waited. I had only a semi hard-on when she touched
me. I let it grow under her hand which was resting immobile.
Gradually I felt the pressure of her fingers, then a firm grasp, then
a squeezing and stroking, all very quietly, delicately, almost as if she
were asleep and doing it unconsciously. When it began to quiver
and jump she slowly and deliberately unbuttoned my fly, reached
in and grabbed my balls. Still I made no move to touch her. I had
a perverse desire to make her do everything herself. I remembered
the shape and the feel of her fingers; they were sensitive and expert.
She had cuddled up like a cat and had ceased to look at the screen.
My prick was out of course, but still hidden under the overcoat. I
watched her throw the coat back and fasten her gaze on my prick.
Boldly now she began to massage it, more and more firmly,
more and more rapidly. Finally I came in her hand. 'I'm sorry,'
she murmured, reaching for her bag to extract a handkerchief. I
permitted her to wipe me off with her silk kerchief. Not a word
out of me. Not a move to embrace her. Nothing. Just as if I had
watched her doing it to someone else. After she had powdered her
face, put everything back into her bag, I pulled her to me and glued

my mouth to hers. Then I pushed her coat off her lap, raised her
legs and slung them over my lap. She had nothing on under her
skirt, and she was wet. I paid her back in her own coin, doing it
ruthlessly almost, until she came. When we left the theatre we
had a coffee and some pastry together in a bakery and after an
inconsequential conversation parted as though nothing had
happened.

'Excuse me,' she said, 'For being so long. I felt like getting into
something comfortable.'

I came out of my reverie to look up at a lovely apparition hand-
ing me a tall glass. She had made herself into a Japanese doll. We
had hardly sat down on the divan when she jumped up and went
to the clothes closet. I heard her moving the valises around and
then came a little exclamation, a sigh of frustration, as though she
were calling to me in a muted voice.

I jumped up and ran to the closet where I found her standing on
top of a swaying valise, reaching for something on the top shelf. I
held her legs a moment to steady her and, just as she was turning
round to descend, I slid my hand up under the silk kimono. She
came down in my arms with my hand securely fastened between
her legs. We stood there in a passionate embrace, enveloped in her
feminine frills. Then the door opened and Dolores walked in. She
was startled to find us buried in the closet.

'Well!' she exclaimed with a little gasp, 'fancy finding *you* here!'

I let go of Irma and put my arms around Dolores, who only
feebly protested. She seemed more beautiful now than ever.

As she disengaged herself she broke out into her usual little
laugh which was always slightly ironical. 'We don't have to stay in
the closet, do we?' she said, holding my hand. Irma meanwhile
had slipped an arm around me.

'Why not stay here?' I said. 'It's cosy and womblike.' I was
squeezing Irma's ass as I spoke.

'God, you haven't changed a bit,' said Dolores. 'You never get
enough of it, do you? I thought you were madly in love with . . .
with . . . I forget her name.'

'Mona.'

'Yes, Mona . . . how is she? Is it still serious? I thought you were never going to look at another woman!'

'Exactly,' I said. 'This is an accident, as you can see.'

'I know,' she said, revealing more and more her smothered jealousy, 'I know these accidents of yours. Always on the alert, aren't you?'

We spilled into the living room, where Dolores threw off her things—rather vehemently, I thought, as though preparing for a struggle.

'Will I pour you a drink?' asked Irma.

'Yes, and a good stiff one,' said Dolores. 'I need one . . . Oh, it has nothing to do with *you*,' she said, observing that I was looking at her strangely. 'It's that friend of yours, Ulric.'

'What's the matter, isn't he treating you well?'

She was silent. She gave me a desolate look, as though to say— you know very well what I'm talking about.

Irma thought the lights were too strong; she turned out all but the little reading lamp by the other divan.

'Looks as though you were preparing the scene,' said Dolores mockingly. At the same time one felt that there was a secret thrill in her voice. I knew it was Dolores whom I would have to deal with. Irma, on the other hand, was like a cat; she moved about softly, almost purring. She was not in the least disturbed; she was making herself ready for any eventuality.

'It's good to have you here alone,' said Irma, as though she had found a long lost brother. She had stretched herself out on the divan, close to the wall. Dolores and I were sitting almost at her feet. Behind Dolores' back I had my hand on Irma's thigh; a dry heat emanated from her body.

'She must guard you pretty close,' said Dolores, referring to Mona. 'Is she afraid of losing you—or what?'

'Perhaps,' I said, giving her a provocative smile. 'And perhaps I'm afraid of losing *her*.'

'Then it is serious?'

'*Very*,' I answered. 'I found the woman I need, and I'm going to keep her.'

'Are you married to her?'

'No, not yet . . . but we will be soon.'

'And you'll have children and everything?'

'I don't know whether we'll have children . . . why, is that important?'

'You might as well do it thoroughly,' said Dolores.

'Oh, stop it!' said Irma. 'You sound as though you were jealous. I'm not! I'm glad he's found the right woman. He deserves it.' She squeezed my hand, in relaxing the pressure, she adroitly slipped my hand over her pussy.

Dolores, conscious of what was going on, but pretending not to notice, got up and went to the bathroom.

'She's acting queer,' said Irma. 'She seems positively green with jealousy.'

'You mean jealous of *you*?' I said, somewhat puzzled myself.

'No, not of me . . . of course not! Jealous of Mona.'

'That's strange,' I said, 'I thought she was in love with Ulric.'

'She is, but she hasn't forgotten you. She . . .'

I stopped her words with a kiss. She flung her arms around my neck and cuddled up to me, writhing and twisting like a big cat. 'I'm glad I don't feel that way,' she murmured. 'I wouldn't want to be in love with you. I like you better this way.'

I ran my hand under the kimono again. She responded warmly and willingly.

Dolores returned and excused herself lamely for interrupting the game. She was standing beside us, looking down with sparkling, mischievous eyes.

'Hand me my glass, will you?' I said.

'Perhaps you'd like me to fan you too,' said she, as she put the glass to my lips.

I pulled her down beside us, stroking the half-exposed limb which protruded from her dressing gown. She too had taken off her things.

'Haven't you got something for me to slip into too?' I asked, looking from one to the other.

'Why certainly,' said Irma, springing to her feet with alacrity.

'Oh, don't pamper him like that,' said Dolores, with a pouting smile. 'That's just what he loves . . . he wants to be made a fuss over. And then he's going to tell us how faithful he is to his wife.'

'She's not my wife yet,' I said tauntingly, accepting the robe which Irma offered me.

'Oh, isn't she?' said Dolores. 'Well, then it's worse.'

'Worse, what do you mean *worse*? I haven't done anything yet, have I?'

'No, but you're going to try.'

'You mean you'd like me to. Don't be impatient . . . you'll get your chance.'

'Not with *me*,' said Dolores, 'I'm going to bed. You two can do what you like.'

For answer I closed the door and started undressing. When I returned I found Dolores stretched out on the couch and Irma sitting by her side with legs crossed, fully exposed.

'Don't mind anything she says,' said Irma. 'She likes you as much as I do . . . maybe more. She doesn't like Mona, that's all.'

'Is that true?' I looked from Irma to Dolores. The latter was silent, but it was a silence which meant affirmation.

'I don't know why you should feel so strongly about her,' I hastened to continue. 'She's never done anything to you. And you can't be jealous of her because . . . well, because you weren't in love with me . . . then.'

'*Then*? What do you mean? I was never in love with you, thank God!' said Dolores.

'It doesn't sound very convincing,' said Irma playfully. 'Listen, if you never loved him don't be so passionate about it.' She turned to me and in her blithe way she said: 'Why don't you kiss her and stop this nonsense?'

'All right, I will,' said I, and with that I bent over and embraced Dolores. At first she held her lips firmly shut, looking at me defiantly. Then, little by little, she surrendered, and when at last she pulled away she was biting my lips. As she pulled her lips away she gave me a little shove. 'Get him out of here!' she said. I gave her a look of reproach in which there was an element of pity and disgust. She became at once repentant and yielding again. I bent over her again, tenderly this time, and as I slipped my tongue into her mouth I put my hand between her legs. She tried to push my hand away but the effort was too much.

'Whew! it's getting close,' I heard Irma say, and then she pulled me away. 'I'm here too, don't forget.' She was offering her lips and breasts.

It was getting to be a tug of war. I jumped up to pour myself a drink. The bathrobe stood out like a stretched tent.

'Do you have to show us that?' said Dolores, pretending to be embarrassed.

'I don't have to but I will, since you ask for it,' I said, drawing the robe back and exposing myself completely.

Dolores turned her head to the wall, mumbling something in a pseudo-hysterical voice about 'disgusting and obscene.' Irma on the other hand looked at it good-humouredly. Finally she reached for it and squeezed it gently. As she stood up to accept the drink I had poured for her I opened her robe and placed my cock between her legs. We drank together with my cock knocking at the stable door.

'I want a drink, too,' said Dolores petulantly. We turned around simultaneously and faced her. Her face was scarlet, her eyes big and bright, as though she had put belladonna in them. 'You look debauched,' she said, her eyes twitching back and forth from Irma to me.

I handed her the glass and she took a deep draught of it. She was struggling to obtain that freedom which Irma flaunted like a flag.

Her voice came challengingly now. 'Why don't you do it and get done with it?' she said, flinging her words at us. In wriggling about she had uncovered herself; she knew it too and made no effort to hide her nakedness.

'Lie down there,' I said, pushing Irma gently back on the divan. Irma took my hand and pulled. 'You lie down too,' she said.

I raised the glass to my lips and as it was slipping down my throat the light went out. I heard Dolores saying—'No, don't do that, *please*!' But the light remained out and as I stood there finishing the drink I felt Irma's hand on my prick, squeezing it convulsively. I put the glass down and jumped in between them. Almost at once they closed in on me. Dolores was kissing me passionately and Irma, like the cat, had crouched down and fastened her mouth on my prick. It was an agonizing bliss which lasted for a few seconds and then I exploded in Irma's mouth.

PHILIP ROTH

from

Portnoy's Complaint

Published in 1969, Philip Roth's 'Portnoy's Complaint' is one of the funniest and most uninhibited books about sex ever written. Roth describes the coming of age of a Jew in New Jersey through his exploration of his own sexuality.

ANOTHER gentile heart broken by me belonged to The Pilgrim, Sarah Abbott Maulsby—New Canaan, Foxcroft and Vassar (where she had as companion, stabled in Poughkeepsie, that other flaxen beauty, her palomino). A tall, gentle, decorous twenty-two-year-old, fresh from college, and working as a receptionist in the office of the Senator from Connecticut when we two met and coupled in the fall of 1959.

I was on the staff of the House subcommittee investigating the television quiz scandals. Perfect for a closet socialist like myself: commercial deceit on a national scale, exploitation of the innocent public, elaborate corporate chicanery—in short, good old capitalist greed. And then of course that extra bonus, Charlatan Van Doren. Such character, such brains and breeding, that candour and schoolboyish charm—the ur-WASP, wouldn't you say? And turns out he's a fake. Well, what do you know about that, Gentile America? Supergoy, a *gonif*! Steals money. Covets money. Wants money, will do anything for it. Goodness gracious me, almost as bad as Jews—you sanctimonious WASPs!

Yes, I was one happy yiddel down there in Washington, a little

Stern gang of my own, busily exploding Charlie's honour and integrity, while simultaneously becoming lover to that aristocratic Yankee beauty whose forebears arrived on these shores in the seventeenth century. Phenomenon known as Hating Your Goy And Eating One Too.

Why didn't I marry that beautiful and adoring girl? I remember her in the gallery, pale and enchanting in a navy blue suit with gold buttons, watching with such pride, with such love, as I took on one afternoon, in my first public cross-examination, a very slippery network PR man . . . and I was impressive too, for my first time out: cool, lucid, persistent, just the faintest hammering of the heart—and only twenty-six years old. Oh yeah, when I am holding all the moral cards, watch out, you crooks you! I am nobody to futz around with when I know myself to be four hundred per cent in the right.

Why didn't I marry the girl? Well, there was her cutesy-wootsy boarding school argot, for one. Couldn't bear it. 'Barf' for vomit, 'ticked off' for angry, 'a howl' for funny, 'crackers' for crazy, 'teeny' for tiny. Oh, and 'di*vine*.' (What Mary Jane Reed means by 'groovy'—I'm always telling these girls how to talk right, me with my five-hundred-word New Jersey vocabulary.) Then there were the nicknames of her friends; there were the friends themselves! Poody and Pip and Pebble, Shrimp and Brute and Tug, Squeek, Bumpo, Baba—it sounded, I said, as though she had gone to Vassar with Donald Duck's nephews . . . But then my argot caused her some pain too. The first time I said fuck in her presence (and the presence of friend Pebble, in her Peter Pan collar and her cablestitch cardigan, and tanned like an Indian from so much tennis at the Chevy Chase Club), such a look of agony passed over The Pilgrim's face, you would have thought I had just branded the four letters on her flesh. Why, she asked so plaintively once we were alone, why *had* I to be so 'unattractive'? What possible pleasure had it given me to be so 'ill-mannered'? What on earth had I 'proved'? 'Why did you have to be so pus-y like that? It was so un*called*-for.' Pus-y being Debutante for disagreeable.

In bed? Nothing fancy, no acrobatics or feats of daring and skill; as we screwed our first time, so we continued—I assaulted and she surrendered, and the heat generated on her mahogany four-poster (a Maulsby family heirloom) was considerable. Our one peripheral delight was the full-length mirror on the back of the bathroom door. There, standing thigh to thigh, I would whisper, 'Look, Sarah, look.' At first she was shy, left the looking to me, at first she was modest and submitted only because I wished her to, but in time she developed something of a passion for the looking-glass, too, and followed the reflection of our joining with a certain startled intensity in her gaze. Did she see what I saw? *In the black pubic hair, ladies and gentlemen, weighing one hundred and seventy pounds, at least half of which is still undigested halvah and hot pastrami, from Newark, NJ, The Shnoz, Alexander Portnoy! And his opponent, in the fair fuzz, with her elegant polished limbs and the gentle maidenly face of a Boticelli, that ever-popular purveyor of the social amenities here in the Garden, one hundred and fourteen pounds of Republican refinement, and the pertest pair of nipples in all New England, from New Canaan, Connecticut, Sarah Abbott Maulsby!*

What I'm saying, Doctor, is that I don't seem to stick my dick up these girls, as much as I stick it up their backgrounds—as though through fucking I will discover America. *Conquer* America—maybe that's more like it. Columbus, Captain Smith, Governor Winthrop, General Washington—now Portnoy. As though my manifest destiny is to seduce a girl from each of the forty-eight states. As for Alaskan and Hawaiian women, I really have no feelings either way, no scores to settle, no coupons to cash in, no dreams to put to rest—who are they to me, a bunch of Eskimos and Orientals? No, I am a child of the forties, of network radio and World War Two, of eight teams to a league and forty-eight states to a country. I know all the words to 'The Marine Hymn,' and to 'The Caissons Go Rolling Along' and to 'The Song of the Army Air Corps.' I know the song of the *Navy* Air Corps: 'Sky anchors aweigh/ We're sailors of the air/ We're sailing every-where—' I can even sing you the song of the Seabees. Go ahead, name your branch of service, Spielvogel, I'll sing you your song! Please, allow me—it's my money. We used to sit on our coats, I remember, on the concrete floor, our backs against the sturdy walls of the basement corridors of my grade school, singing in unison to keep up our morale until the all-clear signal sounded—'Johnny Zero.' 'Praise the Lord and Pass the Ammunition.' The sky-pilot said it/ You've got to give him credit/ For a son of a gun of a gunner was he-e-e-e!' You name it, and if it was in praise of the Stars and Stripes, I know it word for word! Yes, I am a child of air raid drills, Doctor, I remember Corregidor and 'The Cavalcade of America,' and that flag, fluttering on its pole, being raised at that heartbreaking angle over bloody Iwo Jima. Colin Kelly went down in flames when I was eight, and Hiroshima and Nagasaki went up in a puff, one week when I was twelve, and that was the heart of my boyhood, four years of hating Tojo, Hitler, and Mussolini, and loving this brave determined republic! Rooting my little Jewish heart out for our American democracy! Well, we won, the enemy is dead in an alley back of the Wilhelmstrasse, and dead because I *prayed* him dead—and now I want what's coming to me. *My* GI bill—real American ass! The cunt in country-'tis-of-thee! I pledge allegiance to the twat of the United States of America— and to the republic for which it stands: Davenport, Iowa! Dayton, Ohio! Schenectady, New York, and neighbouring Troy! Fort Myers, Florida! New Canaan, Connecticut! Chicago, Illinois! Albert Lea, Minnesota! Portland, Maine! Moundsville, West Virginia! Sweet land of *skikse*-tail, of thee I sing!

From the mountains,

To the prairies,

To the oceans, white-with-my-fooaahhh-mmm!

God bless A-me-ri-cuuuuhhhh!

My home, SWEET HOOOOOHHHH-M!

Imagine what it meant to me to know that generations of Maulsbys were buried in the graveyard at Newburyport, Massachusetts, and generations of Abbotts in Salem. *Land where my fathers died, land of the Pilgrims' pride* . . . Exactly. Oh, and more.

Here was a girl whose mother's flesh *crawled* at the sound of the words 'Eleanor Roosevelt.' Who herself had been dandled on the knee of Wendell Willkie at Hobe Sound, Florida, in 1942 (while my father was saying prayers for F.D.R. on the High Holidays, and my mother blessing him over the Friday night candles). The Senator from Connecticut had been a roommate of her Daddy's at Harvard, and her brother, 'Paunch,' a graduate of Yale, held a seat on the New York Stock Exchange and (how lucky could I be?) played polo (yes, games from on top of a horse!) on Sunday afternoons someplace in Westchester County, as he had throughout college. She could have been a Lindabury, don't you see? A daughter of my father's boss! Here was a girl who knew how to sail a boat, knew how to eat her dessert using two pieces of silverware (a piece of cake you could pick up in your hands, and you should have seen her manipulate it with that fork and that spoon—like a Chinese with his chopsticks! What skills she had learned in far-off Connecticut!). Activities that partook of the exotic and even the taboo she performed so simply, as a matter of course: and I was as wowed (though that's not the whole story) as Desdemona, hearing of the Anthropapagi. I came across a newspaper clipping in her scrapbook, a column entitled 'A Deb A Day', which began, 'SARAH ABBOTT MAULSBY—"Ducks and quails and pheasants better scurry" around New Canaan this fall because Sally, daughter of Mr and Mrs Edward H. Maulsby of Greenley Road, is getting in practice for small game season. Shooting—' with a gun, Doctor—'shooting is just one of Sally's outdoor hobbies. She loves riding too, and this summer hopes to try a rod and reel—' and get this; I think this tale would win my son too—'hopes to try a rod and reel on some of those trout that swim by "Windview" her family's summer home.'

What Sally couldn't do was eat me. To shoot a gun at a little quack-quack is fine, to suck my cock is beyond her. She was sorry, she said, if I was going to take it so hard, but it was just something she didn't care to try. I mustn't act as though it were a personal affront, she said, because it had nothing at all to do with me as an individual . . . Oh, didn't it? Bullshit, girlie! Yes, what made me so irate was precisely my belief that I was being discriminated against. My father couldn't rise at Boston & Northeastern for the very same reason that Sally Maulsby wouldn't deign to go down on me! Where was the justice in this world? 'Where was the B'nai B'rith Anti-Defamation League—! 'I do it to you,' I said. The Pilgrim shrugged; kindly she said, 'You don't have to, though. You know that. If you don't want to . . . ' 'Ah, but I *do* want to— it isn't a matter of 'have' to. I *want* to.' 'Well,' she answered, 'I don't.' '*But why not?*' 'Well,' she answered, 'I don't.' 'Shit, that's the way a child answers, Sarah—"because"! Give me a reason!' 'I—I just don't do that, that's all.' 'But that brings us back to why. *Why?*' 'Alex, I can't. I just can't.' 'Give me a single good reason!' 'Please,' she replied, knowing her rights. 'I don't think I have to.'

No, she didn't have to—because to me the answer was clear enough anyway: *Because you don't know how to hike out to windward or what a jib is, because you have never owned evening clothes or been to a cotillion* . . . Yes sir, if I were some big blond *goy* in a pink riding suit and hundred-dollar hunting boots, don't worry, she'd be down there eating me, of that I am sure!

I am wrong. Three months I spent applying pressure to the back of her skull (pressure met by a surprising counterforce, an impressive, even moving display of stubbornness from such a mild and uncontentious person), for three months I assaulted her in argument and tugged her nightly by the ears. Then one night she invited me to hear the Budapest String Quartet playing Mozart at the Library of Congress; during the final movement of the Clarinet Quintet she took hold of my hand, her cheeks began to shine, and when we got back to her apartment and into bed, Sally said, 'Alex . . . I will.' 'Will what?' But she was gone, down beneath the covers and out of sight: blowing me! That is to say, she took my prick in her mouth and held it there for a count of sixty, held the surprised little thing there, Doctor, like a thermometer. I threw back the blankets—this I had to see! Feel, there wasn't very much to feel, but oh the sight of it! Only Sally was already finished. Having moved it by now to the side of her face, as though it were the gear shift on her Hillman-Minx. And there were tears on her face.

'I did it,' she announced.

'Sally, oh, Sarah, don't cry.'

'But I did do it, Alex.'

' . . . You mean,' I said, 'that's all?'

'You mean,' she gasped, '*more?*'

'Well, to be frank, a little more—I mean to be truthful with you, it wouldn't go unappreciated—'

'But it's getting big. I'll suffocate.'

JEW SMOTHERS DEB WITH COCK, *Vassar Grad Georgetown Strangulation Victim Mocky Lawyer Held*

'Not if you breathe, you won't.'

'I will, I'll choke—'

'Sarah, the best safeguard against asphyxiation is breathing. Just breathe, and that's all there is to it. More or less.'

God bless her, she tried. But came up gagging. 'I told you,' she moaned.

'But you weren't breathing.'

'I can't with that in my mouth.'

'Through your nose. Pretend you're swimming.'

'But I'm *not*.'

'PRETEND!' I suggested, and though she gave another gallant try, surfaced only seconds later in an agony of coughing and tears. I gathered her then in my arms (that lovely willing girl! convinced by Mozart to go down on Alex! oh, sweet as Natasha in *War and Peace*! a tender young countess!). I rocked her, I teased her, I made her laugh, for the first time I said, 'I love you too, my baby,' but of course it couldn't have been clearer to me that despite all her many qualities and charms—her devotion, her beauty, her deerlike grace, her place in American history—there could never be any 'love' in me for The Pilgrim. Intolerant of her frailties. Jealous of her accomplishments. Resentful of her family. No, not much room there for love.

No, Sally Maulsby was just something nice a son once did for his dad. A little vengeance on Mr Lindabury for all those nights and Sundays Jack Portnoy spent collecting down in the coloured district. A little bonus extracted from Boston & Northeastern, for all those years of service, and exploitation.

ANDREA NEWMAN

from

A Bouquet of Barbed Wire

'A Bouquet of Barbed Wire' by Andrea Newman was first published in 1969 and was made into a controversial television series.

THE flat was cool and shuttered, but he was still hot with surprise at finding himself there. The chain of events was simple. Sarah had been as good as her word at the office: punctual, bright, unembarrassed. He had been grateful to her and felt that she deserved some acknowledgement of her attitude so he said, 'Sarah, you're marvellous and I owe you an apology.'

Sarah said matter-of-factly, 'No, you don't. I told you I'd feel the same today and I do. But I've no objection to being told I'm marvellous.' Then she had gone on calmly typing.

At eleven she brought his coffee without any sign of awkwardness and as she put it on his desk he said, 'Sarah, you really are making things very difficult for me.' Her eyes widened in surprise. 'A little outraged indignation would be much easier to take.'

She said, 'I'm sorry but I did warn you.'

He drank some of the coffee. 'I'm supposed to be driving down to Salcombe tomorrow to bring my wife back—she's taken the boys down there to stay with their grandparents.'

'And you're busy this evening?'

He looked up in surprise. 'No.' He saw tenderness and anxiety and hunger in her face and another look also—that suggested she was puzzled by her own behaviour. And that makes two of us, he thought.

She said, 'I can't bear to leave it like this.'

He said, feeling his blood begin to race, 'Sarah, you are either very kind or very foolish, tell me which,' and she said with a kind of desperation, 'Neither, neither.'

He got through the rest of the day in a daze.

About five, by arrangement, they left the office separately and met round the corner. Already they were starting to be careful. He hailed a taxi, trying not to look nervously round for spies, and when they were in it they sat and held hands, not daring to kiss, and smiled at each other.

He said presently, 'You're mad.'

'I hope it's catching.'

'I mean we're mad.'

'That's better. Isn't it lovely?'

The taxi crawled. He took in for the thousandth time every inch of the brown and gold flowered dress above golden-brown knees. Her hair was tied back with a piece of the same material. He said, 'I think you're a miracle.' An authentic feeling of insanity had swept over him: the situation was predestined and right, nothing could spoil it; he had complete trust in the madness of it all.

Sarah said, 'Where are we going?'

'Regent's Park. A flat near Regent's Park.'

'Whose is it?'

'A friend's. They're away.'

He turned her hand over and over in his own. Small and square. Nails shiny-painted, uncoloured. The lines very firm and marked. He said, pretending to read them, 'Ah, a long and happy life.'

'I should hope so.' She smiled back. Her light-hearted lack of guilt reminded him of Prue ('Daddy, I'm going to have a baby.'). Perhaps that was true innocence: if you did not see any harm in something, then for you it was harmless. Or was that rather the corrupt reasoning of the totally selfish, determined to have their own way? The first chill thought. He brushed it aside.

Sudden pressure on his hand. 'Don't be sad.'

'I'm not.'

'You were. I saw it in your face.'

'All right, I was. But it's gone.'

She shook her head. 'It hasn't really. But I'll make it go.' Now she held his hand in both hers. 'Look. This isn't going to make trouble for anyone—you, or your wife or me. I'm quite realistic and I don't expect anything. But I think this is something we need very much. Both of us. I think it would be worse not to do it. Really.'

'You're a witch.' It bothered him that both their minds should run upon the same lines of self-justification.

'No. Just realistic. *Please* don't be sad. Look—if you've changed your mind you can still stop the cab, throw me out. I'll quite understand.'

'Do you want me to?'

'No.'

'Neither do I.'

The taxi drew up before the curving row of white houses. She was impressed. He paid the driver and she said, 'God, they must be very rich, your friends.' Up the steps and inside across endless yards of carpet to the lift: up, purring almost silently. He became apprehensive. None of the neighbours knew him yet, he was safe there, but what if for some crazy reason—anything could have happened—they had returned home unexpectedly?

The flat was silent and empty. Very cool after the taxi and the street. They stood in the hall and looked at it.

Sarah said, 'It's lovely.'

'Yes, it's quite nice. Rather small but otherwise all right.'

'And to be so near the Park . . .' But the chat petered out. 'Oh please—please kiss me or I shall run away.'

He put his arms round her. 'Sarah, Sarah.' He found he wanted to use her name more and more as if it expressed and held within itself all the words of love he could not (yet?) use. 'It's all right, it's all right, do you hear? You can't run away now, I want you so much, I need you. Sarah—beautiful Sarah.'

They kissed for a long time, until Sarah, drawing breath, said, '*Please* can we go to bed now or I shall fall over,' and indeed as he loosened his hold on her she swayed against the wall. The bedroom gave him an odd qualm, a sense of intrusion, of invitation almost, but strongly mixed with a sensation of triumph and justice. He watched her as they undressed and she was very beautiful; he said so. She said, 'Don't, you'll make me cry,' and he took her in his arms to lie down, saying, 'You're a funny girl,' and she said, 'It's no good pretending I don't do this often, because I do; but it's also no good pretending this isn't special, because it is.' And after that they did not talk much.

They took time to explore each other; he felt that he owed her a lot and must control his impatience. Her pleasure repaid him amply; she did not hide anything and her movements and the look on her face were enough to reward an eternity of effort. When he paused to take precautions (a lunch-hour visit to the chemist, the first in God knows how many years) she stopped him, saying, 'No, that's all taken care of,' and when he entered her they both groaned with delight and relief at achieving something so long delayed. He tried to make it last, tried to be controlled and expert, but it was soon too much for him and she seemed so nearly ready that he could not wait. It was not perfect, in the end, but for a first time it was remarkable. With her he felt free to let go, which amazed him; in the few extra-marital affairs of his life he had always felt a last veil of reticence, even in extremity. He had never known if this was a hard core of fidelity to Cassie or a buried resentment towards his partner of the moment. But he did not feel that with Sarah. Perhaps it was the confidence with which she entrusted herself to him. When he had regained his breath he kissed her all over her face and her shoulders and neck and said, 'Sorry, not perfect,' and she said, eyes closed and a rapturous smile on her face, quite sufficient to drive him out of his mind, 'No, but still *super*.' He laughed then with relief, and said, 'What a child you are.'

She made a face. 'Funny children you know,' and they both began to laugh hysterically, quite out of proportion to the joke. It was a long time since he had laughed so much after making love, and it brought it all back, the crazy hysterical well-being and goodwill. It was youth, or novelty, or love, or a blend of all three, but she had made him remember it and it was intoxicating. He played with her hair; he had never seen it all loose before. It made her look younger. They drew apart and admired each other. She was golden all over except for the pale bikini imprint; he said, enviously, 'You've had a holiday,' and she said, 'Yes, in May. In Italy.' He was suddenly quite sick with jealousy and said, knowing he had no right, no right in the world, 'Did you make love there?' and she said simply, 'Yes,' and he wished she had lied. It was a time when nothing could be concealed: not just that their eyes gave them away but their very skin seemed transparent and revealing. She said, 'I'm sorry you mind but I never pretended to be pure,' and he did not answer. He made a great thing of lighting a cigarette and lay there admiring her honesty and hating her for it. She said, 'Go on, say it,' and he pretended not to know what she meant. 'Go on, tell me that's why I'm here, call me names if you like,' and he pulled her to him, close, and kissed her shoulder and said. 'Oh, Sarah, Sarah,' because it was at that moment the most beautiful name in the world. She said in a muffled voice, 'I'm terribly afraid I'm going to fall in love with you, but I won't let it interfere with my work,' and suddenly they were laughing again and it was all right. He did not even mind that his body next to hers was pale and there was a thickness round the middle that he was ashamed of, whereas she was all bones and correctly placed curves. Her breasts were more full than he had expected and her waist curved in sharply; her hip bones stuck out either side of a flat little stomach. He looked all the way down and found beautiful legs and the most tiny perfect feet, like the feet of a child who has never worn shoes. Naked, he thought she was as neat and precise as she was with her clothes on. He remembered her saying that her room was always tidy and he thought that in some way her body was tidy, too.

*   *   *

Sarah said, 'Shall I make coffee or get us a drink or something? Would your friends mind?' He was so silent that she wondered if he had fallen asleep and as usual she was beginning to feel restless now the languid phase had passed. In a little while she would be hungry. This was the unfailing, predictable pattern and it was reassuring that this still remained, for there seemed little else to be sure of. She had not expected anything to happen between them, not expected to be here, most of all not expected to feel so much. She could not remember such immediate involvement with anyone since the boy in the sixth form (when she was in the fifth form) who had touched her up pretty thoroughly behind the science block one dark night at a school dance. She had adored him after that, as a god (for surely anyone who could produce such sensations must be a god?) and waited, trembling, scarcely breathing, for him to approach her again for a date. But he never did. Term ended and he left and she never knew if he was embarrassed, disgusted, indifferent, or merely absent-minded. It had taught her a sharp lesson, intensified by other later lessons, yet somehow perhaps the most important because it was the first, because she was only fifteen. The glorious sensations behind the science block, her gratitude to him for evoking them, her desperation to go out with him—all this she had obviously failed to transmit; or, if transmitted, it simply did not interest him. Perhaps he regarded her as cheap. Perhaps he laughed about her to his friends. (This thought was too terrible to contemplate: that he might be boasting of what she had 'let' him do, even now while she was recalling the beauty of it all.) Lying awake at night crying—but softly so as not to alert her parents—or staring at him in Assembly, willing him to smile at her, writing his name on pieces of paper to admire the sheer poetry of it (and then tearing them up), walking a discreet distance behind him and his friends to admire what seemed to her the easy grace of his movements, so casual, so self-possessed—all this was clearly ridiculous and achieved no good at all. She had made the mistake of caring. Not to care was the answer. If you did not care they came running, all the people you did not care about. They jostled each other to dance with you, walk with you, buy you chocolates and take you to the cinema—one had even left flowers on her doorstep and then run away—and all you had to do was permit the occasional kiss (or, later, make love). As long as you did not care, back they came. So what was she doing now, letting all this feeling creep in? For it was not, she decided, what you *did* behind the science block that counted, it was how you felt. If you did not care, they could not hurt you; in fact they would not even try. For eight years this policy had worked for her; what on earth made her think it was safe to abandon it now?

She turned her head on the pillow to look at him and said softly, 'Peter Eliot Manson.'

'What?'

'I thought you were asleep.' It was nice to speak as tenderly as she felt. She had forgotten how nice it was.

'No.' He opened his eyes and they gazed at each other. 'Why did you say my full name like that?'

'I don't know. Well, I've typed it often enough but I've never said it.' And making love she had not called him anything: while the 'Sarahs' multiplied, she had not called him Peter or darling, or anything.

'Well, now you have.'

'Yes.' She considered it. 'It's a lovely name. Very formal. Rather Victorian. I like it. But I don't feel it's mine to use.'

'You don't know me well enough, hm?'

They smiled.

'Well, in a way, no. And tomorrow it's Mr Manson again so I better not get in bad habits.'

Tomorrow was Cassie and Salcombe. Tomorrow was office. Tomorrow was reality, making now into only last night. 'Don't remind me,' he said.

She said easily, 'Oh, it will be all right, you'll see. Don't worry. And I love the way you say Sarah.'

'Sarah.'

'Yes.'

'You're a beautiful girl, Sarah.'

'Am I? Did I please you?'

'Yes. Very much.'

'You pleased me too. Very much.'

Somehow this exchange frightened them both: it was too absolute, it seemed final, marking the end of something. Sarah said,
'Well. Shall I get us a drink or some coffee? I asked you before but
you didn't answer so I thought you were asleep.'

'No. I was thinking.'

'Not sad thoughts. Please. I promise you it's all quite all right.'

He said, 'No, not sad thoughts.' He chose his words carefully. 'I
was thinking I care for you.'

'You don't have to say that, you know.'

'No. I know.' Strange how tenderness tipped into anger.

'But I care for you, too. That's the trouble. I've broken a rule.'

'What rule?'

'My own rule.' She stroked his shoulder. It was funny seeing
him naked and tousled, and remembering his office suit, his hair
immaculately brushed. She was glad he had plenty of hair. 'My
rule not to care.'

'What kind of a rule is that?'

She smiled, feeling sad. 'The first law of survival. Don't you
know it?'

'It sounds like death to me.'

'Does it?' She sat up. She suddenly felt much older than he, and
protective. 'Then you must be very brave.'

He put a hand on her arm. 'Don't be cynical, Sarah, it doesn't
suit you.'

'Doesn't it?'

'No.'

'Why, because I'm so *young*? That's got nothing to do with it. I
know about me. If I care I get hurt and behave badly.'

'I'm not going to hurt you.'

'No, of course not.'

'I mean that.'

'I know you do.'

'And I can't imagine that you could ever behave badly.'

She sighed. 'Why do you think I'm so nice? You don't know me at all.'

He said seriously, 'Are you wishing we hadn't done this?'

'Oh no. *No.*'

'Then why all the sadness?' He pulled her back, down to him and wrapped his arms round her. She buried her head in his shoulder, wanting to hide. He said, 'Darling, listen,' and she stiffened, ever so slightly, at the word. 'You're lovely and precious and you've made me so happy I can never repay you. *Please* don't be sad, or I shall feel I've taken advantage and behaved like an old-fashioned cad. Last night I called myself names all the way home. If I can't make you happy all the names will be true.'

She said, 'Oh, you can make me happy, you have. You do,' her voice muffled against his skin. 'It's just—I never imagined this happening.'

'Neither did I. But now that it has we must make it work. We mustn't make anyone unhappy, even ourselves. That's my rule, if you like, though I've only just thought of it. Heads everyone wins and tails nobody loses. Isn't that a good rule?'

'That's the best kind of rule.'

They kissed. Sarah said, 'By the way, you still haven't told me whose flat this is.'

He hesitated. The temptation to tell the truth was strong, perhaps to set a seal on their relationship. But the temptation to lie was stronger, representing safety and self-preservation. 'Just friends of mine. No one you know.'

'A couple? Married and all that?' She sat up.

'Yes.'

'But they don't mind? Us in their bed and everything?'

'Well, we're not exactly *in* it.' They were lying on top of the bedspread and he had been careful to spread a towel.

'No, but the principle's the same. The married are generally on the side of the married, aren't they?'

He wondered how she knew that. 'They're my friends, not Cassie's.' Deeper and deeper in. It felt odd to speak her name in these circumstances. Unlucky.

'And you're sure they won't mind?'

He felt irritated by her questioning and his own thoughts. 'I told you. Why go on about it?'

'Sorry.' She sounded very innocent. 'But it's odd to be in their flat, in their bed, and not know anything about them. It makes me feel strange. I feel I *ought* to know more. For instance are they young or old, happy or unhappy?'

'Young and happy.'

She studied his face. 'You sounded bitter when you said that. Do you envy them?'

'Yes, I suppose I do.' He had been mad to bring her here and mad, having brought her, not to lie properly and make a thorough job of it.

She got up, wandered over to the dressing-table, smoothed her reflected hair and opened a drawer. 'Don't,' he said sharply, a reflex.

She stared at him in the mirror. 'Why not?'

'I'd rather you didn't, that's all.'

She said slowly, 'It's your daughter's flat, isn't it? I think I knew all the time.'

ERICA JONG

from

Fear of Flying

Erica Jong's 'Fear of Flying' was published in 1973. John Updike called it 'the most uninhibited, delicious, erotic novel a woman ever wrote'.

CHARLIE FIELDING ('Charles' when he signed his name) was tall and stoop-shouldered and looked like the Wandering Jew. His nose was enormously long and hooked and had flaring nostrils, and his small down-turned mouth always wore a sour expression, somewhere between contempt and melancholy. His skin was sallow and unhealthy-looking, and had been ravaged by acne which still troubled him from time to time. He wore expensive tweed sport coats which hung on his shoulders as if on wire hangers and the knees of his trousers bagged. The pockets of his old Chesterfield were distended with paperback books. From his worn pigskin briefcase, the point of a conductor's baton protruded.

If you had seen him on the subway or eating a solitary dinner in Schrafft's (where he charged the bills to his father's account), you would have supposed, from his expression, that he was in mourning. He was not—unless he was mourning in advance for his father (whose money he was due to inherit).

Sometimes, while waiting for his dinner to arrive (creamed chicken, hot fudge sundae with chocolate ice cream), he would take an orchestral score from his briefcase and, holding his baton in his right hand, would begin to conduct imaginary musicians. He did this with perfect unselfconsciousness and apparently without any desire to be conspicuous. He was simply oblivious to the people around him.

Charlie (his mother had named him for Bonnie Prince Charlie, and Charlie was, after all, a Jewish prince) lived alone in a one-room apartment in the East Village. The same neighbourhood his poor ancestors had lived in two generations before. The venetian blinds were laden with greasy black soot, and grit crunched under your feet as you walked across the bare floor. The surroundings were Spartan: a pullman kitchen whose cupboards were always bare except for boxes of dried apricots and bags of hard candy, a rented piano, a single bed, a tape recorder, a portable record player, two cartons of records (which had never been unpacked since he brought them from his parents' house two years before). Outside the window was a fire escape overlooking a sooty courtyard and across it lived two middle-aged lesbians who sometimes neglected to draw the blinds. Charlie had that defensive contempt for homosexuals which people often have when their own sexuality is an embarrassment to them. He was horny all the time, but he was terribly afraid of being vulgar. His Harvard education had been designed to extinguish all the vulgarity glowing deep down in his genes, and though he wanted to get laid, he did not want to manage it in a way that would make him appear crude—either to himself or to the girls he tried to seduce.

I've noticed, anyway, that unless a man is a bona fide genius, a Harvard education is a permanent liability. Not so much what they learn there, but what they presume about themselves ever after— the albatross of being a Harvard man: the aura, the atmosphere, the pronunciation problems, the tender memories of the River Charles. It tends to infantilize them and cause them to go dashing about the corridors of advertising agencies with their ties flapping behind them. It causes them to endure the dreadful food and ratty upholstery of the Harvard Club for the sake of impressing some sweet young thing with the glorious source of their BA.

Charlie had this Harvard impediment. He had graduated with a straight C- average and yet he always felt incredibly superior to me with my Phi Beta Kappa from grubby déclassé Barnard. He felt that at Harvard he had been touched with the brush of refinement, that despite all his failures in the world, he was still (a Gilbert and Sullivan chorus should sing out this phrase) a Harvard Man.

Most mornings, Charlie slept until noon, then got up and had breakfast at one of the dairy restaurants left over from the old immigrant-neighbourhood days. But two mornings a week he dragged himself out of bed at nine and took the subway uptown to a music school where he taught piano and conducted a choral group. The money he earned from this work was negligible, but he lived mainly on the income from a trust fund his father had set up for him. He was terribly furtive about the amount of his income, as if it were a dirty secret. Still, I always assumed that if it hadn't gone against the grain of his stinginess he could have lived somewhat less grubbily than he did.

There was, however, a dirty family secret and maybe that was what made the money so embarrassing. Charlie's family had met with money by way of Charlie's Uncle Mel—the famous pseudo-WASP ballroom dancer who glided through the 1930s with patent-leather hair and a fixed nose and a dancing *shikse* wife. Mel Fielding had made a life-long career of keeping his Jewishness secret, and he agreed to share his wealth with the family only on the condition that they fix all their noses too and change their names from Feldstein to Fielding. Charlie refused to comply with the nose, but took the name. Charlie's father, however, *did* amputate half his nose (with the result that he wound up looking like a Jew with an absurdly small nose). But the main thing was that the Feldsteins left Brooklyn and turned up in the Beresford (that gilded ghetto, that pseudocastle) on Central Park West.

The family business was a world-wide chain of dancing schools which sold life memberships to lonely old people. It wasn't exactly a racket any more than psychoanalysis or religion or encounter groups or Rosicrucianism can be said to be rackets, but, like them, it also promised an end to loneliness, powerlessness, and pain, and of course it disappointed many people. Charlie had worked in the dance studio business for a few summers during college, but this was only a token gesture. He hated any kind of everyday job—even if it consisted of gliding across the dance floor with an eighty-year-old lady who had just become a life member to the tune of several thousand dollars. When I knew him, Charlie was very sensitive on the subject of ballroom dancing. He did not want it generally known that this was what his father did for a living. Nevertheless, he dropped his famous uncle's name frequently among his friends and mine. Ambivalence is a wonderful tune to dance to. It has a rhythm all its own.

But what did Charlie do? He prepared himself for greatness. He daydreamed about his conducting debut—which otherwise he did nothing much to hasten—and he began symphonies. They were—every one of them—unfinished symphonies. He also began sonatas and operas (based on works by Kafka or Beckett). These were unfinished, too. He began jazz songs—which never got beyond the first few bars (but which he always promised to dedicate to me). Perhaps to others he was a failure, but to himself he was a romantic figure. He spoke of 'silence, exile, and cunning'. (Silence: the unfinished symphonies. Exile: he had left the Beresford for the East Village. Cunning: his affair with me.) He was going through the initial trials of all great artists. As a conductor, he had not yet had his break and was further handicapped, he thought, by the fact of not being a homosexual. As a composer, it was a question of learning to cope with the crisis of style which bedevilled the age. That too would come in time. One had to think in decades, not years.

Dreaming at the piano bench or over a plate of cherry blintzes in Ratner's, Charlie thought of himself as he would be when he finally made it—greying at the temples, suave, and eccentrically dressed. After conducting his own opera at the Met, he would not be above running down to the Half Note for a jam session with aspiring jazz musicians. College girls who recognized him there would besiege him for autographs, and he would put them off

with witty remarks. In the summers he would retire to his country
house in Vermont, composing at a Bechstein under a slanting skylight, emerging from his studio to make clever conversation with
the poets and young composers who followed him there. He
would devote three hours a day to writing his autobiography—in
a style he described as somewhere between Proust and Evelyn
Waugh (his favourite authors). And then there would be women.
Wagnerian sopranos with great dimpled asses out of Peter Paul
Rubens. (Charlie had a great partiality for plump—even fat—
women. He always thought I was too skinny and my ass too small.
If we'd stayed together I probably would have become elephan-
tine.) After the fat sopranos came the literary ladies: women poets
who dedicated books to him, women sculptors obsessed with
having him pose in the nude, women novelists who found him so
fascinating they made him the central figure in their *romans á clef*.
He might never marry, not even for the sake of having children.
Children (as he often said) were *boring*. *Boring* (pronounced as if in
italics) was always one of his favourite words. But it was not his
ultimate condemnation (nor was *banal* though he favoured that
too). *Vulgar* was his ultimate word of scorn. People, of course,
could be vulgar, as could books and music and paintings—but
food could also be vulgar with Charles. As he once said when his
famous uncle took him to Le Pavillon: 'These crepes are *vulgar*.'
He pronounced it with a great gap between the two syllables—as
if between *vul* and *gar* he was trembling on the brink of a releva-
tion. Pronunciation was also a big thing with Charles.

After all this, I have neglected to say the most important thing
of all—namely, that I was madly in love with him (with the accent
on the *mad*). The cynicism came later. To me he was not a pomp-
ous, pimply young man, but a figure of legendary charm, a future
Lenny Bernstein. I knew that his family (with their champagne-
silk, decorator-decorated living-room-under-plastic-covers) was a
hundred times more vulgar even than mine. I sensed that Charlie
was more snobbish than he was intelligent. I knew he never
bathed, never used deodorant, and wiped his ass inadequately (as if

he were still hoping his Mommy would come to the rescue), but I was crazy about him. I let him condescend to me. After all, he was a devotee of the most universal of the arts: music. I was a lowly, literal-minded scribe. Most important, he was a piano player like my piano-playing father. When he sat down at the keyboard, my underpants got wet. Those continuos! Those crescendos! Those sharps! Those flats!

You know that awful expression 'tickle the ivories'? That was how Charlie drove me wild. Sometimes we even used to fuck on the piano bench with the metronome going.

We met in a funny way. On television. What can be funnier than a poetry reading on television? It isn't poetry and it isn't television. It's 'educational'—if you'll excuse the expression.

The programme was on Channel 13 and it was a kind of salad of the seven arts—none of them lively. Why it was considered educational was anyone's guess. There were seven young 'artists' each of whom had four minutes to do his (or her) stuff. Then there was a puffy-eyed, pipe-smoking old fart with a name like Phillips Hardtack who interviewed each of us, asking us incisive questions like 'what, in your opinion, is Inspiration?' or 'what influence did your childhood have on your work?' For these questions (and about ten others) another four minutes was allotted. Apart from hosting shows like this Hardtack hacked out his living writing book reviews and posing for whiskey ads—two occupations which have more in common than appears on the surface. The Scotch was always 'light' and 'mild' and the books were always 'stark' and 'powerful'. All you had to do was crank Hardtack up and out came the adjectives. Sometimes, however, he got them confused and called a book 'light' and 'mild' while he called the Scotch 'stark' and 'powerful.' For twenty-year-old Scotch and geriatric authors who had published memoirs, Hardtack reserved the word 'mellow'. And for young authors and Brand X's Scotch, Hardtack had this automatic response: 'Lacks smoothness'.

Most of the 'artists' on that show deserved Hardtack. There was a young fool who called himself a 'cinemaker' and showed four minutes of shaky, overexposed film of what looked like two (or possibly three) amoebas dancing pseudopod to pseudopod; a black painter who called himself an activist-painter and only painted chairs (a strangely pacifist subject for an activist-painter); a soprano with very yellow, very buck teeth (Charlie was there to accompany her four minutes of trembling Puccini); a one-man percussion section named Kent Blass who jumped round spastically, playing drums, xylophones, glass fish tanks, pots and pans; a modern dancer who never said the noun 'dance' without using the definite article; a social-protest folksinger whose native Brooklynese had been laced with elocution lessons, with the bizarre result that he pronounced God, 'Garrd'; and then there was me.

They had rigged me up inside a gray plywood picture frame for my four minutes of poetry, and in order to reach it, I had to perch on a kind of scaffolding. Charlie was right below, sitting at the piano and staring up my skirt. While I read my poetry, his eyes were burning holes in my thighs. A day later he called me up. I didn't remember him. Then he said that he wanted to set my poems to music, so I met him for dinner. I've always been very naïve about ploys like that. 'Come up to my apartment and let me set your poems to music' and I always come. Or at least go.

But Charlie surprised me. He looked scrawny and unwashed and hook-nosed when he came to my door, but in the restaurant he displayed his gigantic knowledge of Cole Porter and Rodgers and Hart and Gershwin: all the songs my father had played on the piano when I was a kid. Even the obscure Cole Porter songs, the almost-forgotten Rodgers and Hart songs from obscure musicals, the least-known Gershwin songs—he knew them all. He knew even more of them than me—with my total recall for catchy lines. It was then that I fell absurdly in love with him, transformed him from an unwashed hook-nosed frog—into a prince—a piano-playing Jewish prince at that. As soon as he recited the last stanza of 'Let's Do It' and got the words all *right*, I was ready to do it with him. A simple case of Oedipussy.

We went home to bed. But Charlie was so overwhelmed by his good luck that he wilted.

'Conduct me,' I said.

'I seem to have lost my baton.'

'Well then, do it like Mitropoulos—with your bare hands.'

'You're a real find,' he said, thrashing around under the covers. But, hand or baton, it was hopeless. His teeth were chattering and great shudders were shaking his shoulders. He was gasping for breath like an emphysema patient.

'What's the matter?' I asked.

'It's just that you're such a find, I can't believe it.' He seemed to be sobbing and choking alternately.

'Will you see me again in spite of this?' he pleaded. 'You promise you won't hold this against me?'

'What kind of ghoul do you think I am?' I was astonished. All my maternal instincts had been roused by his helplessness. 'What kind of creep would throw you out?'

'The last one this happened with,' he moaned. 'She threw me out and tossed my clothes to me in the hall. She forgot one sock. I had to go home on the subway with one bare ankle. It was the most humiliating experience of my life.'

'Darling,' I said, rocking him.

I guess I should have been tipped off about Charlie's emotional instability by his sobbing and choking and shuddering—but not me. For me this only confirmed his sensitivity. The Prince and the Pea. It was understandable. Opening nights got him down. We could always sing Cole Porter together instead of fucking. But instead he fell asleep in my arms. He slept like no one I've ever known. He wheezed and sputtered and farted and thrashed. He groaned and shuddered. He even picked his pimples in his sleep. I stayed up half the night watching him in utter amazement.

In the morning he woke up smiling and fucked me like a stud. I had passed the test. I had not thrown him out. This was my reward.

STEPHEN VIZINCZEY

from

In Praise of Older Women

On Happiness with a
Frigid Woman

'This book is dedicated to older women and addressed to young men—and the connection between the two is my proposition', writes András Vajda, the hero of Stephen Vizinczey's classic erotic novel. First published by the author himself in Canada in 1965, 'In Praise of Older Women' is a memorable account of growing up in post-war Hungary and a young man's sexual education.

I WAS so sick of myself that I became attracted to a woman who showed absolutely no sympathy for me. Although Paola was writing an apparently endless series of articles about Hungarian students, her personal indifference to us wasn't affected by exposure to our company day after day. As I interpreted for her every afternoon in the dim lobby of the Albergo Ballestrazzi, I tried to guess her age. It could have been anywhere between twenty-eight and thirty-six: there were fine lines on her forehead and neck, yet her pale blue eyes shone with the unperturbed innocence (or ignorance?) of a young girl. When she walked into the lobby, wearing some clinging silk or knitted dress, strikingly elegant, her body looked as if it had been massaged into perfect shape by a long line of ardent lovers. But as she came closer, the warm glow turned into cold grace. She had a slim, distant face, the pale oval of a Byzantine madonna, and I began to wonder whether she would come to life if I touched her.

'You know,' I said to her one day, 'I'm really quite an experienced interpreter. I did a lot of it when I was a small boy.' I hoped, of course, that she would ask me where and why. At times when I didn't believe in myself, I used to exploit my American Army camp stories quite shamelessly as feelers and stimulants. But Paola wasn't interested. I also tried to impress her with my talent for languages, switching from English to Italian whenever I could, to show off each new word I had learned. She didn't react. Most of the boys excused themselves from her company as quickly as they could, and I was often left alone with her before she'd found out all she needed to know for the following day's instalment. I tried to help her, although my boil was throbbing and my whole body shivering with fever, and sometimes I alluded to my sufferings. She received such personal remarks with a raised eyebrow, as if I'd asked her to write a front-page story about my state of health.

'I'm sorry, but I'm afraid I'll have to leave you too,' I told her one day, thoroughly fed up, and in plain English. 'I feel so sick, I think I must be dying.'

'Now, try to say that in Italian,' she urged, in Italian. 'You shouldn't be so lazy—you should practise the language you know the least.'

Too weak to grind my teeth, I repeated in humble Italian that I was dying.

'Excellent!' Paola exclaimed, and actually smiled. 'See you tomorrow then.'

Infuriated, I went for a walk to calm myself. At the end of the Via Veneto stands one of the gates to the Villa Borghese, which is set in a luxuriant yet ordered park of ancient trees and fresh flowers, wild nature in a frame of carefully detailed artistic design, as much a forest as a garden. There is a small lake, there are exquisite paths winding past white marble statues, and everywhere (as the park occupies one of the Seven Hills of Rome) it offers glimpses of church domes, palace walls—a breath of the Renaissance. I'd never seen anything so magnificent and yet so soothing as the Borghese Gardens, and as I walked around I became sufficiently relaxed to realize that the fresh air and exercise had cleared my head and cooled my fever. Yet if it hadn't been for Paola's outrageous indifference to my sufferings, I would have spent the afternoon brooding in the hotel. Indeed, this sort of cause and effect turned out to be the pattern of our relationship: Paola used to make me furious, but I ended by feeling healthier and brighter afterwards.

'I'm not an outgoing personality,' she observed after our last interview in the lobby, when we were left by ourselves again. 'And I concentrate on what I'm doing. I noticed your friends don't like me.'

'They think you're humourless, bloodless and insensitive,' I informed her.

'That sounds pretty astute.' She was impressed, as if we were talking about someone else. 'I must say, I was favourably impressed by most of you,' she added in the spirit of objectivity. 'You're all too wrought up about politics, but at least you're not like Italian men—you're not obsessed with sex.'

I don't know how the other boys would have reacted if they'd been present to hear the compliment, but its effect on me was profound. Once when I was in hospital at the age of nine with a ruptured appendix, I heard the doctor advising my mother to make arrangements for my funeral, and I was back on my feet in two weeks. Paola's remark affected me the same way. I asked her whether she would show me around Rome, in return for my services as an interpreter; she agreed, and we made an appointment for the following day. After she left I went up to my room, did ten push-ups, had a bath, and resolved to make love with that woman as soon as my boil disappeared.

It was on our second date, about the middle of January, that I began to make verbal passes at my guide. She was leading me through a small museum, and I kept insisting that she was more beautiful than any of the paintings or statues she pointed out to me. In her reddish-brown dress, with her blonde hair combed sleekly upward from her slim, impassive face, she looked like a royal Egyptian mummy, enamelled in russet and ochre—whatever period she conjured up, it was never the present. She didn't acknowledge my flattery, except by raising her eyebrows. Was it a childhood habit of hers, I wondered, to express surprise and disapproval in this way? Had she tried for years to get rid of the habit, and finally given up in despair? I imagined everything I could that might have made her more human and likeable.

When we were about to part, in front of the museum, I tried my luck.

'Do you know, I've never been invited for a meal in an Italian home?'

'You haven't missed anything—the hotels have the best food in Rome.'

'Still, it's not the same as a home-cooked meal.'

'What's got into you today? For one thing, I'm married. For another, if I want to have you for dinner, I'll ask you.'

That was definite. I held out my hand. 'Well, it was nice knowing you, maybe we'll meet again if I stay in Italy.'

Paola took my hand, but didn't let it go. Some women shouldn't be rude, if they don't want to end up being kind, out of uneasiness over their bad manners. 'I suppose if I don't invite you for dinner you'll think it's because you're a refugee.'

'Not at all,' I protested, pressing her long, smooth fingers. 'I realize it's simply because you don't like me personally.'

She withdrew her hand and looked around to see whether any of the passers-by were watching us. 'I've nothing at home but canned food.'

'I love canned food.'

She narrowed her eyes this time, though it may have been on account of the sharp sun. 'All right, but remember—you asked for it.'

As Paola led me into her apartment, I kissed the back of her neck. Her skin was so fair that it seemed to radiate light in the windowless alcove. She stood still for a moment, then removed her body and the smell of her perfume to a bright, modern kitchen.

'I'd be the wrong woman for you,' she said firmly, 'even for a casual affair.'

Still, our situation was becoming more intimate. She heated up some canned ravioli and we sat down at the kitchen table to an uninspired meal, just like an old married couple. Which reminded me that Paola had said she was married. 'Where is your husband?' I asked anxiously. I'd quite forgotten about him.

'We haven't been living together for the past six years,' she admitted with an apologetic half-smile. 'We're legally separated— that's what we have in Italy instead of divorces.'

'Why did you leave him?'

'He left me.'

The answer didn't invite further questions, and it was just as well, for had Paola told me more I would probably have lost my nerve and retreated to the Albergo Ballestrazzi. We began to talk about politics and she explained to me the differences between the various factions of the ruling Christian Democratic Party, in a relaxed manner, as if she'd taken for granted that I understood that all I was going to get was canned food. Inspired both by piqued pride and by the smell of her perfume (I'd somehow been unaware of it on other occasions, though now it overpowered even the ravioli), I could hardly wait for the end of the meal, and I declined her offer to make coffee, as it would have involved an intolerable waste of time. I asked her to show me the apartment, but it impressed me only as a blue and green background to her figure, until we came to a huge round bed. Paola let me kiss and hold her, without responding; but when I began to unbutton her dress, she tried to push me away with her elbows and knees. The tight dress frustrated her efforts as much as I did, and at last I succeeded in releasing her breasts, which swelled up as they emerged from the brassiére. Neither of us had spoken, but when my head bent over her white bosom she remarked, with a tinge of malice in her voice, 'I'm frigid, you know.'

What was I to do, standing against her, with her bare breasts cupped in my hands? 'I've just come from a revolution,' I declared manfully, but without showing my face, 'you can't scare me.'

At that Paola raised my head and gave me a strong passionate kiss. While we were undressing each other, I began to hope that this mysterious Italian woman had been lying to test me. Hadn't Nusi warned me that she wouldn't sleep with me for at least a month, not an hour before we first made love?

Unfortunately, there are few happy parallels in life. When we had got rid of our clothes, Paola gathered hers together piled them neatly on the bureau, and hung her dress in the closet. Then she went to the bathroom to brush her teeth. I watched her with a mixture of disbelief, fear, and longing. Naked, her buttocks were larger than they had seemed under the dress, but they only gave an exciting, firm centre to her tall, slim body. As she turned from the washbasin, the combination of her long blonde hair and the short blonde tuft between her thighs brought back the painful cramps of my boyhood. But she walked towards me, in the glorious strangeness of her naked body, as casually and deliberately as if we'd been married for ten years. She stuck out the tip of her tongue— then walked right past me to take off the bedspread, which she folded three times and deposited on the chair. Terrified that she would spend the whole night puttering about like this, I grabbed her by her cool buttocks.

'They're too big,' she commented soberly.

I squeezed them with the violence of my frustration and it must have hurt, for she bled me in turn, sinking her teeth into my tongue. Only the fact that I'd been without a woman for over two months enabled me to get through the next quarter of an hour. Paola behaved more like a considerate hostess than a lover: she raised and twisted her body so attentively that I felt like a guest for whom so much is done that he can't help knowing that he's expected to leave soon. I didn't feel at home in her, and couldn't come for a long time. At the end, I ran my hands over her body, still not quite believing that there could be such perfect form without content.

'Did you enjoy it?' she asked.

As all else had failed, I tried to soften her with words. 'It was wonderful.'

'Oh, I'm glad, glad, glad.'

'I love you.'

'Don't talk like that,' Paola protested She pulled the blanket up to her neck, preventing me from hovering over her body. 'You make me feel I should tell you the same thing. And I can't say I love you. It wouldn't be true.'

'Let's lie then!'

'Maybe you can lie, but I can't.'

While thinking out some polite way of leaving, I reached down between her legs and began playing with her, almost mechanically—only to discover that she liked this better than our lovemaking.

'Aren't we having a good time without making things up?' she asked comfortably.

Was she one of those women who could only come in a roundabout way? Never one to leave well enough alone, I hopefully pulled off the blanket and turned myself around to reach the source of her mystery. But she pushed my head away and shoved me violently in the chest, almost rolling me off the bed. 'Don't! It's unclean to do a thing like that.'

'But you're clean. You smell so good!'

'I'm not a pervert—I like it the normal way.'

'You mean, when you don't come?'

'I'd be ashamed.'

'Do you know,' I told her, 'one of the most common endearments in Hungarian is *my sweet flesh*. Nobody is ashamed to say it. Lovers call each other *my sweet flesh* in front of everybody.'

'You would be disgusted.'

I tried to persuade Paola that she was perfect in all her parts, but she was stubborn. The more we talked about it, the less it mattered. Finally, I looked around for my clothes on the grey broadloom—it was getting dark—then got up and began to dress.

'Why are you getting dressed?' she asked, annoyed.

'I think I should be going—it's getting late.'

Paola was silent for a while, then burst out unexpectedly, 'You men are all vain monkeys. You don't enjoy women, you don't even enjoy your own orgasm. The only thing you really want is to make a woman go off with a big bang. It had to be men who invented the atomic bomb.'

'Maybe you'd have a bang, if you'd only try.'

'Oh, God, I'm thirty-six years old, Andrea. I've tried enough.'

I turned on the light to find my shoes.

'Did I tell you about my husband?' she asked, propping herself up on her elbow. 'He's a lawyer—he ran for Parliament twice on the Monarchist ticket, and was defeated, of course. He thought he lost because I was frigid. I had destroyed his self-confidence. He read a lot on psychoanalysis and decided that I must be a masochist, so he took to beating me with a wet towel every time we made love. I got so sick of that towel, I finally told him maybe we should find out whether I was a sadist.'

'What did he say?'

'He actually wanted to try it. I did hit him one evening, he insisted, but I didn't enjoy that either, in fact I hated it. So I said there'd be no more experiments.'

I sat down on the edge of the bed to tie my shoelaces. 'None of your lovers were any better?'

'Oh, it's always on the basis of friendship. There's an editor on the paper, he comes up sometimes. But he doesn't want to mess around like you do. He's fifty-one.' I hated the idea of trespassing on an elderly gentleman's territory, and it must have showed. 'What are you thinking about?' she asked, reaching out to brush my hand affectionately. A most contrary woman.

'I was wondering what's going to happen when the Italian government gets tired of keeping us in the hotel,' I lied. But when I'd said the words I did begin to fret again about what was going to become of me. 'The worst of it is, I really don't have the faintest clue. I got a list of Italian universities from the Red Cross and sent off a bunch of applications—but even if they accept my degrees here, they probably won't let me teach, with my Italian. And I want to be a teacher, I've been preparing for it too long to give it up now.' I already saw myself as a waiter in a cheap café, taking small tips.

'Oh, you'll get something. And in the meantime, you're in Rome, staying in a hotel that would cost you ten thousand lire a day if you had to pay for it. Why don't you just relax and enjoy yourself? I noticed you're awfully tense.'

How would I be otherwise, in her company? 'It's easy for you to talk,' I complained bitterly. 'You have a steady job, you're in your own country, you don't have to worry what'll happen to you tomorrow.'

Paola got up and began to dress. 'Nobody knows what'll happen to him tomorrow. You like to feel sorry for yourself.' Now that we were discussing a problem that she could handle with pure reason, she regained her confident manner. And she must have felt relieved, as I did, that we both had our clothes on again: it was certainly more appropriate to the nature of our relationship. 'A lot of people,' she added briskly, 'would commit murder to have your problems.'

'I shouldn't be talking to you, you only remind me that I'm absolutely alone in this world.'

'Who isn't?'

For some reason—perhaps because she went back to the bathroom to comb her hair, with slow dreamy movements of her arm, as if we'd had a great time—I felt compelled to convince her that I had every reason to feel rotten. I'd made my whole past simply irrelevant by leaving Hungary, didn't she understand that? Nothing I'd done in my life meant anything any more. I told her about the Russian tank which drove over me every night.

'Because you keep brooding over what you've been through. You spend all your time feeling sorry for yourself.'

'I wouldn't dare in your presence.'

'You're a student of philosophy—you should know that life is chaotic, senseless and painful most of the time.'

'That's exactly why I'm so miserable,' I protested.

'At twenty-three, aren't you too old to get upset about such obvious things?'

I tried to prove that I knew more about the absurdity of existence than she did, and we began to argue about Camus and Sartre. While we talked I wandered from room to room, so as not to be too close to that mean woman. When would I have an apartment like hers, I wondered. It was a truly extraordinary place. There was none of the oppressive stinginess of most modern apartments about it, although the building was only a few years old. The ceilings were high, the rooms enormous and they had the most exciting layout. The bedroom was round and had a big semicircular window, at which stood a half-moon-shaped desk with a portable Olivetti on it. The only other furniture was the huge round bed, which Paola had quickly made up again with its gold quilted cover. The adjoining grey-marble and gilt bathroom was the size of a small public bath. The blue and green living room was shaped like a capital S, and this wavy line gave it an illusion of movement, in spite of the large and solid armchairs and sofas, which were made to fit the curves of the wall.

'I'm not surprised,' I told Paola, 'that you can accept the absurdity of existence with such equanimity.'

'I've had to move out of this place twice because I couldn't afford the rent. I haven't got a car.'

'Doesn't your husband pay you alimony?'

'Well, he's supposed to according to law, and he can certainly afford it, but I couldn't very well go to court and force him to support me, considering the miserable time I gave him.'

I wasn't inclined to contradict her. The time had come to say goodbye, but before I could introduce the subject of our parting, she put her arm through mine with a confident gesture. 'Let's go for a walk, Andrea.'

Did she think I planned to go on seeing her? When we were in the elevator, she drew my head to hers and whispered, 'You know, I enjoy it in my own little way. You made me feel like a real woman.' Which was Paola's best argument to convert me to a stoical view of life: instead of feeling sorry for myself, I began to feel sorry for her.

But I showed up on our next date mainly because I had received a letter from the Monsignor at the University of Padua. He informed me that Italian universities in general required more credits in Christian philosophy than I seemed to have; that at the moment they had no funds available to grant me a scholarship for the time I would require to perfect my Italian and complete my doctoral thesis; and that I should perhaps apply to the American foundations. The Monsignor also advised me, since I spoke German and English, to enquire at universities in West Germany and the English-speaking countries. It didn't sound as if Italy had any use for Signor Andrea Vajda with his *cum laude* degrees from the University of Budapest.

As I was reading and re-reading the letter, I had a sudden desire to hear Paola telling me that it was nothing to complain about, and that there were people starving to death in Sicily. Besides, I began to wonder about the fact that, in all her thirty-six years, no man had been able to get through to her. What if I could make all the difference? Back home in Budapest, I wouldn't have conceived such an ambition. By the time I recovered from my hopeless love for Ilona, I had learned that there were more important obstacles to overcome in this world than a difficult woman. As I began to take my studies seriously, I invested my ego in becoming a good teacher and, possibly, the author of a few worthwhile philosophical essays; and my masculine craving for excitement, conflict and danger was satisfied by the Security Police. Much as I loved women, all I wanted from them was straight affection, and I came to avoid those whose behaviour suggested complications. But in Rome, where I was fed, housed and bored, reduced to the uncertain and purposeless life of the undisposed refugee, Paola offered the happiness of constant challenge.

We began to spend most evenings together—sometimes the night, in Paola's apartment. Being with her was like living on a high plateau. The air was clear but thinner, one had to slow down one's responses, breathe lightly, be cool and careful and avoid excitement. For obvious reasons, conversation was a very important element in our affair.

Once when we were in bed and I wanted to try a way which she found strange, Paola leaped out of bed and returned with a pile of books by and about Sartre. 'I've been thinking,' she said, 'you must be depressed with nothing to do here. You must work on something. You know, there's no reason why you shouldn't write your thesis, just because you don't know yet where you're going to submit it. And I can help you to get the journals and papers you need.' It was impossible not to see that Paola had brought me the books to evade a struggle on the bed, but this didn't make her suggestion any less appealing. We spent the rest of the evening poring over the books, and the next day I began to make notes on *Sartre's theory of self-deception as it applies to the body of his own philosophy*, for which the University of Toronto granted me a PhD three years later. It appeared in the second issue of *The Canadian Philosophical Review* (Volume 1, Number 2, pages 72–158) gaining me whatever standing I have in my profession. At any rate, thanks to Paola's way of evading our most personal problem, I became involved in something I enjoyed doing and thought useful—which did a great deal to steady my nerves. I stopped having nightmares, and began to fit into the world again.

However, the novelty of my spiritual well-being wore off after a while. No longer starved for either sex or companionship, I missed increasingly what Paola couldn't give, and began to lose hope of ever changing her. At the beginning we used to leave the lights on in her bedroom, but we gradually got into the habit of turning off all the switches before touching each other. I was especially incensed by her violent throes and sighs. As she grew fond of me, she wanted to show that I made her enjoy herself in her own little way, but her pretences only served as incessant reminders that she was having an indifferent time and going to the trouble of acting for it. I was bitterly conscious of being a joy-parasite, a sexual free-loader. All of which made me obsessed with her stubborn vagina, that pine-smelling fountainhead of our predicament. I often tried to kiss it, but she always pushed me away. If I argued, she became desolate.

'I was happy as long as I was a virgin,' she once complained bitterly. 'Then it was enough that I was a good-looking, intelligent, nice girl. Ever since, it's always the same story. What a sexy-looking woman, let's lay her. And when she finally gives in, sick to death of being pestered, what a big disappointment! I wish I were ugly, then everybody'd leave me alone and I wouldn't have to listen to complaints.'

'Who's complaining? Don't talk nonsense.'

'You wanted canned food, remember?'

We made love then the normal way, simulating enjoyment in unison. Our bed grew damp with the sweat of remorse, and there was nothing we could do about it. At first I thought she would welcome my attempts to give her joy, but she took them as an admission that I held it against her that she couldn't satisfy herself. Of course I tried to convince her that there was more to sex than pleasure—much more, indeed!—and that it was facile, idiotic, to make a fetish of orgasm. She agreed. But whatever is sanctioned by society as a principal good also becomes a moral imperative (whether it's the salvation of the soul or the body) and we can't fail to attain it except at the peril of our conscience. Paola couldn't help feeling guilty about her frigidity any more than she could have felt righteous about making love in the Middle Ages. In fact, I sometimes wished us back into the twelfth century, when her coldness would have been the pride of her virtue and she would have felt sinful only for the delights of the flesh, whereas now she was doomed to feel guilty for her painful frustration. Nor could I help sharing her guilt. If she had been younger and not yet convinced that her misfortune wasn't her lover's fault, we might have ended up strangling each other (even among frigid women, older women are preferable), but though we both knew I wasn't the cause, I was still accessory to her suffering. And my attempts to relieve it only made matters worse. On the other hand, to ignore the despairing excitement and let-down of her body would have meant denying even the bond of elementary sympathy between us. We were getting lost in a desert of impossibilities.

Paola said that I made her feel like a real woman by wanting and enjoying her, and at times she was the blissful mother of my pleasure. But the mistress couldn't have endured her smouldering expectations which never caught fire, except in a state of vigilant despair. There would be very few sexual problems if they could all be ascribed to inhibitions, yet at first I took it for granted that Paola refused to consent to any unfamiliar love-play out of modesty. However, her violent resistance showed not shyness but fear. It leaped through the blue of her eyes and hung over her long white body—the fear of false hopes and deeper defeats.

Even a sentimental glance put Paola on her guard. She had a horror of being carried away, or rather of forgetting that she couldn't be. On a mild evening late in March we sat at the edge of a sidewalk cafe, watching the flow of human splendour, and as Paola seemed relaxed and cheerful, I began to eye her as pleadingly as if she were a strange woman I was trying to pick up. She raised her eyebrows and turned her head away. 'Your trouble is that you love yourself too much.'

'How could you possibly love anybody, if you don't even love yourself?'

'Why should I love myself?' she asked with her casual and depressing objectivity. 'Why should we love anybody?'

We might have been able to cope with her lack of physical satisfaction, but the metaphysical consequences were opening a void between us. They made it difficult—in fact, for a long time impossible—to test my hopeful guess at an easy way to free us from the sting of her husband's wet towel.

Late one Saturday morning, I was awakened by the heat. The sun was shining into my eyes through the curved window panes and gauzy white curtains, and the temperature in the room must have been at least ninety degrees. During the night we had kicked off the blanket and the top sheet, and Paola was lying on her back with her legs drawn up, breathing without a sound. We never look so much at the mercy of our bodies, in the grip of our unconscious cells, as when we are asleep. With a loud heartbeat, I made up my mind that this time I would make or break us. Slowly I separated her limbs: a thief parting branches to steal his way into a garden. Behind the tuft of blond grass I could see her dark-pink bud, with its two long petals standing slightly apart as if they, too, felt the heat. They were particularly pretty, and I began smelling and licking them with my old avidity. Soon the petals grew softer and I could taste the sprinkles of welcome, though the body remained motionless. By then Paola must have been awake, but pretended not to be; she remained in that dreamy state in which we try to escape responsibility for whatever happens, by disclaiming both victory and defeat beforehand. It may have been ten minutes or half an hour later (time had dissolved into a smell of pine) that Paola's belly began to contract and let up and, shaking, she finally delivered us her joy, that offspring not even transient lovers can do without. When her cup ran over she drew me up by my arms and I could at last enter her with a clear conscience.

'You look smug,' were her first words when she focused her critical blue eyes again.

We had one friend in common: a Hungarian-Italian painter, Signor Bihari, a tall, sporty-looking gentleman in his sixties. He always wore an elegant ascot scarf of his own design, and used to assure everyone that his main ambition in life was to stay as young as Picasso. He had started his career as a reporter in Budapest, but his paper had sent him on a two-week assignment to Paris in 1924 and he hadn't been back in Hungary since. His wife was a French lady whom he used to drag along to the Albergo Ballestrazzi so that she could at least hear Hungarian conversation and find out how her husband's mother-tongue sounded. She would stand at his side, bewildered, while he talked with the refugees. Signor Bihari knew not only Paola but also the editor who'd been friendly with her, and it was thus I learned that Paola had broken off with the man telling him that she was in love with a young Hungarian refugee.

I quoted the statement back to Paola, curious whether she would acknowledge such an affectionate confession.

'Don't you believe it,' Paola said. 'I wanted to get rid of the man peacefully, and you can't get rid of anybody by telling him the truth of the matter.'

'And what's the truth of the matter?'

We were in her kitchen and she was cooking dinner for us, wearing only a bra and a light skirt, for it was already summer. I sat by the kitchen table, smelled the delicious food and watched her moving about, with a stirring of all sorts of appetites.

'Well,' she said, her attention still on her steaming pots and pans, 'the truth of the matter is that in ten years or so I'm going to quit working and retire to our old house in Ravenna. My parents'll probably be dead by then, and I'll live there with some old maid. Our noses will get sharper every winter, I suppose.'

'Maybe I'll be teaching in Ravenna.'

'There are enough philosophy teachers in Italy to fill the Adriatic. You'll emigrate to some other country sooner or later. Which will be just as well, because it'll save me from the unpleasant experience of having you get bored with me.'

Her prediction that I would get bored with her seemed most improbable. There was now less tension between us than with most of the women I'd ever known, and our relaxed happiness used to remind me of the bad times I'd experienced with all my other lovers. I remembered the moments of anxiety when I used to recite historical dates in my head while we were making love, so that I wouldn't enjoy myself too much and too quickly for my lover's convenience. With Paola, I had no reason to regulate my response. She used to receive me when already shaking and flowing—which somehow made her more desirable each time. We got along famously. We were happy.

But I couldn't get a job, and the Albergo Ballestrazzi was to be given back to paying guests at the beginning of August. If I went to live with Paola, she might have to support me for a very long time. So she turned out to be right about my leaving Italy. Signor Bihari had a friend at the Canadian Embassy who had friends in Toronto who promised me a job at the university there, and I didn't have the courage to refuse.

On August 16, Paola accompanied me to the airport. We were rocking in the back of an ancient taxi and, as I was gloomy and speechless, she pulled my hair.

'It isn't that you're sorry to leave me,' she said accusingly, "you're scared of going to Canada.'

'Both,' I admitted, and began to cry, which I believe made our parting easier for my unsentimental lover.

After we said goodbye at the gate of the runway, Paola turned to leave, then came back and gave me another hug.

'Don't worry, Andrea,' she said, quoting our private joke with a serious smile, 'every road leads to Rome.'

SUBNIV BABUTA

from
The Still Point

Subniv Babuta's first novel, 'The Still Point', was published in 1991. This extract shows why it was hailed as the work of an exceptional new talent.

For Max and Imogen, India brings to their loving, a burning intensity. Nine centuries earlier Srivastava, the court architect, dreams of the future and of the passion of two young Europeans.

ALL alone in the afternoon heat, with only the fighting dogs for company, Max and Imogen caressed each other with passionate hands. They were soaked in perspiration. The salty taste as they kissed heightened their appetites and as their desire increased, so they became oblivious of their surroundings. As Max unfastened the buttons down the front of Imogen's blouse, she breathed deeply, pressing herself against him. His lips still fastened to hers, Max pulled the shirt off her back, feeling her firm breasts press gently against his chest. He could feel her damp nipples rubbing against his own skin. Holding her face with his hands, Max followed the contours of her chin and neck with his lips, descending slowly, finally taking her hardened nipple into his mouth. Imogen groaned, raising her face upwards to the sky, her eyes firmly closed, feeling the passion surge through her arteries.

Srivastava had never dreamt such visions, even when he was a virile young man. He was back amongst the temples, but the

painful heat and sunlight of the desert had given way to a cool
amber haze, covering everything with its deep sunset hues. As the
craftsman wandered in and out of the sacred halls and courtyards,
the stones began to speak. But theirs was not a language of words.
Srivastava turned; behind him, a young girl had sighed, yearning
with impatience for her lover. As his eyes focused in the soft light,
he saw in a distant courtyard two lovers, locked in embrace. The
girl's golden hair was swept lightly by the evening breeze as her
face, held softly by her partner's hands, stared at the crimson sky,
lost in its own passion. Her lover, with an ardent thirst, pressed his
lips firmly to her breast, caressing her with an eager tongue.
Srivastava stared, transfixed by the image. Who were these lovers,
transported by irresistible passions? As he gazed at the couple, a
cloud of mist blew through the courtyard, enveloping the young
man and his partner. Slowly, it cleared, and the court was empty
once more.

Max urged Imogen backwards, pushing her gently with his lips,
until she lay back. He stretched out alongside her slim body, his
hand caressing her waist, moving softly across her stomach, and up
into the cleft between her breasts. Imogen stared willingly into
Max's eyes, silenced by the strength of her own desires. As his hand
continued its hypnotic massage, his face moved closer to hers, and
once more their lips sealed together. Imogen dug her sharp finger-
nails into Max's neck, pulling his mouth tighter into her own. Max
widened the circle of his massage, and his hand began to reach the
boundary formed by the waistband of her white cotton skirt.
Impatiently, Imogen turned onto her side. Max stroked the small
of her back, and pushed his hand further down. The crinkled
waistband was tightly fastened, too tight for him to slip his hand
beneath it. Dextrously he undid the buttons running down the
side of the skirt, one by one, relishing the ritual. As each button
gave way, Imogen's breathing quickened in anticipation; the skirt
loosened, open at the side down to her thigh. Max ran his hand
along her leg, slowing teasingly just beneath her waist, but

choosing to continue its upward motion, coming to rest on her breast. He saw Imogen's nostrils widen perceptibly and felt her body shift uneasily from the waist down. A warm, fishy aroma rose into Max's head, making his eyes close in a narcotic trance. He yearned for the taste on his lips.

In his dream, Srivastava walked on, venturing ever further into the outer chambers of the temple. Not a soul stirred. High above his head, a million tiny eyes, forever fixed in the saffron firmament, kept watch as the old sculptor wandered alone amongst the desert sands. He had now reached one of the most ornate halls, desolate and cold without the life that filled it during the waking hours. As Srivastava stepped over the threshold, he heard the impatient touch of a young man's hand caressing his lover. The sculptor stopped and gazed into the deep, orange shadows. There, once more, were the lovers he had seen earlier, now in a new pose, the youth lying alongside his beloved. His hand gently touched her thigh, nervous and hesitant. The mixture of trepidation and impatience and yearning drawn across the young man's face hypnotized Srivastava. Would he ever be able to recapture it in stone? He drank in the frozen image, relishing its every savour, committing each nuance to memory. A moment later, a veil of fine sand swept across the hall, its tiny motes flashing in the shafts of light. And once more, the phantom lovers were gone.

Like Max, Imogen too responded to the smell, and to the sticky dampness between her legs. As she felt Max stir, she moved her body closer to his, letting her skirt slip further, pressing and caressing his erection with her thigh. Imogen moved her hands down to Max's belt, and unfastened it. As the waist eased, she felt for the buttons down the front. One by one she worked her way down, slowly, letting her hand press firmly and deliberately against Max's white cotton shorts. As she loosened the last button, she put her hand inside the opening she had made, found the cut in the boxer shorts, and released him, throbbing with a mixture of pain and ecstasy. She ran her delicate fingers along the ridges and contours, excited by her power to enrage, then soothe. As she felt along the full length, Imogen tightened her grip a little, and grasped Max firmly within her hand, watching his eyes close. She felt a single drop ooze onto her fingers. Instinctively, she rubbed the juice between her finger and thumb, then lifted her hand to her lips. The bitter taste made her body tighten.

As he wandered about the halls on the periphery of the temple, Srivastava thought of his own youth, far away in his hometown by the sea. He too had been a passionate lover in his time, had made women lose themselves in mazes of delight. The sculptor smiled to himself as he recalled the hot lusty days spent in secret caves high above the waters of the Indian Ocean. In his dream, he could almost feel the roar of the incoming waves, smell the froth of the surf, hear the hiss as the water died, and receded. Still contemplating these images, Srivastava walked through an archway, and turned. He had come through six similar arches, each smaller than the one before it. Now, as he looked back along the length of the avenue, he saw at its far end, bathed in light, the young lovers wrapped around each other, their limbs intertwined, so that Srivastava could not ascertain which belonged to the young man, and which to the girl. As they held each other, the dreamer studied the perfect features of the young woman's face. Surely, this was some goddess: only divinity could possess such fair skin, such faultless eyes, such a delicate brow. And only in the imaginations of ancient artists had such magnificent breasts ever taken shape. The girl held her face up to the light, letting her hair fall freely towards the ground. It seemed aflame as the cool sunlight bathed its silken strands. Only the amber granite of the Kashmir caves could possibly capture this fiery crown, thought the sculptor. As he continued to watch, the light grew brighter, until the glare, white hot, blinded the old man. Then it abated, returning once more to its gentle orange, lighting up the shafts of dust in the empty archways.

Max stopped kissing Imogen, and laid his head on her chest, his lips resting open on her breast, his eyes fixed on the gap between her skin and the top of her skirt. He let his hand run slowly down Imogen's body, over her stomach, underneath the open waistband, down the gentle undulation, and onto the small ridge of hair. He lingered there, massaging the soft follicles, running his finger along the boundaries of the v-shaped clump. At the lower end, he could feel that the hair was soaked, and the individual strands clung together in damp knots. The feel of the moisture between his fingers fascinated Max, and he continued to trace the outline of the hair. He could hear Imogen's heart pumping frantically. Its pace quickened as Max allowed his hand to explore further down. The clumps of hair gave way to warm, damp flesh, which retracted with a reflex action upon touch. But the contraction was only momentary. The more Max stroked, the more Imogen relaxed, and the more the juices flowed. His hand was soon bathed in dampness. He looked up, intrigued by the blush rising in Imogen's breasts, the crimson flooding through the pale skin. Imogen put her own hand down beneath her skirt, and gently pushed aside Max's inquisitive fingers. Then, she plunged her fingers into the crevice, covering them with the moisture. Carefully lifting her shining hand out from underneath the white cotton, she rubbed the cream onto Max's erection. Unable to wait any longer, Max moved onto Imogen. He stared for a moment at her usually gentle face, distorted by the force of her passion. Imogen pulled Max into her. He felt the base of his stomach contract deeply, and he let out a deep sigh.

There was no mistaking it that time: Srivastava had not imagined the gasps of the stones. His wanderings had brought him now to the inner courtyards, where the glimmering light of the outer rooms had gradually been replaced by a deeper hue. It was as he entered one of the innermost chambers of the temple that the old sculptor had heard the sigh. He looked about him, searching the shadows for another sight of his playful lovers. The perfect corners of the room cast long, tenebrous streaks across the marble floor, forming a new mosaic unimagined by the craftsmen who had laboured day and night to decorate the halls. Srivastava looked up at the open sky, trying to locate the position of the sun which was giving out such magnificent light. But there was no sun, only a warm glow, spread deeply, casting its reflections upon the temple beneath. Yet the shadows must have a source. Unable to accept the logic of dreams, Srivastava looked down at the floor, calculating the direction of the shafts of lights. Each alcove, each window, seemed to have its own private source, a dozen suns, casting a multitude of shapes onto the holy ground. As he stared at the intricate shadows, Srivastava saw two of the dark outlines merge, and form one. The pattern rotated, and there, before his eyes, Srivastava saw the silhouette of the amorous pair whose presence filled the temple. The virile youth now straddled his partner, their bodies joined beneath the waist, forming one thick tail. At the other end, two chests and two heads blossomed out, two buds from one branch. The old artist beheld the display, all the time imagining the long, slim boulder inside which he would find the image of this union. The shadows merged, and became once more the central pillar of the latticework that criss-crossed the ground.

Max held his whole weight on his outstretched arms, one each side of Imogen's face. Slowly, he found the pulsating entrance, streams of honey running down the passageway. Max pushed himself in, feeling Imogen's muscles tighten, then expand to accommodate him. She pulled him in, closing her eyes with a sharp intake of breath as she felt the dull pain of collision inside her.

The two bodies tumbled together on the dry grass, striving to push ever deeper into each other. Imogen's white skirt was now completely gathered at her waist, her long, tanned legs winding themselves high around Max's back. As he thrust deep and hard, Imogen's legs moved up and down the small of his back. For ten, fifteen minutes, the eager pounding continued, the lovers' breathing keeping pace with the increasing rhythm, perspiration running off their limbs and faces, making it difficult to retain a firm grip. The bodies slithered and slipped on each other: Max could feel Imogen's breasts undulating beneath his chest, her nipples hardening as his torso rubbed them up and down. His legs were burning from the thighs down, his waist caught up in its own automatic gyrations. He could never get deep enough. Imogen felt the body on her quicken in its movements. She closed her eyes and concentrated on the dramatic surge of feelings taking place within her. It was as if a tiny firefly had found its way into her womb, and was now flying rapidly to all the different, most sensitive parts of her body, setting them aflame. The fiery whirlwind was gathering force, scorching its way through Imogen's arteries, into the network of capillaries, into each and every individual cell. She could hear nothing except the frantic sound of their own breathing, and the ebb and flow of blood rushing in waves past her eardrum.

She felt a rising urgency in Max's thrusting. With a soft but determined push from her waist, Imogen eased Max onto his side, their bodies still joined. For a moment they rested, side by side, staring hungrily at each other. Then, in one smooth movement, Imogen pushed Max underneath her, rising to a crouching position above him. From his new vantage point, lying flat on his back, Max could see Imogen's face dripping, almost a silhouette with the sun behind her. He let his eyes wander down, to rest on her flushed breasts, and his hands came up to fondle them, cupping them, then softly massaging the nipples. The gentle movement of his hands brought Imogen back from her reverie. She threw her head back, holding her face up to the sky, and began to rise and fall rhythmically above her lover. Holding her arms tightly by the biceps, Max kept Imogen in position, pushing her up and pulling her down. At one point, she bent her face down to within an inch of him, her eyes staring straight into his. Like a cobra hypnotizing its victim, she held his gaze, her frantic breathing recovering its normal pace, her hair dripping salt water straight onto his forehead and cheeks. Max was deep inside her, as deep as she could possibly

pull him in, and he felt her muscles contract around him. He tried
to thrust up, but he was already at his limit, so Imogen's whole
body shifted upwards. She continued to hold his gaze. Then, without any warning and keeping her upper body as still as possible,
Imogen began to thrust from her waist, plunging and pulling long
and deep, testing her lover's strength. Max had no choice. Imogen's
body pinned him down, her violent undulations preventing any
movement on his part. He loved the sensation of being trapped,
was excited beyond measure by the strength of Imogen's slender
body. Yet he could feel an irresistible stirring inside him. His
inability to move heightened the tension, and Max felt totally out
of control. At the last minute, as if reading his mind, Imogen
stretched back, pulling Max up from the ground, off his back, and
falling backwards herself, the two of them forming a wild see-saw.
Still they remained joined together. Clutching him towards her,
Imogen once more lay back onto the grass, her legs open wide
enough to enclose Max within her.

Srivastava had arrived at the deepest chamber of the holy temple,
the hall reserved for the most venerated priests, the most enlightened scholars. Here, the amber light of the other chambers had
been replaced by a dark blue, the deep cool shade of a summer's
day at dusk, just before the monsoon. The room was empty. As the
guiding hand of his dream forced the sculptor to enter, a shiver
descended his spine, the cold air of the interior enveloping him.
Every corner, each crevice, was suffused with the violet rays.
The room drew the long-awaited craftsman inside. Almost immediately, Srivastava heard the passion of the couple making love. But
where were they? He looked about him for the now familiar sight,
but saw nothing, just the perfect, smooth blue walls of the inner
sanctum. There was only one alcove in this room, illuminated by
a direct pillar of blue light. Instinctively, Srivastava knew that this
would be the most challenging of the commissions. The old man
was tired, and the pounding he had heard grew louder by degrees,
accompanied by occasional gasps and sighs. Perhaps he was already

too old for the task. The presage of mortality depressed Srivastava. He sat down on the cold marble floor, glad to rest his weary legs. Leaning back against the wall, the craftsman stared at the alcove, its emptiness accusing him, impatient, mocking the artist's lack of vigour. Although he knew he was dreaming, Srivastava closed his eyes once more, listening to the ever louder pounding. Suddenly, a new noise joined the symphony. Srivastava opened his eyes, and looked over to his left, searching for the dog that had yelped.

The old man was still in the inner chamber, in the midnight desert near the Prince's palace. It was very cold, and the sculptor was beginning to shiver. For a moment, he imagined that the wall he had leaned against was gone and the room he had entered was no more than a derelict shell, the marble of the floor broken into a thousand tiny pieces, grass and sand protruding through the fissures. Was this a tree that had taken root in the corner of the chamber? The old man looked closely at the decrepit trunk, with its geriatric limbs erupting through the ceramic of the floor. His eyes had deceived him—he was beginning to confuse the shadows with reality. Srivastava knew he would have to wake up, knew that he was alone in his bed, knew he was an old man with only imaginings of passion. But he would hold on to his dream a moment longer. And all the time, the sound of two dogs fighting filled his head, mingling with the vehement sighs of the lovers. It was difficult to separate out the frenzied snarling and howling from the orgasmic gasps. Yet, try as he might, Srivastava could not bring the images out of the sounds. He looked about him, scanning each corner of the room, lingering over every shadow, but there appeared neither beast nor lover. The alcove was still there, empty as before. Disappointed, the sculptor let his eyes fall from the arched shelf to the patch of ground at its foot. He must have one more vision, one final image, to furnish that reproachful emptiness. Gradually, as the dreamer fixed his eyes on the empty patch of ground, the pool of light darkened and began to form a shape. The sounds Srivastava heard inside his ears separated: the dogs were now behind him, some ten feet away, in the corner where the imaginary tree had taken root. And the lovers' yearnings? The light had now coalesced into a definite pattern, and there, clearer than ever before, were the lovers Srivastava sought.

Max knew he was being watched. But he often had this feeling when making love to Imogen, and it was never anything more than a figment of his imagination. He was, once again, above her. He could see her perfectly, his own shadow shielding her face from the fierce sun above them. Max bent down and kissed her, searching her mouth with his tongue. Moments later, he pulled away, and let his tongue begin to explore her neck, which Imogen stretched to its full length as she arched her body backwards. She tasted bitter, and the saline savour, coupled with the aroma rising from lower down, quickened Max's desire. As he traced a path with his tongue between her breasts, he slid his whole body down. Over the ridges he continued, sucking the skin until the blood rose to the surface. Imogen held onto Max's shoulders, restraining him. Then she released him, and he worked his way down, pushing his tongue into the crevices formed beneath each breast, then going on to trace intricate invisible patterns on Imogen's stomach. He felt her hands urging him to go lower, but he waited, resting his cheek on her waist. Max closed his eyes, breathing in the juices deeply, feeding on their promise. Then, almost imperceptibly, he began to descend. Max's tongue moved from the smooth surface of Imogen's womb, into a tiny thicket of soft hair. Slowly and deliberately, he licked each strand dry. Eventually, he reached the crevice between his lover's legs and, frantically, Imogen pressed his head into her, twisting strands of his hair in her fingers. With his tongue, Max pushed aside the soft folds of flesh, feeling at last the warm fluid flowing over his lips.

Imogen relaxed. As soon as she relinquished her hold over herself, the tiny disparate fires that the firefly had set alight inside her suddenly gathered force, and exploded. Wave after wave of fire rushed through Imogen's body. She held Max's head down, drawing it in with her thighs. As he sucked deeper and deeper, so Imogen surrendered to the raging within her.

Srivastava felt the dream slipping from him. The image of the lovers was beginning to fade, and he knew that soon he must leave this place and return to the world of his labours. He was satisfied that he now possessed the visions he would sculpt. He turned to leave the hall through the archway he had entered. But something held Srivastava back. On an impulse, the old man turned back again, and keeping his eyes fixed on the empty alcove on the wall, walked over to it. He touched the smooth plaster. It was still soft and supple, and the sculptor's finger left a tiny trench where he had traced it. Srivastava caressed the wet wall softly, as if stroking a delicate animal. As his eyes looked down, he noticed a pebble at its base. Instinctively, he bent down and picked it up. Its sharp point formed a perfect nib with which to inscribe the plaster. Srivastava smoothed the wall with his hand just below the base of the alcove. Here, deliberately, and with a craftsman's practised care, he took the pebble and began to cut the intricate outlines of Sanskrit characters into the stonework. The pebble sliced easily through the smooth skin. One by one the shapes appeared. Srivastava knew that such a liberty with the Prince's temple would be forbidden him in reality, but here, in his sleeping vision, the old man was master. With a steady hand, Srivastava finished off the word that he had been compelled to write. VIDHI. As the sculptor stepped back to examine his handiwork, his lips formed the sound. 'Vidhi,' he whispered silently to himself. Destiny.

Max pushed further and further into the soft flesh. Imogen had begun to convulse gently, pulling him in, then pushing him away in a regular rhythm. Her hands grasped Max firmly, afraid that he might withdraw. He could feel her gasping for breath. But now Imogen pulled him up sharply, guiding his head the full length of her body, forcing him to shift his body awkwardly and rise once more onto her. As he covered her, Max felt Imogen pull his still glistening mouth hungrily onto her own. At the same time, her hand searched lower down, beneath their waists. Gradually, her firm sensitive fingers tightened on Max, guiding him once again inside her. He felt her thighs shuddering against him. Her gasping became desperate, yet she refused to release her lover's mouth. Her heart pounded with a deafening rhythm.

As Max thrust, and thrust again, Imogen rushed to the edge of the precipice, and looked down into the chasms of fire at her feet. Yet she clung for a moment longer. Together, they would plunge into the inferno. Each tiny movement brought Max closer. He felt her waiting for him. Higher and higher he pushed. Still she waited. Finally, Max too could see the edge of the precipice: as he caught sight of the blazing sea beneath the cliff, he rushed forward with a final explosion of energy, grabbed Imogen as she waited on the edge, and leapt into the chasm.

For a moment, the two bodies, fused together on the dusty patch of grass, stopped. All sound ceased. The breeze did not blow, the dust froze. Even the birds, hiding from the sun in shady nooks, arrested their fidgeting. The shadows on the ground, lengthening each second, held their shapes one instant longer. Into the stillness a shot was fired. The noise tore through the silence, and sound rushed back in through the hole in the vacuum. Birds, startled by the explosion, took off, flapping their wings frantically. The sand began its meanderings once more, blown into flurries and eddies by a new wind. The sun continued on its relentless journey, and the shadows lengthened once more.

Imogen felt the surge deep inside her, and screamed silently. Though audible to no human ear, her cry reached every corner of the derelict temple. The carvings, motionless and inert, safe within their alcoves, heard the song, and for a moment their own sculpted passion came to life. As Imogen cried out her satisfaction, an orgiastic ecstasy filled the wilderness of Madhya Pradesh.

Acknowledgments

The publisher is grateful to the following for permission to reproduce copyright material from:

Les Liaisons Dangereuses by Choderlos de Laclos, translated R. Aldington. Reprinted by permission of Peter Owen Publishers, London.

Lady Chatterley's Lover by D. H. Lawrence. Reprinted by permission of Laurence Pollinger Ltd and the Estate of Frieda Lawrence Ravagli. Copyright © 1961.

The Group by Mary McCarthy. Chapter 2 from THE GROUP, copyright © 1963 and renewed 1991 by James Raymond West, reprinted by permission of Harcourt Brace Jovanovich, Inc and George Weidenfeld and Nicolson Ltd, London.

Story of O by Pauline Réage. Copyright © 1972 Société Nouvelle des Editions Pauvert 1954, 1972.

Sexus by Henry Miller. Copyright the Estate of Henry Miller. Reproduced with permission of Curtis Brown Group Ltd, London.

Portnoy's Complaint by Philip Roth. Copyright © 1969 by Philip Roth. Reprinted by permission of Jonathan Cape Ltd and Random House, Inc., New York.

A Bouquet of Barbed Wire by Andrea Newman. Copyright © Andrea Newman. Reprinted by permission of the Peters Fraser & Dunlop Group Ltd.

Fear of Flying by Erica Jong. Copyright © 1973 by Erica Mann Jong. Reprinted by permission of Henry Holt and Company and Martin Secker and Warburg Limited. First published in the UK 1974.

In Praise of Older Women by Stephen Vizinczey. Copyright 1990 by Stephen Vizinczey. This chapter reprinted from the 41st English-language edition of the novel. *In Praise of Older Women* published in 1990 by The University of Chicago Press, 5801 Ellis Avenue, Chicago, Illinois 60637–1496.

The Still Point by Subniv Babuta. Copyright © 1991. Reprinted by permission of George Weidenfeld and Nicolson Ltd, London.

All Pan books are available at your local bookshop or newsagent, or can be ordered direct from the publisher. Indicate the number of copies required and fill in the form below.

Send to: Pan C. S. Dept
             Macmillan Distribution Ltd
             Houndmills Basingstoke RG21 2XS
or phone: 0256 29242, quoting title, author and Credit Card number.

Please enclose a remittance* to the value of the cover price plus: £1.00 for the first book plus 50p per copy for each additional book ordered.

*Payment may be made in sterling by UK personal cheque, postal order, sterling draft or international money order, made payable to Pan Books Ltd.

Alternatively by Barclaycard/Access/Amex/Diners

Card No.

Expiry Date

Signature:

Applicable only in the UK and BFPO addresses

While every effort is made to keep prices low, it is sometimes necessary to increase prices at short notice. Pan Books reserve the right to show on covers and charge new retail prices which may differ from those advertised in the text or elsewhere.

NAME AND ADDRESS IN BLOCK LETTERS PLEASE:

....

Name

Address

6/92